C000103867

By the same author

ALL WE CANNOT LEAVE BEHIND

IAIN KELLY

The Book Guild Ltd

First published in Great Britain in 2024 by
The Book Guild Ltd
Unit E2 Airfield Business Park,
Harrison Road, Market Harborough,
Leicestershire. LE16 7UL
Tel: 0116 2792299
www.bookguild.co.uk
Email: info@bookguild.co.uk
Twitter: @bookguild

Copyright © 2024 Iain Kelly

The right of Iain Kelly to be identified as the author of this
work has been asserted by them in accordance with the
Copyright, Design and Patents Act 1988.

All rights reserved. No part of this publication may be
reproduced, transmitted, or stored in a retrieval system, in any form or by any means,
without permission in writing from the publisher, nor be otherwise circulated in
any form of binding or cover other than that in which it is published and without
a similar condition being imposed on the subsequent purchaser.

This work is entirely fictitious and bears no resemblance to any persons living or dead.

Typeset in 11pt Minion Pro

Printed on FSC accredited paper
Printed and bound in Great Britain by 4edge Limited

ISBN 978 1916668 140

British Library Cataloguing in Publication Data.
A catalogue record for this book is available from the British Library.

For
Chloe Dawn and Caden Daniel

and
Dad

PROLOGUE

THE CANAL

1905

It was his favourite part of the day. The sun dipped below the trees, glinting through the bare autumn branches, a hush descended, a calmness settled, welcoming the oncoming darkness. In the distance, across fields covered in gathering mist, a murder of crows pecked at seeds in the turned soil. A latecomer let out a screeching *caw* and swooped to join them. The horse's heavy steps on the rough path echoed around the cut. The gelding's warm breath formed clouds as he plodded onwards, pulling the barge through the glass-like canal.

'There, there.' Rab patted the matted mane. 'No' much further.'

They had planned to stop at their usual place, next to the Castlecary Inn. It was a night Rab always looked forward to on their route along the Forth and Clyde Canal. Instead of sleeping on the barge, the skipper let them sleep at the inn, where they could enjoy a plate of hot food and the local beer. But all the mooring berths were full, and the banks of the canal were lined with barges.

'We'll carry oan tae the next lock,' the skipper of the *Genevieve* had decided, 'git a hied start in the mornin.'

They would be first in line to get through the series of lock gates at Allandale the next day. Rab and Margaret, the skipper's wife, had shared a look of disappointment as the prospect of a comfortable bed evaporated into the night. Hamish, the skipper, was oblivious to their disconsolation. Rab patted the ageing piebald horse who would also miss out on a warm stable and fresh hay.

'Another night under the stars, Angus. We've no' much tae complain aboot in this weather.' Angus plodded onwards, taking the weight of the barge on the rope attached to his harness.

The mist settled over the canal, the water cooling after a day of sunshine. Banks on either side of the cut held the air still, suspended over the water. The crows leapt into the sky, their harsh calls breaking the restful peace of the evening. Rab shivered, pulling his coat closer around his chest. He tried not to think of the winter months ahead, when the job of treading along the canal paths through rain, mud, sleet and snow became an ordeal. In truth, he was lucky to have the *Genevieve*. Horseboating was rapidly declining, bowing to the industrial age and the steam-powered narrowboats that ran at twice the speed of the horse-drawn boats. Rab knew he would soon have to work on such a vessel and looked forward to the noise, acrid smell and belching smoke even less than the prospect of a cold, wet winter trudging along the banks. Perhaps he would be forced to leave the canals altogether, as more freight switched to the ever-expanding railway and the iron horses that sped across the land. The tracks between Edinburgh and Glasgow ran alongside the canal here, following the same valley floor through the rolling hills. Some railwaymen swore there was romance in the steam engines and metal rails. For Rab, it would never compare to the narrowboat gliding along the canal, pulled by the docile beasts that paced along without complaint.

He looked across to the narrowboat. Hamish and Margaret had moved inside and the smell of supper being prepared came from the small stove in the living area.

Donald had taken over at the tiller, guiding the boat through the narrow channel. 'After the next corner,' he called to Rab, letting him know to start slowing Angus after the next bend. Embankments rose on either side, obscuring the view of the countryside beyond. The trapped mist thickened to a fog. Rab raised his cap in acknowledgement and allowed himself to start thinking about the warm cup of tea that awaited him, and the heat of the stove on his chilled hands.

The path turned, following the contour of the canal and the black gates of the lock revealed themselves through the deepening gloom. Rab gave Angus another clap and pulled gently on the harness. 'Slow doon, boy. Easy does it.' Angus came to a halt and the rope grew slack. Rab unhitched the harness as the boat slid onwards. Donald steered away from the middle of the channel towards the bank. Beneath the lock, mooring cleats lined the stone wall bank. They would tie up here for the night. Hamish appeared through the door at the front of the barge and began unravelling a rope, ready to throw it to Rab.

Just as the narrowboat was coming to a gentle stop, Rab heard the splash. The noise was loud enough to disturb the crows across the field, triggering another round of cawing. Rab paused, straining to hear anything further. He peered through the hanging mist. There was a soft bump as the barge nestled against the bank. A heavy mooring rope landed at Rab's feet.

'Stoap standin' there lik' an eejit, boy. Grab the rope.' Hamish shouted. 'Whit are ye daein'?'

Rab ignored him. He bent down and held the rope, continuing to stare ahead, towards the lock gates. He could sense movement ahead. Someone was in the water.

'Rab!' Hamish shouted again.

A high-pitched scream pierced through the fog. A woman's voice, shrill and desperate. 'There's somewan in the watter!' Rab yelled and dropped the rope and ran along the path towards the noise. Donald leapt from the back of the boat onto the path and sprinted after him.

Rab climbed the rise that led to the top of the lock gates.

The woman's voice shouted, 'What have I done?'

He stared down into the pool of water held between the two gates, a black rectangle shrouded in mist. Donald arrived next to him.

'There!' Donald pointed, and now Rab could see it too: a disturbance in the water. A dark shape was thrashing around, throwing up foam and spray. The shape evolved until Rab could make sense of it. It was a person, their arms flailing, their head struggling to stay above the surface.

'Come oan!' Rab removed his boots and shirt. 'Hawd oan, we're comin' tae git ye!'

'Jesus Christ,' muttered Donald.

The woman choked and spluttered, gasping for breath, fighting to stay afloat. The thrashing weakened, and her head disappeared under the dark void. Rab took two paces back and threw himself off the lock wall, landing in the water next to where he had seen the head disappear from view.

The force of hitting the water and the shock of the freezing cold temperature forced the breath from his lungs. He could see nothing through the thick black water. He groped around with his hands and kicked his legs until he broke through the surface and sucked in oxygen. There was a loud splash as Donald landed next to him in the canal.

'Anythin'?'

Donald gasped and spat out a mouthful of brown water. 'Nothin'.'

Rab took in a gulp of air and ducked under the surface again. He felt Donald next to him as their legs clashed. He tried pushing himself further through the water, his arms outstretched. His chest screamed for air and he was about to push himself towards the top again when his hand hit something and became entangled in clothing. A hand grabbed his arm, pulling him down deeper. Then another, clawing at him. She was pulling them both down in her panic. He reached out and found the trunk of her body, and pinned her arms to her side. He kicked as hard as he could, desperately trying to push them towards the surface. They hovered for a moment, balanced between life and death. Then they were moving upwards, being pulled towards the dim light above.

They broke through the water and Rab gasped and gulped. The woman in his arms was a dead weight. Donald was holding her with one arm. It was he who had hauled them to the surface. In Donald's other hand, he grasped the end of a bargepole. Rab looked to the bank and saw Hamish.

'Grab oan,' he called down to them. 'Ah'll pull ye o'er tae the ladders.'

'Take her,' Rab called to Donald, and released the woman's inert body. They drifted away from Rab as Hamish pulled them to the wall of the lock. Running up the side were metal rungs bolted into the bricks. Donald gripped onto the one above the water level. Rab swam over to them. He held the woman while Donald got a foothold on the ladder and between them managed to heave the woman up and onto Donald's shoulders. He began climbing, one step at a time until he was close enough for Hamish to reach down from above and take the woman from him. Rab followed them up the rungs.

Donald lay on his back, gasping for air. Rab, ignoring the coldness of the water on his skin and clothes, went to help Hamish. He had the woman on her front, hitting her back. Her ghostly pale skin contrasted with her sodden black attire.

'Is she breathin'?'

'Barely. Swallowed a lot a' watter, ah reckon.'

Rab put his arms under the woman's body and hoisted her up, while Hamish thumped her back. 'Come oan, breath wumman.'

She convulsed; her head jerked upwards. She spluttered and coughed and vomited up a lungful of dirty water. Hamish hit her back again. 'That's it, git it aw oot a' ye.' She coughed up more canal water. Her breathing became steadier. Colour returned to her face. 'There ye are, there ye are,' soothed Hamish.

Rab collapsed onto the cold, hard bricks and looked up at the stars in the black night sky.

Margaret appeared with a police officer and several locals and boatmen in tow. She had gone to the inn at Castlecary to alert them. The policeman assumed control of the situation. Margaret fetched warm blankets and spare clothes from the *Genevieve,* and got the woman out of her drenched dress and into dry garments. The woman remained silent. Rab and Donald changed into dry clothes on the narrowboat, then came back to give statements to the officer.

As they were recounting their version of events, one of the locals from the inn, standing looking into the canal water in the lock, gave out a sharp cry. 'There's somethin' else in the watter there.' He pointed. Everyone moved to the edge of the lock. There was a grey object floating on the surface. Hamish pushed his way through with the bargepole and hooked it out of the water.

'It's jist the lady's shawl,' said the policeman after a quick inspection of the drenched cloth. But when the woman saw it, she let out a scream, similar to the one that had alerted Rab and Donald to her plight, and fainted to the ground.

The excitement over, the crowd began to disperse, heading back to the inn. Hamish and Donald secured the barge for the night and Margaret rescued the meal she had abandoned earlier. The policeman commandeered Angus in order to carry the weak woman back to the village. Rab went with him in order to return with the horse. As they walked, Rab was able to see the woman for the first time as she lay draped across Angus's back and withers. Her hair, which he had thought to be black, turned to a dark red copper as it dried. Her skin was pale, her lips and cheeks a soft pink. She was slight and underweight, even malnourished. He reckoned her to be no more than seventeen or eighteen years of age. He stayed with the woman until they reached the house of the local doctor. He was not best pleased at being interrupted as he sat down to his evening meal, but agreed to take the woman in and care for her until the morning.

'Whit'll happen tae her noo?' Rab asked the police officer as he turned Angus in the road and prepared to return to the boat.

'Ah'll collect her in the mornin', wance she's rested. Tak' her doon tae the station an' find oot who she is an' whit happened.'

'An' then whit?'

'Depends. If she fell in by accident, ah guess there'll be nothin' mare tae be said.'

'Ye think it wisnae an accident?'

'Plenty try tae take their lives jumpin' intae the canal. She widnae be the first. Could be she's fae a nice home that'll take her back an' care fir her. Could be she'll be aff tae the loonie bin. Most likely, lookin' at her claes and her general appearance, she'll be back in the poorhoose afore this time th'morra. She'll probably try it again if she's determined enough, an' she might nae be lucky enough tae ha' a passin' boatman tae save her next time.'

Rab returned to the *Genevieve* and tied Angus up for the night. The next morning, the lock-keeper appeared, unaware of the drama that had occurred the previous night, and opened the wooden mitre gates. Before the sun had crested the hills across the fields, the barge was through the lock and other narrowboats were queued up ready for their turn; their engines sending the crows into the blue, crisp sky. Rab hitched Angus to the rope once more and another day began along the Forth and Clyde Canal.

It was two days later that a passing cartman, travelling along the canal path at the lock, noticed a white piece of cloth sticking out from under an overgrown bramble. He bent down and picked it up.

'Wid ye look at that,' he muttered. 'Whit wumman wid drap their shawl an' no' notice it.' He glanced around to make sure he wasn't being watched. 'Weel, if she's well aff enough tae no' miss it, there's nae harm in takin' it, ah reckon.' He stuffed the shawl into the pouch on the side of his horse and carried on his way.

1

THURSDAY, 11 NOVEMBER

1920

In the centre of the village of Liberton, at the junction of Kirkgate and Kirk Brae, sat the two-storey building that housed The Liberton Inn. The upper floor exterior was made of sandstone brick, while the walls of the lower half of the establishment were painted with whitewash that needed a fresh coat. The publican, Arthur Melchin and his wife, Rose, lived above the inn and spent their evenings and weekends working behind the bar. The public could enter the lounge room through a door on the Kirkgate side of the building, while the standing bar, with stools and low window seats, was accessed via a door on Kirk Brae. On the wall above this door, in large gold lettering against a black background, the sign for The Liberton Inn was garishly painted, adorned with Rose's well-tended hanging baskets at either end. Inside, the inn was like any other local hostelry, with dark oak wood panels around the walls, a deep red worn carpet that had seen brighter and better days and windows of frosted glass covered with wooden shutters that remained closed, allowing only a glimmer of sunlight to enter through narrow slits. The bar formed a U-shape, protruding into the room from the back wall, behind which a staircase led to the living quarters above. At the midpoint of the bar, a panelled oak wall separated the lounge room from the standing bar. In the middle of this wall was a door with a frosted glass pane. There was no official rule excluding women from the standing bar, but it was accepted that they should keep themselves to the lounge room and allow the men their own space in the bar. The exception to this unwritten rule was Rose, who served drinks to customers on both sides of the divide. The men in the standing bar were sensible enough to prefer having their thirst sated in good time rather than insisting that only Arthur serve them.

It was through the door on Kirk Brae that Doctor Thomas Stevenson stepped into the standing bar on a cold November evening. He had made the short walk from the sanatorium, up Lasswade Road, passing the row of sandstone cottages on the right and the farmhouse on the left just before the crossroads. His own house lay farther down Kirkgate, opposite the church, which lent its name to the street. Every evening, the warm, welcoming gas lamps of The Liberton Inn were impossible for him to resist as he passed. Tonight, he wished to salve his tired and melancholy mind and clear the clinging grip of death and chronic illness that had surrounded him for the past two hours. That afternoon, he had made his weekly visit to the sanatorium to check up on his patients who were convalescing there, alongside those whom he knew would not leave there until they had taken their last breath. With winter drawing on and nightfall descending in late afternoon, leaving the sick house and entering the black night served to heighten his gloom. The only bright thought this winter was the absence of any Spanish Flu outbreak, which had blighted the last two years.

Unlike the clear night sky outside, where the stars could already be seen and a frost was beginning to form, the inside of the inn was shrouded in a cloud of smoke which hung in the air. Thomas approached the bar, nodding a greeting to the regulars he was unsurprised to find occupying a window seat.

'Joseph, Malachy.'

'Doctor,' the men replied in unison, half-raising their pint glasses towards him. 'A cauld wan the night.'

'It is that.'

'Nothin' a fine warm ale willnae protect ye fae though, eh?'

'Just the one now, Joseph. I hope you're remembering what I told you on your last visit.'

'Richt ye are, Doctor,' replied Joseph, and as if on cue, he let out a series of hacking coughs. Thomas had warned him to quit smoking cigarettes to allow his chest to clear, otherwise he risked the onset of consumption of the lungs. He was not unsurprised to find his advice had been ignored. Although he had been the local general practitioner in Liberton Village for two years now, since arriving in the suburb to the south of Edinburgh at the end of the war, he still had a way to go to earn the trust of those who had spent their whole lives within the small community. All he could do was administer his medicine and advice as he saw fit. Joseph Burns, the groundskeeper at Liberton House, was one such untrusting patient, nearing fifty years old, and having lived in the village since he was born there.

He couldn't be too critical, given his own reliance on alcohol. He knew he was drinking too much, turning to the comfort of it every evening in order to settle his mind and allow him to get a modicum of sleep each night.

'I'll keep him right, Doctor,' said Malachy, the young Irish immigrant who had been taken on at the House to help Joseph with his duties.

'You'll more than likely lead him further astray,' Thomas replied.

'Whatever would give you that idea now?' said Malachy, a broad smile across his face.

Thomas turned to the bar, where Rose had appeared from the lounge side of the inn.

'Guid evenin', Thomas. Whit kin ah get ye?'

'The usual, Rose.'

'Richt ye are.' She poured him a pint of ale and a measure of whisky. Rose Melchin was in her late forties, a petite woman whose youthful looks had started to fade as her hair turned from brown to grey and her smooth skin began to wrinkle and yellow. The years of inhaling smoke in The Liberton Inn had not helped her. Through the haze she placed his drinks on the bar. Thomas handed over the money to pay for them. As a local and a regular, he could have joined Joseph and Malachy in having a running tab with Rose and Arthur, but Thomas preferred to pay as he went. That way he ensured he never drank more than he could afford. Rose pocketed the coins in the front of her apron. 'Ye two need another roun' yet?' she called to the other men.

'Jist savourin' this the noo,' Joseph called back. The quality of the local ale was their running joke, although they consumed enough each night to suggest they had no complaints.

'Any problems ye kin tak' up wi' Arthur.' Rose left and returned to the lounge, where a continuous hum of voices suggested it was busy this evening.

'Ye tell Arthur we're perfectly happy,' called Joseph after her as she went. Arthur Melchin, unlike his small wife, was a giant of a man, standing well over six feet tall and broad-shouldered, with a large bushy beard and a barrel chest. The Liberton Inn had never had much trouble with rowdy patrons once they had seen the stature of the landlord.

Thomas took his drinks and sat on a low window seat on the wall away from Joseph and Malachy. The regulars knew the doctor liked to have a peaceful drink, and although not hostile to having the odd word in passing, preferred to sit on his own in contemplation. They assumed he was deep in thought about his patients, which was sometimes the case. This Thursday though, for men of Thomas's generation, had been a particularly sombre day. Two years ago today, the war had finally ended.

He raised the whisky to his lips and offered a silent thought to those who had not come home. He couldn't offer a prayer or go to church. Others had found solace and comfort in faith, searching for some way to make sense of the horror they had witnessed. Thomas had no argument with those that turned to the church; he envied those that had found some way to deal with the trauma. He had found no such respite, with the exception of a drink each night. He swallowed the whisky in one gulp, letting it hit the back of his throat and feeling the burn as it slid down his gullet. He shut out the images that haunted him. Many had returned physically unharmed from the battlefields, but no one, Thomas was sure, had returned without the mental scars.

There had been a service at the kirk that morning, and at the war memorial that had been unveiled two months ago in the cemetery. Thomas had been invited, along with the other men who had served, but he had declined. In September, when Brigadier General Gordon-Gilmour had arrived to unveil the memorial, Thomas had attended. It brought back too many memories. This morning, he had declined, insisting he had too many patients in need of his attention. Whether his excuse was believed or not by the local minister, no ill will would be directed towards him, though he was sure there would be disapproving comments behind his back from some. There were those who felt it was inappropriate for the local doctor to spend his evenings in the local inn. He knew his living arrangements continued to cause a stir within the close-knit, small community of Liberton.

After the Allied victory on the Hindenburg Line, Thomas returned to the place of his birth, the town of Stewarton in North Ayrshire, halfway between Kilmarnock and Glasgow, and found he could not settle back into his previous life. His parents had passed away before the war, leaving him with no close family. All that was left were empty spaces where the friends he had grown up with had once been. When he walked down the main street and was met by the cripples, widows and mothers who had lost their sons, all he felt was a void. He needed a fresh start. He sold the family home and left his practice with the elderly Doctor Ludlum, who had manned it in his absence for the duration of the war. He had thought to move to the capital city, expecting to find plenty of work and opportunity to set up another practice, but the noise and bustle of Edinburgh proved too much for his shattered nerves and he soon found himself looking for a place that combined a calmer pace of life with enough patients to run a successful practice.

One afternoon, drinking in a pub in the Old Town, down the cobbled street from the castle, he picked up a copy of *The Scotsman* that had been discarded. There he read the advert for a doctor required at short notice in the village of Liberton, three miles to the south of the city centre. The previous practitioner had not returned from the battlefields of Europe. He packed up his meagre belongings and headed south, skirting past the university and The Meadows until he reached Inch Park and joined Liberton Road, which brought him to Kirk Brae. He found lodgings for the night at the hotel on Lasswade Street and first thing the next morning knocked on the door of a small cottage opposite the church. He was offered the practice that afternoon and was soon thrust into the life of the village, occupying the rooms and clinic of the previous incumbent, who lay somewhere in an unmarked grave in France.

As he settled into his new life, he learned more about his new home. The name was derived from old English and was thought to be a contraction of 'Leper Town', named after a leper colony that had once occupied the site. That name belied the tranquillity that Thomas felt there. Monks had settled on the site as far back as the 12th century and the tower, a landmark at the foot of the

Braid Hills to the west, dated from the 15th century. Thomas had ventured out that way on many occasions, passing the grand Liberton House and the tower, to wander up the Braid Hills, from where he could look north and take in Arthur's Seat and the full skyline of Edinburgh. More recently, Liberton had become known for being a former home of Arthur Conan Doyle, who had spent his student years living in Braid Burn on the northern edge of the village. *His Last Bow* was published during the war. It detailed Sherlock Holmes's escapades against the Germans and was often mentioned by patients who learned of their new doctor's own war service.

Thomas found it helped his recovery to stay occupied, never allowing his mind to wander back to his memories of Europe. As well as running his practice, he volunteered at the local sanatorium, helping to look after less fortunate war veterans. He visited the poorhouse at Alnwickhill, next to the reservoir to the south-west, which had become the Edinburgh Industrial House for Fallen Women. Despite the attitude of the local gentry to the immorality of the women who ended up there, Thomas always found their company enjoyable and their medical needs genuine. It was there that Thomas had met Louise. He did not know exactly how she had come to be staying at the home, but she lived there and helped with the housework, the cooking, the cleaning, and caring for the disadvantaged women who arrived from the city seeking shelter. They had shared many conversations in the homely kitchen over cups of tea during his visits. Agnes, the formidable woman who ran the home, had passed away last year, another victim of the flu pandemic. After her death, the home had been closed and the building divided and converted into living quarters. Thomas overcame his own reservations and asked Louise to move into his house. She became his assistant, volunteering to help in the practice, although many patients, particularly the women who knew her past, preferred her not to be present when they visited.

She began to help out at a local school and her rehabilitation into the community took another step forward.

Thomas heard the gossip about the prostitute who lived with the doctor. He had never been confronted by anyone, but he had noticed the looks that followed him, especially when accompanied by Louise. If anyone had asked him, he would have given them an honest answer, not that it was any of their business. He and Louise were friends who lived together, but there had never been any romantic involvement. They had separate bedrooms, sharing only the living room and kitchen, and he had never questioned her in depth about her past. He did not know if she had once worked on the streets of the city, and he did not wish to know. He knew that she had a troubled past, and he suspected that she had suffered. Beyond that, he wished to know no more. He suppressed any romantic feelings towards her. She had never shown any reciprocal feelings towards him, and he was reluctant to upset the arrangement into which they had settled. They were two tortured souls who had found a measure of peace together, and for Thomas, after the horror of the war, that was enough.

Arthur appeared through the doorway at the back of the bar and nodded a good evening to Thomas, Joseph and Malachy. The Kirk Brae door opened and disturbed the smoke cloud. Robert Plenderleith, the owner of the lodge at Mount Vernon, entered. Plenderleith was a loud man, and one that Thomas was not keen to spend much time with. His entrance was Thomas's cue to head home, but only once he had finished his pint of ale.

'Evening Doctor,' Plenderleith shouted across the room to Thomas. Plenderleith was not the sort of man who needed an invitation to enter into a conversation with anyone.

'Robert,' Thomas replied, raising his glass slightly and relieved that Plenderleith didn't come and join him.

'Malachy, Joe,' Plenderleith turned to the other two men, who both nodded in return.

Thomas watched the new arrival settle his wide posterior into a stool at the bar. 'A pint, Arthur.'

'Certainly,' Arthur replied and began pouring.

Plenderleith withdrew a folded newspaper from the inside pocket of his coat and spread it across the bar. Thomas knew what was coming. It would only be a moment before a story would catch Plenderleith's eye and he would start sharing his views about it with the rest of the room. Sure enough, just as Arthur was placing a pint glass in front of him, Robert Plenderleith began giving a summary of the headlines to his captive audience.

'They've a picture of that Pankhurst woman in jail.' He took a full mouthful of beer, gave a contented sigh and wiped the froth from his mouth. 'Best place for her, and the rest of her Communist friends.' Thomas racked his memory of past Plenderleith bulletins and recalled something from a fortnight previously about the suffragette Sylvia Pankhurst being charged and jailed for encouraging workers to strike in London.

Undeterred by the lack of response from his listeners, Plenderleith took another swig of beer and continued. 'Miners are back at work too, and not before time.' He turned a page and gave a dismissive grump. 'More about the boundary expansion. Leith voted against it and still they press ahead.' The expansion of Edinburgh to include the parishes of Leith and Liberton, along with Corstorphine, Cramond and Colinton would more than double the area of the city. It was not popular among the majority of those who would suddenly find themselves living in a city instead of a suburb. Plenderleith had already exhausted his arguments against the decision on several previous evenings. He was resigned to the inevitable occurring now, as all those in Liberton were, though that wouldn't stop him returning to the subject in the future, Thomas was sure.

'Prohibition vote next month, Arthur. Will you be able to serve us water?'

Arthur had to respond to this. 'The day we Scots vote tae ban the drinking a' alcohol is the day Hell will freeze o'er.'

Plenderleith laughed, 'Don't worry, Arthur. You can rely on the vote of everyone in this room. Isn't that right, Doctor?'

Thomas raised his almost-finished glass. 'That you can, Arthur.'

Despite the Temperance Act of 1913, which allowed local districts to ban the consumption of alcohol, hardly any areas of Scotland had taken up the legislation. The stories coming across the Atlantic from America, a year into its experiment with prohibition, did little to garner enthusiasm for the cause. It seemed the prohibition of alcohol was leading to more problems instead of doing any good. Thomas wondered how he would cope in the unlikely event that his only legal comfort should become unavailable to him. He thought of the locked cabinet in his surgery back at his house. He had found himself staring at it on more than one occasion, tempted by the painkillers that would offer him a stronger dose of relief. He had resisted so far, but he was finding the volume of drink needed to settle his nerves creeping up, and if he carried on as he was, how long before he turned to something stronger?

Thomas stood and returned his empty glass to the bar. 'Another measure for the road, Arthur.'

'Richt ye are, Doctor.'

'Another bairn gone missing in the city,' remarked Plenderleith, draining the last dregs from his pint glass and passing it to Arthur for it to be refilled.

Thomas leaned over towards him and looked at the newspaper, searching for the story that had prompted this last remark. He found it halfway down the inside page, underneath an article about the impending merger of Leith with Edinburgh. The headline read: 'THIRD WOMAN CLAIMS CHILD TAKEN'. Below that, there was a smaller subheading: 'POLICE APPEAL FOR WITNESSES AT EDINBURGH POORHOUSE'.

Plenderleith noticed him leaning over his paper. 'Have a read for yourself, Doctor. I'll pay a visit to the lavatory.' He manoeuvred his large bulk down from the stool and headed through the door to the lounge, at the back of which was situated the single, newly installed flush toilet. The sound of the busier room next door, including women's laughter, amplified for a moment until the door swung closed.

Thomas turned the newspaper round and read the short article underneath the headline:

A third woman in as many weeks has reported to police that her baby has been abducted. The woman, Abigail MacPherson, known as Abi, had taken refuge in the Craigleith Poorhouse on Crewe Road to the north-west of the city, on the evening of Monday 8 November, along with her six-month-old son. The following morning, she claims, she awoke to find her baby missing. As Miss MacPherson became hysterical, the city police were called.

Miss MacPherson is the third woman to report a missing child from the poorhouses in the city. Two weeks ago, a Miss Fitzpatrick suffered a similar circumstance at the Edinburgh City Poorhouse at Craiglockhart, when her daughter disappeared. Last week, a Miss Symons reported her son missing at the Queensberry House of Refuge and Night Refuge in Canongate.

Detective Inspector McHarg, leading the investigation, briefed reporters on the details of the case at the Abbeyhill Police Station on Wednesday afternoon.

'We are treating these disappearances with all due seriousness, including the possibility that there could be a link between the three cases. At this time, we would request anyone staying at these establishments on the nights in question to come forward with any information they may have that could assist our investigations.'

Inspector McHarg went on to reject a claim from a journalist at The Herald that the initial complaints had not been taken seriously due to the lowly status of the women. Miss Fitzpatrick has already stated the police did not attach any importance to her claim when she first reported her baby missing. McHarg did, however, concede that the nature of the poorhouses, with their transitory inhabitants and poor record-keeping, meant it had been difficult to determine exactly who had been staying in the establishments on the nights in question.

'It has been difficult to establish whether these women, who suffer from many problems, including alcoholism and mental delusions, did indeed have children in their care when they entered the establishments in question. Now that we see a pattern emerging that causes us some concern, we are giving this matter our full attention.'

The areas around each of the poorhouses have been searched by the police, but no evidence or clues as to the whereabouts of the missing children has so far been found. The investigation continues.

The article ended with a telephone number for people to call with any information. As Thomas reached the end, Plenderleith returned through the lounge door and retook his seat at the bar. Thomas turned the newspaper back to him. He glanced at the article Thomas had just read.

'It'll be another Jessie King; you mark my words.'

'Pardon?' Thomas asked.

'The baby farmer. You might not be old enough to remember. The woman who killed babies that she was meant to be looking after. Over in Stockbridge.'

A vague memory stirred in Thomas's mind. It had been a scandal in Edinburgh. A woman called Jessie King, known as a 'baby farmer', who took unwanted newborns from their mothers to care for them or to find them new homes with families who wanted children, had instead been murdering the babies. Baby farmers had been known to take children from the poorhouses from women in poverty in order to sell them to those willing to pay for a child. An investigation had shown that many children were murdered by those that were meant to care for them. The practice had effectively been ended at the turn of the century when new legislation had been brought in to protect these vulnerable children.

'Last woman to be hanged in the city,' Plenderleith continued. 'Mark my words, this'll be something similar.'

'You think someone has taken these infants in order to sell them to other families?'

'Wealthy people who can't conceive, perhaps. Rich folk think they can buy anything, even families.'

'There are plenty of orphans in need of a good home, there's no need to steal children from their mothers.'

Plenderleith shrugged, 'Orphans come with a certain stigma though, don't they. It's that or some lunatic killing them for fun. Probably one of those traumatised chaps back from the war.' He paused, then added, 'No offence.'

Thomas knew it was not worth arguing with a man like Plenderleith and politely said no offence had been taken. 'Let's hope they are found safe and well,' he said, while picking up his coat and putting it on. 'Goodnight, Arthur. Gentlemen.'

'Doctor,' Joseph replied from the window seat.

Thomas stepped out the door into the fresh chill air of the November evening. Plenderleith's conversation had riled him. The people of the village would pay little attention to missing children in the city. Despite being incorporated into Edinburgh, Liberton was still a world away from the big city it was now attached to, and the bustle and lack of morality that festered there. The locals, many of whom still carried an air of superiority around with them, would resist being pulled into the gutter of the urban sprawl for as long as they could. He walked along the pavement and crossed the road towards his home. Out of nowhere, an automobile roared through the junction and sped past him, causing Thomas to jump back to safety. The modern internal combustion engine vehicles still took some getting used to. Thomas found their loud noise unsettling.

When the engines misfired and let out a sharp crack, it took him back to the gunfire of the trenches and the terror that came with those memories.

He made his way up the short path to the front of the house. The door was unlocked. In the hallway, he took off his coat and hung it on the coat stand. To the left was the small waiting room and office where he saw patients. On the opposite side was the living room. He looked in and saw the fire had burned down to a few glowing embers. There was no noise in the house. It was Louise's habit to retire to her bedroom at an early hour. At the end of the hallway were three doors, one that led to the small kitchen and beyond the small back yard and outdoor toilet. The other two doors led to bedrooms at either side of the rear of the house. Through the small gap at the bottom of the door to Louise's room, he saw the orange glow from the oil lamp that would be flickering on her bedside table. She would be sitting reading in bed, or perhaps had already drifted off to sleep. He stopped and listened. He could hear her faint, regular breaths. She was asleep. He knew better than to enter to extinguish the oil lamp. Louise never slept through the night. She would wake later and turn the lamp out herself. Thomas had heard her disturbances during the night. He never pried into what made her dreams so unsettled.

He turned away and entered his own bedroom, feeling his way around the familiar furniture in the darkness. He undressed and slipped under the covers. Sleep would not come immediately. He lay in the quiet stillness and let his nightmares overtake him.

2

TUESDAY, 16 NOVEMBER

1920

She added a final dab of the powder to her cheek, covering up the blemishes on her skin. She took in her reflection in the mirror. She sat up, straightening her spine, pushing her shoulders back, turning her head to the side. She could still not get used to this new image of herself, the fuller cheeks and chin, the rounder shoulders. Ever since she had left home as a girl, she had been rake thin. Her reflection smiled back at her. She preferred her healthier, rounder face to the angular, emaciated ghost she had once been. The powdered make-up helped too, hiding the marks that the hard years had imprinted, adding colour to her pale complexion.

Louise picked up her hairbrush and combed out her long, black hair. That had changed too, shinier and fuller than it had once been. She enjoyed the smooth feel of it running through her fingers, appreciating the cleanliness and softness of it. It took her back to childhood and the smell of the soap and her mother's hands rubbing her scalp while she sat in the warm bath water. That memory remained ingrained within her, a bittersweet reminder of what she had once had. She wondered about her mother. Was she still alive? Did she ever think about the daughter she had lost? Had she ever tried to search for her? Louise felt no inclination to find her parents. They were part of a past life she did not want to revisit. The worry that her past may somehow catch up with her, that she would be returned to it, still lingered.

This morning was not a time to revisit those worries. She tied her hair into a loose bun and pinned it into place. She picked up the dark skirt from the bed where she had laid it out and stepped into it and pulled it up to cover her stockings. She pulled a dark blouse over her slip, buttoning the high neckline all the way to the top. She looked once more in the mirror. She had thought she would never know happiness like her childhood in this world again, but she could admit that, at this moment, she was content.

She picked up her gloves and bag from the dressing table and left her bedroom. In the hallway, she could smell fried bacon and eggs coming from the kitchen. She couldn't stomach the heavy breakfast Thomas always insisted upon. Her stomach, after years of undernourishment, could not cope with a full plate of stodgy food. She opened the door and saw him at the stove, with his back to her, in his shirt and braces.

He turned as she entered. 'Toast'll be two minutes, just turned it over.'

'Thank you.' She took a seat at the small table and saw that he had already poured her a cup of tea. This was their morning routine. He knew she liked just a slice of toast with butter and a piece of fruit. Then he would sit opposite her and eat, with only the occasional remark about the day ahead. Content, she thought once again, they were content. She watched him as he sat at the table. He was ten years older than her, in his early forties. His black hair was thinning and greying, adding a distinguished air to his appearance. His blue eyes were kind, but she often noticed the haunted look that would pass over them. She knew it was the war.

She knew not to ask him about it. He knew she had a troubled past of her own and never asked her to tell him what happened to her before she ended up in the House for Fallen Women. It was a mutual understanding that suited them both. She knew that he drank in the evenings, sometimes too much, but unlike other men she had known, when he drank, he became quiet and insulated rather than angry or violent. If he needed to drown his memories, then it would not be her that told him to stop. She only hoped he was not harming himself. In the year since he had met her in the House, she had grown to care for him greatly. When he had first suggested she move in with him, she had been reluctant. Men had been the source of all the trouble she had faced in her life, and few of them had ever shown her true kindness. But practicality outweighed doubt. Agnes had passed away and the House for Fallen Women was to be closed. All that was offered to the women staying in the house was a bed in another of the poorhouses in the city. Louise knew she could not return to that way of life, so when the doctor offered her a room and board, she had little option but to accept. She was thankful that, for once, her decision had proved to be a good one. Some would no doubt frown upon their living arrangement without knowing the truth about their situation. Thomas had never shown her anything but kindness and politeness. He had never shown any intention towards her other than friendship. Once she had settled into her bedroom, he had never suggested the arrangement should change. He had never made an unwelcome advance upon her. He seemed to understand that she was fragile, without needing to know why that should be. He had heard her disturbed sleep during the nights and had asked if she was okay, but he never pressed her for more detail. She may have called out names and words that made him wonder what had happened to her, but the next morning he never questioned her. For her part, she had heard his nightmares from across the hallway. She had heard him stumble in drunk from the pub in the evening.

She had heard the crying in the night. Enough stories had been told, enough people in the village had lost sons and husbands, for Louise to form an understanding of his suffering.

She found herself staring across the table at him as he read the morning newspaper and ate his breakfast. Could there ever be more than friendship between them? That would require them both to open up about their pasts, lay bare the full details of their lives. Would any relationship be able to survive that? It was safer to carry on as they were.

Thomas noticed her looking at him. 'Everything okay?' he asked, swallowing a piece of bacon.

Louise shook her head. 'Sorry, I was miles away.'

'School today as normal?'

'Yes, I'd better get a move on.'

'I'll be back late, I imagine.'

'Do take care. I worry this might be too much for you.'

'It does me good to talk to those that went through the same things I did. They understand me as much as I understand them. And it feels like I'm helping. Making some sort of difference.'

Each Tuesday, Thomas volunteered at a clinic for soldiers who had returned from the war. Although he helped as best he could with the physical injuries that these men had sustained – scarring, burns, amputations – it was the mental trauma that he was keen to explore and understand. He had told her about the men he had seen so far, how he recognised similar symptoms to his own: the involuntary shaking, the frayed nerves, the fear of loud noises and busy places, the reliance on alcohol and other drugs to calm those symptoms. 'It's something that needs to be investigated more,' he told her. 'It needs to be recognised as a condition. These men can't simply be left to carry on as though everything is normal after everything they have been through. We can't expect them to just go back to an ordinary life, with those mental scars to carry with them.' Although he was talking about the veterans of the war he had seen at the clinic, she knew he was also referring to his own experience.

'Of course. Just promise me you won't forget to look after yourself as well.'

She pulled her shawl together across her chest as she walked along Kirkgate. At the junction, she looked across at St Hilda's School for Girls, further along Kirk Brae with its dormer windows, the multiple chimney stacks and twin spires, one topped with a weathervane that was still on this November morning. When she had decided to look into helping out in a local school, she had first applied to the boarding school for girls run by Mrs Rosa Brodie. Louise was told in no uncertain terms that a woman with her background would not be allowed to corrupt the young, respectable girls of St Hilda's. Her past at the House for Fallen Women preceded her. What would the parents say if they found out the new teaching assistant was once a woman of the street? Redemption was apparently not part of the curriculum that Mrs Brodie taught.

Louise turned her back on Mrs Brodie and walked down Lasswade Street, past the farmhouse and Liberton Cottage and turned up the tree-lined path that led to the grand building that housed the Edinburgh Original Industrial School for Boys. Mr Alex Russel, the superintendent in charge, was less disposed to worry about who the local gossips deemed suitable to teach the neglected boys of the boarding school. The boys were vagrants or came from impoverished homes and had been taken into care by the local authorities. Already corrupted in their youth, they could not learn any new sins from, or be shocked by, Louise's past. She belonged with them.

The path was covered by a carpet of crisp yellow-orange leaves. The ash, elm and oak trees stood naked, their exposed branches reaching into the grey sky. The main entrance of the school was on the south side of the building, a tall three-storey sandstone edifice with a steep, slanting black slate roof, punctuated by windows that looked onto the large green fields of farmland beyond. Inside, the school formed a square, with buildings running along all four sides and a central courtyard used for outdoor activities. The buildings on the north and east sides of the square housed the dormitories and washrooms, while the large building to the south was split into the various classrooms and workrooms of the school. The north-west corner was the preserve of the school matron, Mrs Henderson. It was to her that Louise reported at the start of each day. Mrs Henderson ensured the clockwork running of the school kitchens and laundry, and delegated work to the cleaning staff. She shared the space with Mr Tod, the school janitor. Unlike Mrs Henderson, Mr Tod was genial and good-natured and had a laid-back attitude towards the discipline of the boys, treating them as friends with whom he could share a joke. Mrs Henderson brooked no such latitude and was strict with her young charges, though Louise knew that she cared deeply for each of them as if they were her own children. In her time assisting at the school, Louise, too, had come to care for the boys. She recognised their unfortunate plight, although they were younger than she had been when she found herself homeless and penniless. Their ages ranged from only five or six years old to teenagers who had been boarding at the school for as long as they could remember. Louise had benefited from her parent's love and care while she was young. Only later did she face the hardships that the boys of the Industrial School faced up to from the start of their lives. She had started to recognise a few of the faces and learn their names. Like any children, they were wild and boisterous when left to their own devices, but under the watchful eyes of the teaching staff they had learned to behave.

Breakfast time was just ending in the dining room when Louise entered the front door and the boys were walking in an orderly line along the corridor to their classrooms. She greeted them with a polite 'good morning' as they passed. She was still unused to being referred to as 'Miss Stuart' by those who returned her greetings. Some of them, particularly the older boys, were self-conscious and turned their eyes away as they passed. Louise was aware that women of her age were not common in their lives. Mrs Henderson was in her sixties, the school cook was rarely seen, and the only female teacher at the school, Madame Prentice, was unattractive and dour. There were two young girls, Betsy and Florence, who lived in the staff quarters and comprised Mrs Henderson's staff. They were under Mrs Henderson's supervision at all times and were never left alone with any of the young pupils. Most of the adults the boys knew were strict and serious men. Like the jovial Mr Tod, in Miss Stuart they recognised a kinder adult who they could relate to as someone other than a teacher or master. And she had a mysterious past, with rumours swirling round the dorms at bedtime about the debauched and illicit life she had led before arriving at the school.

The noise of youthful chatter faded as classroom doors were closed and lessons began. Louise found Mrs Henderson supervising the post-breakfast clear-up in the dining hall, checking the tables after Florence had wiped them clean, while Betsy piled empty plates onto a trolley and wheeled them away to the kitchen.

'Good morning, Miss Stuart.'

'Mrs Henderson.'

'Laundry first thing for you. Linen needs folding and then bedsheets changed in the east wing dorms.'

At this time in the morning Mrs Henderson was all business. Louise knew it was not a sign of intolerance towards her. Later on, after the lunchtime rush, there would be time to talk, as they took their allotted tea break around the table in the back of the kitchen. It was Mrs Henderson who had helped to secure Louise's position at the school. She was a patient of Thomas's. At an appointment a few months ago, she had complained of an aching back. Thomas had prescribed a remedy to help and suggested that it was time for her to take on less work around the school. She was after all, he delicately put it, not getting any younger. Rest was what her aching back needed. Mrs Henderson thought this quite impossible. Who else could ensure the smooth running of the school? It couldn't be left to Betsy and Florence, mere lassies still learning what was required to keep a house in order. It was then that Louise had seized her opportunity.

'I could help out two or three days a week,' she suggested as she caught the end of the conversation between doctor and patient.

Mrs Henderson eyed her up as if noticing her for the first time. She was aware of Louise's past, but unlike others in the village, particularly as she worked with boys who came from a similarly unfortunate background, she believed people deserved a chance. 'Would the doctor be able to spare you?' She directed this to Thomas rather than Louise.

'I think it would be a marvellous idea. I'm not seeing patients here on Tuesdays and Thursdays, so Miss Stuart would be free.' Thomas could tell Louise was excited about the opportunity that had presented itself.

'It would be unpaid, you understand? The school has little enough funds to run on as it is.'

'That's quite acceptable. I would be glad to lend a hand, for the sake of your back if nothing else.'

Mrs Henderson smiled at this. 'Very well. Let me raise the matter with Mr Russel. It will be his decision.'

A fortnight later, a month after being turned down by Mrs Brodie at St Hilda's, Louise began working at the school every Tuesday and Thursday. Soon she was taking on extra days when Mrs Henderson required her, and when Thomas was able to spare her from the practice. Mr Russel had welcomed her without a mention of her past. If Mrs Henderson asked for something from the superintendent, evidently, he was inclined to let her have her way. She started with menial tasks, helping Betsy and Florence with the cleaning and laundry duties and mopping the floors. It was the same work she had done for Agnes in the House for Fallen Women, only on a larger scale. There were around two hundred boys staying in the boarding rooms, all needing to be fed, cleaned and educated, as well as those with behavioural issues that required extra care. Many had never attended school until arriving in Liberton and it took time for them to adjust. Mr Russel believed that no boy was born bad, and no boy was beyond redemption if taught correctly. He instilled this spirit in his staff. A problem child was a child in need of a solution that worked for them. Of course, he and his teachers were not afraid of handing out a punishment if it was deserved. Mr Russel's willow cane was feared by all the boys, but Louise knew he only used it as a last resort.

Treating the boys as individuals was a labour-intensive solution. If a delinquent required extra tuition and guidance, then that was what Mr Russel endeavoured to provide. It wasn't long before the superintendent was enquiring about Louise's education. She could write, she could read, and she could do arithmetic to a satisfactory level. If Mrs Henderson would allow it, could she be spared to take on some teaching duties with small groups of boys? Soon, Louise was taking groups of four or five of the youngest children and teaching them basic spelling and sums. Mr Russel kept a close eye on her until he was satisfied she wasn't corrupting their young minds. While Louise looked forward to the straightforward hard work of the tasks set by Mrs Henderson, it was the time with the boys that she valued the most. Though she never admitted it to anyone, she got as much from the boys as they got from her.

Louise never divulged to anyone the reason she was keen to work with children. In careless moments, she would find herself staring at the older boys, those of sixteen or seventeen years of age. That would have been his age now, if he had lived. What would he have been like if he had survived those early years? Would he have been as boisterous as these boys? Or would he have been a quiet and studious young man, a serious man intent on making his way in the world? She could only speculate, and her daydreams left her despondent. He had never had the chance to learn, to experience life, to discover what sort of person he would become. She still blamed herself. If only she had found an establishment like this Industrial School, she would have given him up if it meant he could have lived. But she was young and helpless at the time, lost and alone in a cruel world with no one and nowhere to turn. Mrs Henderson had found her on more than one occasion staring at a group of boys as they played football on the school playing field, or laughed and shouted their way along the corridor. Had she spotted the tear tracing its way down Louise's cheek? If she had, she made no mention of it.

There was another side to her darker thoughts. These sixteen- and seventeen-year-olds were the same age as she had been when she had been taken advantage of by a boy just like them. She hoped these boys had been taught to behave differently towards girls of their own age. She did not wish anyone to go through what she had.

She spent the first hour of the day in the laundry room, folding the freshly cleaned bedsheets into neat piles and stacking them into the large linen cupboard. She luxuriated in the fresh soap smell of the sheets. Having worked her way through the stack, she piled some onto a wooden trolley and wheeled it along to the dormitories. With so many beds to service, it was a never-ending task to maintain hygiene standards within the bedrooms. Today, it was the older boys who were due fresh linen and Louise spent the rest of the morning making bed after bed, wheeling the trolley back and forth along the wooden floored corridor to collect more sheets. It was no surprise that Mrs Henderson, approaching her twilight years, had suffered aches and pains from the work. As lunchtime approached, she was able to admire a job well done. She returned the trolley to the laundry room just as the bell rang out.

Two hundred hungry, growing boys spilled out of the classrooms and workrooms and converged on the dinner hall. Florence and Betsy had set the places for the midday meal, and Louise now joined them in serving the cook's best effort at vegetable broth soup. Mrs Henderson kept a watchful eye, occasionally barking a reprimand across the hall at a boy who had dared to speak above the acceptable volume. Before the last boy had finished being served, those that had been first in the queue were finishing up and exiting the room. As quickly as they had descended like a plague of hungry locusts, they stripped the hall of all sustenance and flew on. They now enjoyed half an hour of free time in the courtyard that served as a playground. The teachers spent their lunch hour in the staff room, recharging themselves for the afternoon lessons. Only once the lunch dishes had been collected, cleaned and dried, and the tables wiped down and set for the dinner meal to come did Mrs Henderson and her staff get their own break, if time allowed.

They sat around the small table in the back of the kitchen, enjoying their own serving of soup. Florence and Betsy sat together at one end and, as always, spoke to each other in hushed voices, sharing private conversations that always saw them break into giggles and earn a rebuke from Mrs Henderson. If there was nothing that needed urgently mending or cleaned or built around the school, Mr Tod would join them. Louise enjoyed the days when he did. His cheerful gossip lightened the mood, and Mrs Henderson loosened up in his presence, allowing him to entertain them with stories that she would not allow the girls to hear under other circumstances. He would often bring a newspaper with him and comment on the stories of the day, be they politics or world events or sports. Today, he joined them without a newspaper, but with local news that left them in a state of shock. He had been into the village that morning, stopping at the ironmongers. There he had heard the alarming news, which he now related to them across the table.

'Ye've heard aboot the missin' bairns in the city?'

'Only what has been printed in your newspaper,' replied Mrs Henderson.

'Ha' they foun' the children?' Betsy asked.

'No' yet, but ah git talkin' tae Charlie Speedy, he wis in the shop at the same time as me, an' he hid bin speakin' tae Andy Torrance, who is friends wi' Constable Inch, an' Constable Inch telt him that the polis are comin' tae Liberton tae start a search here.'

'What on earth for?' asked Mrs Henderson.

'Inch thinks they must ha' a guid reason. Some sort a' tip aff that the missin' bairns might be here.'

Mrs Henderson tutted, 'I know we are part of the city now, but I think the people of Liberton would still be aware if small children had appeared from nowhere and started living in the village.'

Mr Tod raised his hands in defence. 'Ah'm jist repeatin' whit ah heard. Inch said they will arrive the day an' start searchin' properties an' the fields roun'aboot.'

'It wouldn't be the first time Constable Inch got a hold of the wrong end of the stick.'

Louise and Mr Tod shared a half-smile across the table. Constable Philip Inch was a genial man, and well liked around Liberton, but he was not regarded as having the sharpest investigative mind on the city force. When he had first taken the role of local constable, there had been only a handful of houses in Liberton for him to look after, and Sherlock Holmes had yet to be born. The role of an officer of the law had changed a lot in thirty years, and Philip Inch had resisted much of that change. Most of the locals were thankful for that. The encroachment of the city into their neighbourhood would inevitably mean the end of Constable Inch and younger officers would replace him.

After clearing away their own dishes, they went their separate ways. Louise had an hour of teaching the young boys that afternoon and she made her way along the corridor to the east wing. She tried not to think of Mr Tod's news. She had kept an eye on the newspapers since the story about the children disappearing from the city poorhouses had broken. It brought her own painful past to the fore, not just her own time in the poorhouses of Edinburgh, but of her own lost child. She prayed that the missing children had not suffered the same terrible fate.

Arriving at the door to the classroom, she gathered herself and fixed a bright smile on her face before turning the handle and swinging the door open.

'Right, boys. Good afternoon. How are we all today? Ready to learn our three times table, I hope?'

She was met with eager smiles. The dark past was pushed back into the deep recesses of her memory.

3

TUESDAY, 16 NOVEMBER

1920

Thomas left the house that morning and headed west, along Kirk Brae. It would take him an hour to walk to Craiglockhart, on the other side of the Braid Hills. He took the path which went past Liberton House and through Upper Liberton. At Liberton Tower, he took the fork in the road that slanted to the north and passed the hills to the south. The sun beating down provided warmth to counter the chill of a fresh breeze. The morning frost was melting in the fields, coating everything with a damp carpet. Beyond the old quarry he skirted the edge of the golf course, and was soon going through the built-up area of Greenbank. He crossed the Braid Burn. On the other side loomed the City Hospital, beyond a lawn of green grass, a square and solid building, three-storeys high, with central and corner towers. Beyond the main entrance and reception block lay a network of connected wards and corridors.

As Thomas crossed the front lawn, he glanced to his right, across the road, where the City Poorhouse was located. Also built of sandstone brick, it was smaller than the hospital, adorned with decorative turrets. It was from here that one of the missing children had disappeared. He had expected to see some sign as he passed – a police car outside, a detective inspector making enquiries, a constable posted at the entrance – but there was nothing. It looked the same as it had done a week ago.

The City Hospital, prior to the war, was run by the Craiglockhart Hydropathic Company, providing hydrotherapy to treat a range of maladies with alternative water treatments and offering Turkish baths and massages, alongside facilities for tennis, fine dining, billiards and evening entertainment. In 1916, while Thomas was on the battlefields of Europe, it was commandeered and turned into a military hospital for the treatment of officers suffering from shell shock. The war poets Seigfried Sassoon and Wilfred Owen were treated there. It was Sassoon who had christened the institute 'Dottyville'. When Thomas arrived in Liberton, the war hospital was being wound down. He had heard of Doctor W. H. R. Rivers who had led the study of war psychoneuroses, establishing shell shock as a mental illness that could affect physical ability. Rivers established the principle that brave men could suffer from overwhelming fear during battle. He was also among the first psychologists to adhere to the principle of a 'talking cure' to overcome the neuroses caused by war. Thomas, fresh from his own experience of the war, visited the hospital determined to learn more about the mental issues suffered by veterans, but his plans were scuppered by the winding down of the hospital in 1919. Doctor Rivers had already moved on, returning to England and moving away from his psychology research and into politics. The building had been purchased by the Society of the Sacred Heart, a Catholic organisation, with the intention of using Craiglockhart as a convent and school. However, while the conversion was taking place, it had been agreed to allow one wing of the sprawling building to continue being used to treat veterans.

Those that remained welcomed Thomas's help. He hid his own war trauma from them. Every Tuesday, he made the hour-long walk to Craiglockhart. He listened to the men who were willing to talk and heard their stories of triumph, loss, fear, bravery, cowardice and regret. The remaining staff, led by a young doctor named MacMyn, valued Thomas's first-hand experience of the front line. If they noticed the dark shadow that sometimes crept across his eyes, no one mentioned it. The policy was to let men open up when they were ready to, and Thomas was not yet ready. He doubted he ever would be. With the patients though, his fellow soldiers, he was able to share his recollections of the war and the desperation he had felt in the field hospitals. The men recognised a kindred spirit, someone who could understand what they were going through, who could empathise with them. Thomas discovered he was far from alone in his reliance on alcohol, but he kept his indiscretion secret. These voluntary sessions became his own therapy as he got to know fellow survivors.

A distant church bell was striking nine o'clock as he climbed the stairs leading to the entrance of the main building. Along the corridors, workmen bustled to and fro, continuing the work of turning the hospital into a building suitable for teaching and religious worship. They were a reminder that the psychotherapy unit would soon close. He forced himself to raise his spirits. Those worries were for another day. It helped to start a session with a clear mind, and to give himself fully to the moment being shared by his patients. If they sensed his mind was elsewhere, they would close themselves off, locking their trauma inside.

He had his own room in which to see patients. It was small with basic furniture – a plain desk, a bookcase with medical texts on the shelves, two worn armchairs and a couch. A fresh jug of milk and a plate of biscuits were already on the table, left by Nurse MacKay that morning, along with clean cutlery and mugs. He removed his coat and set out a notepad and pen. Nurse MacKay chapped on the door, punctual as ever, at precisely quarter past nine. She was dressed in her crisp uniform, with her blonde hair tied in a tight bun. She gave Thomas a list of his appointments.

'Private Watt?' Thomas asked, reading the unfamiliar name. It was unusual for someone with the rank of private to be seen. The hospital had existed to serve officers rather than the rank and file.

'He requested you specifically. I thought perhaps you knew him?'

Thomas shook his head. He could not recall anyone called Watt, but that didn't necessarily mean their paths hadn't crossed in the confusion of the battlefield. He had treated hundreds of soldiers; it was possible one of them would remember him, and equally that he had failed to remember them.

The other names on the list, spread out at hour-long intervals, were all familiar to him from previous sessions. Nurse MacKay brought in a boiling kettle and set it down on the side table. 'Shall I bring in Captain Murray? He arrived at nine sharp. He seems a little agitated this morning.'

'Please,' Thomas answered. Captain Murray had been there the first day Thomas had volunteered at the hospital. They had gone over his war experience every Tuesday since. Thomas knew every trauma the Captain had endured. Their sessions started with the Captain experiencing an attack of nerves. After an hour with Thomas, he calmed down, but there was no sign that his condition was improving despite the progress during the sessions. The day they continually returned to was the 1 July, 1916, the opening day of the Battle of the Somme. Captain Murray was due to lead his men out of the trenches in the first wave of attacks by the British Fourth Army. But Captain Murray had suffered the misfortune of being struck by a bullet in the shoulder the day before while scouting enemy positions. While his men led the charge, he was laid up in the infirmary. None of his unit returned alive. The guilt the Captain felt about deserting his men lived with him through the rest of the war. Murray saw it as cowardice. His punishment was to go on living when he should have been dead. No matter how reckless his behaviour after that, he survived the war as others fell around him. He did not see himself as blessed or chosen. He saw it as a dereliction of his duty. He wished to die and be reunited with his unit in the mass graves in the countryside. Why should he have returned home when his comrades did not? He had no family to return to, no wife or children. Men with families had died; why had he not been sacrificed instead?

After Captain Murray had left, promising this time he would not let the depression overwhelm him once again, Thomas saw Major Deakins. Deakins's appointments followed the opposite trajectory of Captain Murray's, beginning in a jocular tone, before the dark clouds of war gathered. Thomas always felt low at the end of their conversations and worried what the Major might do once he had left the hospital. He could only hope that the 'talking cure' was having a positive effect overall. It was a terrible burden to live with, having ordered so many men to their deaths, seeing so many young lives lost in an orgy of violence. Many of the officers pointed to the futility of the trench war. They knew they had a duty to fulfil, they knew the Germans needed to be confronted and stopped, but the constant fighting over inches of ground had become so pointless. There was no logic to the tidal wave of death that achieved nothing. The officers knew it would achieve nothing, yet they still sent men to their deaths. The scars that war had left were deeply ingrained in those that returned.

At midday, Thomas ate a sandwich and scribbled notes on his morning sessions for Nurse MacKay, who would type them up and file them. He took a stroll around the grounds of the hospital to take in some fresh air. He had his own feelings to process after another morning reliving stories of the war that he was still incapable of forgetting or confronting. No matter who he had seen or which stories he heard, Thomas always returned to the same experience. He could suppress the memory when he was occupied with patients, but his mind always turned back to it.

It was the 16 November, 1916, four years ago to the day. The Somme offensive had been raging for four and a half months and was nearing an end. Two days later, General Haig would call a halt to the endeavour, which had failed to make the breakthrough that the Allies had desired. Arguments would rage for years to come about the success or failure of the offensive, but the Battle of the Somme laid bare the futility of the war. Over 300,000 men had died, half among the Allies, half among the Germans. There were more than a million casualties. The slaughter of untold magnitude led, after all that effort and sacrifice, to a meagre seven-mile advancement of the Allied line.

Thomas had been there from the beginning with the Royal Army Medical Corps. The field hospital, designed to be mobile to follow the advancing front line, had become a camp, stagnating in the same muddy field for the duration of the offensive. When the Battle of the Somme had begun, Thomas had been assigned to help those with minor injuries, fatigue and illness. As the full scale of the slaughter began to unfold, he was drafted into the makeshift operating theatres, assisting surgeons with trauma injuries: amputations, gunshot wounds and shrapnel injuries from the tens of millions of shells launched into the trenches and no man's land. As the numbers of casualties grew, the need for more surgeons became desperate and Thomas, a general practitioner, found himself performing emergency surgery by gaslight. He knew a qualified surgeon would have saved some of the men who had died under his hand on the operating table, which was no more than a plank resting on wooden stilts. He knew he was out of his depth, but any concerns he had were brushed aside. Everyone was being forced to do things they wouldn't normally do. Everyone had to do the best they could. If he was no use here, his commanding officer told him, then he could report to the front line and make himself useful there instead.

He soldiered on, improving his knowledge when he could, asking questions about techniques when the surgeons were not elbow-deep in blood. By November, he believed himself to be a competent trauma surgeon. The men who died in front of him now could not have been saved by another surgeon in the field hospital. While never completely inured to the horror that presented itself on a daily basis, he accepted the role into which he had been forced. It was his job now, his duty, his contribution to the effort. He had lost count of how many patients he had seen, of how many had lived and how many had died, but he was sure he had managed to save some. He never asked what had become of the men whom he treated. Some were bandaged up and sent back to the front line, some would never see active service again, and were grateful to be shipped home. Some would die later, lying in the middle of a crowded tent, surrounded by the dying and wounded. The only way to cope was to not think about what happened before or after the soldiers ended up in front of him. He could only control what happened to them in the moment they were under his care, and he strived to do the best for every man who crossed his table. To survive, he had to shut down his own feelings about the men that he met. He would let them talk, scream, rant in delirium at him and he would soothe them with platitudes, concentrating on nothing except doing his job.

On that morning, the 16 November, rumours had begun to circulate that the offensive would soon be halted. The weather had turned again. Another winter in the rain and mud around the commune of Albert beckoned. There was a sharp frost in the air after a clear night, but the gathering grey clouds promised rain. The shelling was sporadic now, unlike the bombardments of the previous months. The effects of the falling bombs were no less violent. Thomas had just arrived at the surgical tent when the first casualties of the day were wheeled in on a string of horse-drawn carts. He watched, taking in the fresh air while he had the chance, as the stretcher bearers jumped into action and began distributing their load. Those left on the carts until the end would go to the temporary morgue. Two bearers carrying a stretcher headed in Thomas's direction. He took a stiff swig from the medicinal alcohol bottle in his hand and stepped inside the tent. His instruments had been laid out in readiness, gleaming in the sunlight that came through the tied-up sides of the tent. Soon they would be coated in blood. He smelled the spirits, the canvas, the fresh earth – the scents that would soon be swamped by the guts and burnt flesh and faecal matter and urine. He nodded to his assistants, already wearing their masks and gowns. They had long ago run out of medical gloves to protect their hands. He pulled his own mask on and tied it behind his head and doused his hands in surgical spirits and wiped them dry.

'Good luck, gentlemen. Let us do our best.' They knew they would not save everyone who landed in front of them that day. Their best effort was all they could promise.

The stretcher bearers burst through the entrance and dropped a soldier onto the table without ceremony. Thomas knew not to admonish them. There was no time for argument and nothing he said would change the pace at which the bearers had to work.

'Morphine,' Thomas ordered. An assistant picked up a syringe and injected the painkiller. 'Try to lie still. Let me have a look at you.' The squirming boy stopped moving, though he still kept his arms wrapped across his midriff. He could have been no older than sixteen. He was definitely not eighteen, the minimum age of conscription. He was covered in mud and debris, kicked up from the ground as a shell had landed close to him. Thomas peeled away his tattered uniform shirt while others pulled off his boots and cut away his trousers. He still had all his limbs. That was a blessing in itself. As he tried to cut the remains of the shirt away, Thomas asked him to unfold his arms.

'Ah cannae,' his terrified voice screamed in reply.

'I need to have a look at you.'

'They telt me tae haud oan tight. Tae haud masel' taegether.'

Thomas heard his Ayrshire accent. 'You can let go now, we'll put you back together, son.' The boy screamed again as another surge of pain ran through his crippled body. Thomas could see blood pouring from somewhere under the shirt. He turned to his assistants. 'Take his arms and hold him down.'

They prised the clenched arms away from the soldier's stomach. Blood spurted upwards, a fountain erupting high enough to leave spray on the tent roof. Thomas clamped his hands over the wound, but as he did so, his heart sank. He was not pressing against skin. The intestines of the boy slithered out from the gaping hole in his abdomen. Another assistant tried to wipe some of the blood away to let them see the damage. Thomas already knew this was a lost cause. 'More morphine,' he shouted. All they could do was make the poor soul comfortable until his life drained away. He saw white specks of fractured and shattered ribs at the base of the exposed rib cage. Something glinted, a metal shard embedded in the gut. He could only see the tip of it, but he guessed there was more buried deep inside, like the tip of an iceberg hinting at the monstrosity that lay beneath the surface. A Voluntary Aid Detachment Nurse had appeared at the boy's side. She wiped his face clean with a damp cloth and whispered comforting words into his ear, holding one of his hands tightly. Thomas watched them. He wondered if this was the youngest soldier he had lost in the war. He took the boy's other hand, which was now lying limp by his side on the table.

'Please, Tam, dae somethin'.' His voice was weak now. The morphine was taking effect as blood and life drained from him. 'Tam, will ye tell ma da ah did ma best.'

Recognition came over him like waking slowly from a nightmare, a gradual creeping horror. He looked at the boy's face, the boy who knew his name. His hair was fiery red, the skin pale and freckled, the eyes, dulling as drugs and injury took effect, were pale blue. Thomas knew the face. It belonged to a fourteen-year-old boy in Stewarton. A patient at his practice. The name came to him. James Napier. The father, also James, was a miner prone to lung infections. The mother, Kathleen, had brought her young boy in with various coughs and colds and cuts. The same young boy who now lay in pieces, dying, in front of him.

'Why are ye no' dain' anythin', Doctor Stevenson?' the boy pleaded with him.

'James, what are you doing here?' Later, he thought how stupid that question was. No answer came from young James Napier. He was not alone in lying about his age in order to fight the Germans. Back home, away from the horror, young men thought there was something heroic about the whole sorry mess. The futility of it only hit them when it was too late, when they were already on the front line.

The nurse was looking up at him now, her eyes wide. 'You know him?' It was bound to happen. Thomas wasn't the only one to have found a familiar face from home alongside him on the frontline. Men from Ayrshire, and all across the central belt of Scotland, had been conscripted in vast numbers. It was only a matter of time. But why now, when the offensive was to be stopped and the war paused? And why him, a young boy with his whole adult life ahead of him? A memory flashed through Thomas's mind. A dressing applied to a skint knee, a stethoscope pressed against a frail back and the metronomic beat of a young, healthy heart.

'We have to save him,' he said, looking at the nurse. No one reacted. He shouted it again. 'We have to save him. Not this one, not this boy.' He sprang forward, dropping James's unresponsive hand. He grabbed the intestines and started pushing them back into the cavity of his abdomen. His hands were covered in the fluid and blood of the boy's insides. He tried to fold him back together. 'Help me.' He pleaded with the staff standing around the table. They watched him, unmoving and unsure. 'Do something.' He grabbed a scalpel. The shard of metal still stuck out from James's inside. He had to get it out. He had nurtured this boy, ensured he had grown up safely. For what? To die, scared and alone in this bloody pointless war? He wouldn't allow it to happen. He cut around the edges of the metal, prising it out. But it kept coming. It was not a small piece of shrapnel. It was an entire section of a shell casing, buried deep, angling up from the abdomen where it had entered and caused such devastation. It had gone through his ribs, and a lung, and the veins around his heart. The metal pulled clear. Thomas staggered backwards. 'It's out,' he cried, 'stitch him up, quickly, before he loses too much blood.'

Nobody moved.

'Fine, I'll do it,' he stepped forward, only to be halted by an assistant who grabbed him around his chest and restrained him.

The nurse stepped between him and the table. 'He's gone, Doctor.'

Thomas tried to break free. 'What's wrong with you? Help him.'

The nurse repeated herself. 'He's dead. There's nothing we could have done.' She lay a calming hand on Thomas's chest.

Thomas felt the tears streaming down his face. When had he started crying? He looked at James Napier, dead on the table in front of him. He could remember his date of birth from the file in Stewarton – 12 January, 1900. He added the date of death – 16 November, 1916.

'Take the rest of the morning off,' the nurse said, though she had no authority to give such an order. He left the tent as they carried James's body away, adding him to the day's dead, lined up in rows under blankets in the field behind the tents. No one stopped him. He could have kept walking away. He could have kept walking all the way back to Stewarton, to James and Kathleen Napier. He could tell them what had happened to their only child, how he had failed to keep their son alive.

He didn't. He got as far as his tent. His campmates found him later that night, behind a small crest away from the main camp. He was drunk. They got him back to his bed and let him sleep it off. The next day he reported to the surgical tent. No one said anything to him. The nurse who had been with him when James had died gave him a sympathetic smile. The next casualty had been dumped in front of them by the stretcher bearers and another day began. Thomas did not speak to anyone about what had happened. He carried the pain inside and buried it with drink. He carried on serving until the end of the war. He was given his campaign medals and thanked for his service and discharged.

He left Stewarton before he saw James and Kathleen Napier. He couldn't face telling them about the pointless sacrifice their son had made, and how he had been powerless to save him. He knew it was cowardly. From the day of his death, James Napier haunted Thomas.

Lost in the ghosts of his past, Thomas entered Craiglockhart Hospital through the main entrance again without looking towards the poorhouse across the road. If he had looked up, he would have seen the wagon arrive and the police constables dismount and head into the building.

4

TUESDAY, 16 NOVEMBER

1920

'Private Watt is here.' Nurse MacKay announced.

'Thank you, Constance. Send him straight in.' He looked at his desk, expecting to see a file. 'No paperwork?'

'Nothing has come through. It was requested by the clerk.'

Thomas shrugged. It wasn't the first time the War Office had failed to comply with a request for a military file. Those in charge did not count the mental welfare of discharged men as a priority, especially now the war was over and the hospital was officially closed. They were under no obligation to provide medical histories, service records or discharge papers.

Nurse MacKay went to the door and held it open, beckoning the man in the waiting area to come through. As he entered, she slipped out and closed the door behind her. Thomas rose from the chair and came round his desk to greet Private Watt with an outstretched hand. The man took the offered hand and shook it firmly.

'Thank you for seeing me, Doctor.'

'Not at all, Private Watt.'

'Duncan, please.'

'Duncan. I'm Doctor Stevenson. Thomas. Please, take a seat.' Thomas showed him into an armchair. He was a head taller than Thomas, which made him just over six feet tall. He had a mop of brown hair, which he continually swept away from his forehead in a nervous gesture. Running down the left side of his face was an angry red scar. Thomas had seen the injury before, likely caused by a slicing blow from a bayonet. Watt had been lucky not to lose an eye. He was lean and muscular, and his hand felt rough, suggesting a life of manual labour. He moved with a slight limp in his left leg, perhaps sustained during the war, too. He didn't have the pale, coal dust look of a miner, rather his skin was healthy and tanned. Thomas speculated he was employed outdoors, perhaps as a farm hand, or a builder.

'Tea, coffee?'

'A glass of water, if that's okay?'

'Of course.' Thomas poured water from the jug that sat next to the kettle. 'You asked to see me?'

'I did, yes.'

'May I ask why? Why me in particular, I mean?'

'I heard some of the lads mention you.'

'The lads?'

'Fifteenth Division.'

'Your battalion?'

'Thirteenth.'

'You don't mind if I take some rough notes, do you? Just for myself, they won't leave this building or be shared with anyone else.' Men from the war were often cautious about the stigma attached to the talking cure. It was seen as a sign of weakness.

'No, on you go.'

Thomas balanced the notepad on his thigh. He noted the Private's well-educated accent. 'A volunteer for Kitchener. You saw a lot of the war then.'

'Almost all of it. Joined up in 1914 in Edinburgh.'

'The Battle of Loos?'

Watt nodded. 'You know your history.'

'I treated many of your fellow infantrymen, in the field and afterwards. Could I ask who in particular recommended me? You understand I'm not a specialist. I'm only a general doctor who volunteers here.'

'I'd rather not say, if you don't mind, Doctor. I wouldn't want to get anyone into trouble for talking out of turn.'

Thomas thought the man's reluctance a little strange, but some men struggled to open up and he didn't wish to start by pushing Watt away from him. 'The Somme?'

'Yes, and Arras.'

'Under Allenby in the Third Army.'

'Yes, with McCraken ordering us about.' Thomas passed over the implied insult about Sir Major-General Frederick McCraken, the highly decorated commanding officer who had led the Fifteenth Division for much of the war and was presently in charge of the Scottish Armies. Some of the men had complained about his leadership during the war already, describing him as a weak leader.

'And disbanded last year, June, was it?'

'Around then, yes. Kicked out with a 'thank you' and be on your way.'

Thomas heard the tone of displeasure in his voice. Many volunteers and conscripts in the service battalions had been given minimal basic training and shipped to the Western Front underprepared. Many never returned. Those that did were discharged from the army in as much haste as they had been signed up, with little support to return to civilian life. 'And since then?'

'It's been hard. I lost my wife; she left me while I was away, thought I wasn't coming back. Can't blame her. No job to return to. No home. I've picked up menial work where I can, harvesting, factory work and so on. But my leg means I can't do the hard work anymore.'

Thomas nodded. At least Watt was not a cripple. He had seen worse cases. 'You're not alone in that, believe me, I have heard that story a few times from your fellow soldiers.' He finished making a note. 'Your limp and scar, both from the war?'

'A shrapnel wound to the thigh at Bullecourt.'

Thomas's pencil paused. He hesitated for a moment, then continued. 'And do the injuries give you any pain?'

'You know what they say, only when the weather turns cold, like it is now.'

Thomas tried to hide his thoughts behind a friendly smile as he resumed writing. Why would this man lie about where he sustained his injury? Better at this stage not to question him. Perhaps he was mistaken, perhaps he had ended up with the wrong battalion at the time. Stranger things had happened in the chaos of the war.

'Aside from your injuries, how are you coping?'

'That's why I'm here, Doctor. You see, I've been having trouble sleeping. Dark thoughts, memories I can't contain.'

'I understand, go on.'

'Well, you know what it's like, don't you? You must've seen some terrible things over there. Friends, comrades.' He paused, looking to the floor. 'Gone in an instant.'

Thomas allowed a moment for reflection. 'You've heard of the term shell shock?'

'Of course.'

'It's a condition of the brain that brings about physical symptoms like tremors, nightmares, shivers, loss of sight or hearing, confusion. Would you say you have experienced any of these?'

'I guess all of them at one time or another.'

'It was recognised as a psychological problem, as far back as the start of the war, and it's been seen in many soldiers, even those who were perhaps fine in the trenches and have since returned home and started to develop symptoms. I'd like to tell you more about it and the treatments we can offer you for it.'

For the next half hour, Thomas explained the talking cure to Private Watt, who listened intently. By then, Private Watt's hour was almost up.

'So, do you think you would like to come again and we can try and start to deal with some of these symptoms?'

'If you think it'll help, Doctor.'

'The nurse will arrange another appointment for you.' Thomas stood, and raised his hand to shake Watt's.

Watt remained in his chair, placing the empty glass on the side table next to him. 'Do you suffer from shell shock, Doctor?'

Thomas's hand dropped. 'Yes, as a matter of fact, I have done.'

'And how do you deal with it?'

'Talking to others has helped.'

Watt cut him off. 'Do you like a wee dram to take the edge off?'

'I wouldn't recommend drink as the solution to a patient.'

'Especially not when you're working with patients, I expect.'

'Exactly, yes.' Thomas felt a shiver run down his spine. The way Watt looked at him from his seat, with a furrowed brow over dark eyes, looked malevolent. The scar that ran down his face added to that feeling.

Then the moment passed. Watt's face broke into a smile, and he stood and offered Thomas his hand. 'Don't worry, Doctor. Your secret's safe with me. No doubt the people of Liberton think you're a fine, upstanding doctor.'

'I would hope so. I'm not entirely sure what you're referring to,' Thomas stammered, failing to hide his discomfort.

'Notwithstanding the company you choose to keep in your house, so I hear. A fine woman, even if she does come with a bit of a tainted past.' Watt gave him a lurid look.

'I think you had better leave, Mr Watt, and it would be best if you sought someone else to continue your treatment.'

Again the sneer dropped, the scar fell; his face was placid once more. 'Don't be like that, Doctor. I've enjoyed our wee chat. I'll talk to the nurse about coming back, shall I?'

With that he dropped Thomas's hand and left, leaving him standing alone in the room. What had just happened? Had he been threatened? How did he know about his drinking? How did he know about Louise, and why did he mention her? He needed a gulp from the hip flask in the desk drawer, but thought better of it. His drinking wasn't out of control. He was sure he had hidden it from his patients. He had never been drunk when seeing them. He only needed a little, a few times during the day, just a mouthful to get him through, to stop the shivers and the nightmares. To stop James Napier from creeping into his thoughts.

He sat down and wiped a film of sweat from his forehead. He looked at his scribbled notes and the question mark he had written next to the word 'Bullecourt'. The Fifteenth Division had not fought there. They had taken Guémappe, ten kilometres to the north of Bullecourt, during the Arras offensive. Was the man mistaken, or was he lying about where he got his injury? And if he was lying, why?

Night had descended when Thomas left the hospital at six o'clock. The rest of his afternoon appointments had passed without incident. His remaining patients called on his skills as a general practitioner: looking at wounds and discomfort, rather than discussing their mental state. They distracted him from the incident with Private Watt. He felt a shake in his right arm, the first sign that he needed something to calm his nerves, having avoided taking a drink all afternoon. He could last until he reached The Liberton Inn. The hospital sat in shadow. Many of the windows had been boarded up while the conversion took place, detracting from the grandeur of the exterior and giving it a look of dilapidation and neglect. The streetlamp outside the entrance shed an orange glow beyond the edge of which was only blackness across the front lawn. Clouds drifted across the moon, casting shadows onto the earth.

Thomas pulled his coat tight across his chest and hunched his shoulders against the chill breeze. There was a commotion across the road. People were gathered outside the City Poorhouse, clustered around the entrance, illuminated by the gas lamps at the side of the doorway. There were police officers in uniform at the top of the steps, trying in vain to usher the crowd back. Thomas saw newspapermen among them, shouting indecipherable questions towards the policemen. Something had happened, and Thomas presumed it was about the missing child that had been taken from the poorhouse. On the edges of the crowd were the homeless and poor of the city who had come seeking shelter for the night. He saw women, young and old, children in tattered clothes and cripples still in their army uniform.

He turned his back and began walking. Whatever had happened, he would read about it in the newspaper tomorrow, or word would already have reached the inn. Plenderleith or Joseph would be able to update him. The thought of a much-needed pint drew him towards home. He started retracing his steps from the morning, this time by the moonlight. As he left Greenbank behind, the empty silence of the night settled over him. In the distance were the faint sounds of the city to the north – a car engine or horses' hooves on the cobbled roads. Thomas was unsettled by the eerie darkness. Too often, nights like this had been full of shell fire and explosions and alarm bells ringing as ambulances and stretcher bearers arrived at the field hospital and orders for the medical staff to get out of bed had been screamed across the camp. His mind wandered. James Napier was there, as he always was. He was joined by the scarred face of Private Watt. The face that had seemed pleasant and humble until it had changed to leer at him, taunting him with some sort of devilment. Was it all in his imagination? Constance MacKay said Private Watt had been perfectly pleasant when he left. He had arranged to be seen again in a fortnight. He had offered her thanks. Were these the actions of a man who wished him ill for some reason?

Further round the foot of the hills, the only sound was his own footsteps crunching along the gravel path. He clenched his left fist in his pocket to still the shakes running through his arm and hand. As he passed the old quarry, a void of blackness against the foothill, he saw a lantern on the path ahead. It wasn't unusual to see others out on the path in the evening, but the lantern appeared to be hovering on the spot, not travelling towards or away from him. He saw other lanterns off to his right, to the south. By their light, he could see they were gathered around Liberton Tower, a square column that had once had a courtyard and been part of a larger castle. Its light-coloured walls with narrow window slits stood out on the flat landscape surrounding it, with the Braid Hills behind it. The landmark had once been lived in, but it had been uninhabited since the 1600s when Liberton House was built as an alternative for the landowners. It was used to store farm equipment now.

As he neared the lantern on the path, it swung round; the holder spotting his approach. It began heading in his direction. The arm holding the lantern raised itself as it drew near, causing Thomas to squint in the light.

'Doctor Stevenson, is that you?'

'Constable Inch?' replied Thomas, recognising the voice.

'This is fortuitous. What are you doing out here?'

'Returning from Craiglockhart, the hospital. What's going on at the tower?'

'Best if you follow me, Doctor. We're only just after sending someone back to the village to collect you. Thought you'd be in the inn as usual at this time.'

'What do you need me for?'

'The Detective Inspector asked for you. Or rather, the nearest medical practitioner.'

'Detective Inspector?'

Inch nodded. 'They've been here since lunchtime, searching the fields, outhouses, farm barns and the like.'

'Searching for what?'

'The missing girl. From Craiglockhart.'

Dread crept upon Thomas. He remembered the crowd outside the poorhouse, and the police presence there.

'They've found something in the tower?'

Inch lowered his voice to a whisper, even though there was no one within hearing distance of them, and leaned towards Thomas. 'A foul business, Doctor. They've found a body.'

5

THE ASYLUM

1908

The solid towers loomed on the horizon as the horse-drawn trap left Gartcosh village behind. A further half mile along the track they turned off the road and passed through the gates of Gartloch Hospital. The sign on the gate read: 'City of Glasgow District Asylum for Pauper Lunatics'. The sky was covered by threatening clouds. McEwan knew he had been sent on a fool's errand by the Chief Inspector, but he was in no position to protest.

Girdwood pulled the reins, and the horse stopped outside the doors of the main building.

'Wait for me here. I shouldn't think this will take long.'

'Ah hope no', replied the driver, glancing at the imposing building which sat alone in the middle of open fields, shrouded in grey. He'd heard tell of horrors within. 'Ah'd like tae be well away fae here before the dark settles.'

McEwan jumped down and pulled his black uniform cloak around his shoulders and straightened his helmet. He looked up, having to bend backwards to see the top of the two towers on either side of the building, topped with turrets. The towers featured detailed carvings and gargoyles with hideous features. McEwan wondered what purpose they served for an asylum. The rest of the building was three-storeys high, built in red sandstone. Smaller buildings lay off to the side, which McEwan guessed housed the nurses and doctors who worked at the hospital. The air was still. There were none of the howls and screams that colleagues had led McEwan to believe surrounded the hospital. 'Best watch yerself, lad,' Constable Chalmers had said, 'filled wi' heretics an' demons an' devils, that place.' The journey from the Low Green Street Central Police Station in Glasgow to the village on the north-east outskirts had taken longer than McEwan had expected and it was now mid-afternoon. Daylight was waning in the early winter gloom. It would be nightfall before they made it back to the city. The return journey would be made along dark trails, in cold autumnal temperatures. The prospect was not a pleasant one, but even less so was what awaited him beyond the heavy oak doors that stood in front of him.

'Are ye goin' in or no'?' growled Girdwood.

McEwan gave the driver a look of disapproval and reached up and pulled the rope that hung from the bell by the side of the door. After a moment without any response, he rapped the metal door knocker, embroidered with another monstrous face of bulging eyes and sharp teeth. The bang echoed around the still fields. The sound of metal bolts being scraped open came from the other side of the door. McEwan withdrew his helmet and tucked it under his arm. He flattened his short, dark hair across his head as the door creaked open.

An orderly dressed in a white medical smock and grey trousers, greeted him. 'Yes?' the tired-looking face inquired.

'Good afternoon, sir. An appointment to see the Reverend.'

'And you are?'

'Constable McEwan.'

'Are you expected, Constable?'

'Yes, I have an appointment,' McEwan repeated.

'Very well, please follow me.' The elderly man opened the door wider and gestured for the Constable to enter. The heavy door closed with a solid thud behind him. 'This way, Constable.'

They passed through a deserted reception hall and along a corridor. Through tall windows on one side of the passageway, he could see the green front lawn and grey skies. On the other side was a row of doors, all closed, with numbers painted onto the dark wooden panels. McEwan assumed they were appointment rooms where doctors met with patients.

At the end of the corridor was a white metal door. The orderly withdrew a large key from his pocket. The lock turned with a reassuring *clunk* and the hinges screeched as the orderly used his shoulder to push it open. McEwan stepped through and waited for him to close and lock the door behind them. Again, he followed, their footsteps echoing along a hard concrete floor. He was being guided deeper into some sort of hellish maze. The walls in this part of the hospital were painted white. The doors along this corridor were metal, with sliding hatches at eye level. Each door had a key hanging on the wall to the side of it. The high windows were covered with metal grilles.

'Are there patients in these cells?' McEwan asked. The orderly only grunted and carried on walking. Ahead of them, another metal door opened. The orderly halted and put an arm across McEwan, pressing him to the wall.

'Stand aside a moment, Constable.'

Through the door came two orderlies, younger and taller than McEwan's guide. Between them they held a gaunt man with a shaved head. His walk was subdued, restrained by the orderlies on either arm. A nurse followed, dressed in a navy cardigan over a white uniform dress and a cap. McEwan's guide stepped forward and picked a key from the wall and opened the cell door opposite them, ready for the patient to be taken into. As they drew level with McEwan, the gaunt man turned towards him, taking in his police uniform.

'Kin ah help ye there, Polis pig man?' he snapped.

McEwan felt spittle in his face and drew back, his back pressing against the corridor wall. The two orderlies huckled him into the cell, pushing him inside and closing the door with a metallic *clang*. McEwan's guide locked the door and replaced the key on the wall.

'I do apologise, Constable. Many of the patients here have reason to dislike the authorities.'

'Quite alright,' McEwan replied, attempting to hide his discomfort and wiping his face with a handkerchief.

'Reverend Peterson is just finishing up his daily rounds. He's just through here.'

The door at the end of the corridor led to a larger room, with chairs spread out and a lectern at one end. Beyond that, they passed a number of offices. The white walls were replaced with wooden panels and the concrete floor with soft carpet. The orderly stopped in front of an unmarked door and knocked, before entering when prompted.

'Ah, thank you Frederick.' Reverend Peterson was a tall man, dressed in black apart from the white dog collar around his neck. His neat black hair was parted to the side. He wore thick spectacles that gave him an owlish nature. The orderly withdrew and left the two men alone.

'I gather from your presence that Detective Constable Ord has decided not to pursue a criminal case against our patient.' The Reverend smiled at McEwan. 'I don't mean to demean your rank, but if there was a crime to be investigated, I assume he would be here in person.'

'No offence taken, Reverend. You are quite correct. There will be no further action taken against the woman. However, Detective Constable Ord wished me to come in person to deliver the details of the search.'

'The search?'

'Of the canal lock. Given the information provided, it was

prudent to empty the canal lock and dredge it for any sign of remains.'

'And was there?'

'As you can imagine, there is a significant amount of accumulated rubbish and dirt at the bottom of a canal, and three years have passed since the incident.'

'But you did find something?' The Reverend's face looked concerned.

'We discovered the remains of an infant, a child around one year old. The body was severely decomposed, making any chance of identification impossible. There were no clothes or distinguishing marks that would have given us a starting point for further investigation.'

'Is it likely to be her child, as she claims?'

'In all probability it is the child she spoke of, but without any actual evidence, there is little point in pursuing it as a criminal matter.'

'Then what she told us was the truth?'

'It would appear so, but we have no way of saying for certain. The patient is not a reliable witness. There is no way to track down any other witnesses unless we have an exact date. It could have happened as she described. Or, it could be that she has knowledge of someone else who disposed of a child this way, or perhaps she was a witness to an incident at this canal lock, which might help to explain her mental illness.'

The Reverend bowed his head in sorrow. 'This is distressing. I assume the remains will be given a proper burial?'

'Once the remains are released by the procurator fiscal.'

'Very well. Doctor Andrews is with her now. We should inform him of the news.'

'Is it necessary that I should accompany you for that?' He thought of the dark ride back to the city that awaited him. He would have liked to have been on his way, and away from this fearful place, sooner rather than later.

The Reverend paused at the door. 'I do hope you don't conform to the wider public view that people with mental disorders are to be shunned and feared by society, instead of helped and treated like any other patient with medical problems?'

'Of course not.' McEwan followed the Reverend out of the door.

Peterson led the way along the carpeted hallway. 'The doctor may have questions that only you can answer. Besides, you've travelled all the way here, Constable, we might take this opportunity to enlighten your mind a little.'

The ward for female patients was at the rear of the main building. They passed along more white-walled corridors with large windows; McEwan felt the claustrophobic atmosphere and oppression. This was where society sent the misunderstood, the damaged, the outsiders they could not understand. Better to lock them away on the outskirts of the city and pretend they didn't exist.

'I only volunteer here, you understand. My ministry is in Garnkirk,' Peterson said as they wound their way up a staircase to the floor above. McEwan had passed the nearby village and estate on the way to Gartcosh and the hospital. 'The doctors are very much in charge of the day-to-day care, but the whole thing relies on benefactors providing funds. Lady MacKendrick gives very generously. You know her, no doubt?'

'Not personally, no,' McEwan answered. He had heard of Lady Sarah MacKendrick, the wealthy widow who was spending her late husband's wealth on various charitable causes, including the Glasgow Police Benevolent Fund. It was rumoured she held sway with many of the powerful men in the city, thanks to her former husband's connections.

'Unfortunately, The State chooses not to protect those it cannot understand. Those that can't contribute to society in the way they would like,' Peterson continued. 'God, however, cannot turn His back on His most needy children. So, I come to offer a service twice a week, and to attend to those who wish some guidance.'

'And that was how you came to know this woman?'

'She seemed to think I belonged to the Roman Catholic faith, a delusion from which she could not be swayed. She insisted on confessing her sins, seeking absolution. Doctor Andrews and I agreed it would do no harm to go along with her notion and let her rid herself of whatever sins were bearing down upon her. We thought it may even help to relieve her malady.'

'And has it?'

'Alas, no. Andrews informs me there has been no significant improvement.'

'And it was in this confession that she informed you about the dead child?'

'Exactly. She grew hysterical as she confessed. She told me she had killed her child, drowned them in a canal at Castlecary.'

'You believed her, despite her illness?'

'Not everyone with mental disorders is a liar, Constable. Some can be too forthright and honest, which is what puts them at odds with society.'

Constable McEwan wished more of the criminals he had to deal with had that particular problem. It would make his job a lot easier.

'I believed her,' Peterson continued. 'I think you would have too if you had been there. There was something about the manner in which she confessed.' He paused as they reached another door, about to push it open. 'She was adamant.'

'You believe the remains we found are those of her child?'

'If I were to speculate, I would think so, but that is not my role here. There are many patients within these walls who have committed many sins.'

They entered a large room. Several women, all dressed in white gowns, milled around. Some sat in groups, some walking back and forth. There was nothing obviously wrong with any of them, and yet when McEwan met their stares, he felt a chill run down his spine. 'These are some of the patients with milder cases,' Peterson informed him. 'They are allowed to socialise with one another.'

'Our patient is not among them?'

'She has good spells and bad. When she is well behaved, she is allowed to join in and take part in some of the group activities.'

'Does she know I am coming?'

'She was told, yes. It is best not to spring surprises on them. They have fragile dispositions.'

'How did she react?'

'There was some agitation.'

Beyond the common room, they entered another corridor of individual cells. Outside one of the metal doors, a doctor stood making notes on a clipboard. He looked up as they entered.

'Ah, Reverend. Well, what news?'

'Doctor Andrews, this is Constable McEwan.' The Reverend informed Andrews of everything McEwan had already told him.

Andrews took a moment to take in the news of the discovered body, his head bowed in thought, his arms crossed, one hand on his chin. 'It would be unlike her to make up anything. Despite all her problems, I have never found her to be untruthful.' He looked to McEwan. 'You say no further action is to be taken against her?'

'Whether we believe her or not, there is no evidence and no reliable witness, only the word of a madwoman.'

Doctor Andrews was used to such misunderstanding from the public. 'We prefer not to use such terms about the patients here, Constable. While Jessie has her issues, she is perfectly lucid most of the time.'

McEwan apologised and continued. 'Detective Constable Ord is inclined to let the matter rest, particularly as the woman is incarcerated here already, and, he assumes, unlikely to be released anytime soon. So long as she remains here, she can be of no risk to the general public.'

'Oh, I don't believe Jessie poses any risk to the public. It is to herself that she poses a risk and from which we hope to protect her.'

'To herself?'

'Perhaps you should see for yourself.' Doctor Andrews slid open the metal hatch in the door. 'Please.'

McEwan looked from the doctor to the Reverend. He had no idea what to expect on the other side of the door. He stepped forward and looked through the small rectangle. Beyond was a white room with padded walls. There was a chair, a small table and a single bed. They were bolted to the floor. Alerted by the noise of the hatch opening, a woman was getting up from the bed. She turned as she did so and stood in the middle of the room. McEwan caught his breath. Whatever he had expected to see beyond the cell door, it was not this.

She was gaunt and malnourished, wearing one of the white gowns like the other patients he had seen in the room before. She was no more than twenty or twenty-one years of age. McEwan had imagined she would be older. Her skin was pale, almost translucent. Her hair, thin and tousled, was a copper red colour, but streaked with premature grey strands. She stared at him. Her eyes were a clear brown. She was undoubtedly beautiful, but there was something about her that unsettled McEwan at the same time as enchanting him, something inhuman.

'You say her name is Jessie?' he asked the doctor, without taking his eyes from her.

'We have only her word for it. We've been unable to trace any family. There is no missing person description that matches her appearance. No family has come looking for her. She calls herself Jessie Bruce. Whether that is her real name or not, we have never been able to confirm.'

'Does she not tell you herself where she came from?'

'She mentions nothing from her childhood. Nothing before this incident at the canal.'

'And no effort has been made to trace her family?'

'We don't have the resources for that sort of thing. We struggle to maintain a service of treating the patients as it is. Perhaps the police could investigate? It seems that would be something more in your line of work, Constable? She talks very little. Her lack of communication is one of the symptoms of her malady. It is something we continue to work on.'

The woman took a step forward, towards the door. McEwan involuntarily stepped backwards.

'You found my son, didn't you?' she hissed the words.

'Settle down, Jessie,' Doctor Andrews called. 'The Constable is here to help.'

'I killed him. Drowned him. Abandoned him.' Her voice grew stronger. 'I won't leave him alone any longer.' She pulled the front of her gown down, exposing her chest. Across her clavicle, from shoulder-to-shoulder passing through her jugular, ran an ugly red band of scar tissue. It stood out against her pale skin, raised and jagged and raw.

'Good God,' exclaimed McEwan. He had seen enough wounds among the victims in the Glasgow gang fights to recognise a knife scar.

Doctor Andrews pushed him aside and closed the hatch. 'Forgive her, Constable. She can have these sudden outbursts. I should have realised your appearance may have triggered a reaction.'

McEwan recovered himself. 'Not at all, Doctor. I hope I haven't caused her any anxiety. She did that to herself?'

The doctor nodded. 'She harms herself when she becomes depressed. She calls it her punishment for what she has done.'

'I'm surprised she survived such an injury.'

'If we did not have a medical ward here, alongside the asylum,

I'm sure she would have died. We were fortunate a surgeon from Edinburgh was visiting at the time, who specialised in trauma medicine.'

'We'll leave you to make sure she is sedated, Doctor.' Reverend Peterson ushered McEwan away, and he did not resist. His duty was done and, despite the strange, beguiling look of the mysterious woman, he wished to be away from this place as quickly as possible.

'Do get in touch if there is anything more we can help you with, Constable,' the doctor called after him. 'Or if your enquiries yield any more information that may help us.'

Constable McEwan didn't look back. He strode through the building, refusing to make eye contact with any of the women in the communal room, and hurried down the stairs and through the hallway. His thoughts were filled with the image of the red scar and pale white skin and what horror could possibly drive someone to do such harm to herself. The answer, he felt sure, was to be found in the remains that had been discovered in the canal lock at Castlecary.

Reverend Peterson struggled to keep pace with him. 'Do not be alarmed, Constable. It is an illness, and one that can be treated with the right care.'

Two minutes later, the orderly closed the heavy door behind Constable McEwan. He took a deep breath in the cold early evening air. Girdwood was on the lawn, smoking a cigarette and letting the horse feed on the grass.

'Everythin' aw right there, Constable?' he called over, seeing McEwan bent double, his hands on his knees.

'Get the bloody horse hitched up,' McEwan ordered.

'Gladly. Dinnae want tae be hangin' aboot this place after dark. Gie's me the creeps.'

McEwan couldn't agree more with the police driver. He took his seat in the trap next to him. Girdwood flicked the reins to get them moving. They turned in the driveway and soon the foreboding Gartloch Hospital was receding into the gloom behind them.

McEwan turned and looked over his shoulder at the twin towers. He shuddered and drew his cloak tight, not against the cold, but to protect him from the sight he had seen in that cell. Her piercing, haunted eyes were burned into his memory. He was not a religious man by nature, but he swore, as he said to Detective Constable Ord the next day, that in the moment the girl had stepped toward him and revealed her scar, she had looked possessed. He had been looking into the face of evil itself.

'If you should be asked to travel to Gartloch again, Girdwood, take my advice and refuse, for I swear the devil himself resides within those walls.'

6

TUESDAY, 16 NOVEMBER

1920

The tower had four levels. They entered by a door into a low-ceilinged entrance room. Thomas, though not the tallest of men, had to stoop to avoid banging his head on the stone ceiling.

'Up?' he asked the officer who was to take him to the Detective Inspector.

'The top floor. I would ask you not to touch anything if you can avoid it.'

A short flight of stone stairs brought them to the next floor. It was a storage room with a wooden ceiling, part of which opened as a hatch with a ladder leading up to it. The officer climbed up first. Thomas felt claustrophobic. His throat gasped for a steadying drink. He felt the shivers running through his arms as he pulled himself up into what had once been the main hall of the tower. On one side was a doorway, which had once been the main entrance to the building. The steps that once led up to it on the outside of the building had been demolished long ago. On the opposite side was another narrow staircase. Gas lamps had been placed around the room. The wind whistled through open window slats. Someone came down the staircase.

'The local doctor, sir.' The officer informed him.

'Thank you. Doctor.' The man offered his hand. 'Detective Inspector George Aitchison,' he introduced himself.

'Thomas Stevenson.'

'Glad you got here so quickly. We want to get the formalities out the way as soon as possible and get everything cleared up before any locals decide to gather. Have you attended a crime scene before?' Thomas shook his head. 'It's not pretty up there.'

Thomas nodded somberly. 'I saw plenty of trauma injuries through the war. I thought Detective Inspector McHarg was in charge of the investigation?'

'I'm happy to let D.I. McHarg deal with the publicity, while I get on with the police work. You served?' Aitchison asked him.

'Medical Corps.'

'Ninth Division, Jock and Springboks.' Thomas recalled the division made up of Scots and South Africans. 'You'll have seen worse than this then, except,' Aitchison paused, leaned in and lowered his voice, 'not on a small child, a baby. One wonders what sort of animal would do such a thing.' The tremors in Thomas's arms increased. He was sure the Inspector must notice. 'I just need you to confirm death and make the basic pronouncement, have a quick look for the cause of death and any evidence you might think helpful. Type of murder weapon, that sort of thing.'

Dear God, thought Thomas, despite his loss of faith, what was he about to walk into?

'Take a deep breath and follow me. Watch your head, low ceiling.'

Thomas followed the detective up the stairs. At the halfway point between floors, they were in pitch blackness. Thomas wished the dark would swallow him. There was no escape. They stepped into a bedroom lit by torches, with an old wooden bed rotting and collapsed in the corner. A wall divided the top floor into two separate rooms. An officer was guarding the internal door that led to the room beyond.

'Through here. Watch your step.' Aitchison took the lead, Thomas followed. They were alone in the second chamber. Four gas lamps had been left to illuminate the scene. At first, Thomas saw nothing unusual. There were a few old sacks in one corner, their contents congealed and spilling out through rips where rats had eaten away the hemp cloth. The floor was bare stone. A broken chair was upturned. Aitchison picked up a lamp and pointed it into the furthest corner, light pushing away the shadows of darkness.

Thomas wanted to scream. He froze. A wave of nausea swept through his gut and throat and threatened to spill from his mouth. He swallowed it, his hand involuntarily brought to his mouth.

'Take your time,' Aitchison advised. 'We've seen similar before, though perhaps not so violent. Mothers who couldn't cope, fathers who didn't want the burden, that sort of thing, but they tend to dispose of their kin more humanly.'

Thomas had seen dead children before, unwanted and unloved and abandoned. It was a fact of life in the industrial world of the early twentieth century, as it had been for centuries before. Married couples who had no need for another child, malformed or disabled babies cast aside, illegitimate offspring. Drowning was common, so was abandonment. Rarely did it involve excessive violence or cruelty.

He forced himself to edge closer. The child was pale, drained of blood. The cause of death was obvious: a slit ran across the throat, crusted red with drying blood. The floor was stained black with a pool of liquid underneath the small body. He knelt down. He took out his handkerchief and covered his mouth and nose. He reached forward and placed his hand on the small bare chest. She was cold. There was no movement from the heart within. She wore only a cloth, tied into a makeshift nappy. He lifted it to confirm the sex of the child. Her small legs were bruised and deformed, broken at an inhuman angle. There were also signs of bruising around her scalp, covered with just a few wisps of fine hair. Thomas could take no more. He turned and left the room. Aitchison followed.

'Sergeant, cover her up and stay on guard at the door.'

Thomas kept walking to the stairs. He had to get out. He plunged into the darkness of the staircase. Images rushed past his eyes. He didn't want to remember what he had just seen. He didn't want fresh, hellish memories to join those that haunted him already. He couldn't breathe, his clothes seemed to strangle him, the dank air suffocated him, he clawed at his throat, his body retching. He reached the main room and kept going. He missed a step on the ladder to the floor below and fell to the floor. He stumbled out the narrow door and down the final staircase and finally burst into the cold evening. He gulped in the fresh air, leaning against the cool stone of the tower. Constable Inch was still there, keeping watch along the path.

Detective Inspector Aitchison came out the door a moment later and stood next to Thomas. He waited for him to gather himself.

Thomas stood up. 'Who would do something like that?'

Aitchison took out a cigarette and lit it with a match, and offered one to Thomas, who took it, even though he was not a smoker. His hands shook as he raised it to his mouth and took a long draw. The detective blew a funnel of smoke out through the side of his mouth. 'I saw things in the war that I thought would not be matched. Terrible things.' He puffed on his cigarette again. 'It's an evil world we live in now.'

Thomas understood what he meant. The war had changed men. The depths of evil that a man could stoop to had been laid bare. Hell had been unleashed on Earth and mankind spiralled ever downwards. The dead body in the tower was evidence of that.

'If I learned anything, it was that there is no limit to the depravity and cruelty man can inflict on a fellow human being.'

'But a child? An innocent baby? How can you be so calm?'

Aitchison gave him a hard stare. 'Do not mistake professionalism for a lack of emotion, Doctor. I have a job to do, to catch the person who would do something like this.' He stepped closer to Thomas, their faces only inches apart. 'And when I do catch him, you can be sure that I will make sure the bastard hangs.' He stepped back. 'Now, can you confirm the details of the crime scene?'

Another detective appeared beside Aitchison, his notebook open and pencil ready. 'Deceased female, not older than six months. Cause of death is a wound to the thorax, done with a thin, sharp weapon, either a small knife, like a soldier's knife, or a scalpel or a bayonet. There are other signs of injury, both legs appeared to be broken and there was bruising around the head.'

'Time of death?'

'I'm not an expert.'

'Roughly?'

'There was no sign of decomposition, so recent. No longer than forty-eight hours ago. Sometime last night would be my best guess.'

'You can't be more specific than that?'

'I'm not an expert.'

'Very well, the police medical officer will be able to be more accurate. Thank you, Doctor. When this comes to trial, you will be called upon as a witness to describe what you have seen. Write down some notes to keep it fresh in your memory.'

Aitchison went back inside. Thomas had been dismissed, his part in the proceedings complete, but it was too late. The horror was imprinted on his mind. He would not need notes to keep what he had seen in his memory. It was there forever now, a fresh nightmare, joining the anguished cries of James Napier and the dismembered limbs and spilled guts and grotesque remains that he carried with him. He walked away, passing Constable Inch on the path. When he had come this way that morning, when the world had been a place he had hoped he could still come to terms with, the body of the baby girl was already lying in the room at the top of the tower. He put his shaking hands inside his pockets and strode on. He needed to get to the inn. He needed to drown the horror. Only then did he remember the date. The 16 November. Four years to the day since James Napier had died in front of him.

Louise heard him enter the house. It must have been long after midnight. He stumbled over the doorstep. She had left the note on the sideboard in the hallway. She couldn't tell if he saw it. His bedroom door opened and closed and there were muffled bangs as he got himself into bed. Then silence.

She rolled over. She wouldn't sleep tonight. She didn't want to sleep tonight, to let her demons back in. They had stirred when Mr Tod had mentioned the police arriving in Liberton to search for a missing child; they had raised their voices to a scream when the police officer had knocked on the door that afternoon.

She had returned from the school. There had been no sign of the police search Mr Tod had described. She had settled in the living room, a small fire on to keep out the November chill. The kettle whistling on the stove had masked the sound of the knocking at the door. The officer was forced to beat on the door before Louise heard him. It was not unusual for a patient to call looking for Thomas at different times of the day, so Louise was caught off guard when she opened the door to the young man in uniform.

'Doctor Stevenson?'

'I'm afraid he's not here today; he's at the war hospital in Craiglockhart.'

'Craiglockhart?' The officer seemed surprised at the mention of the place name.

'Yes, he volunteers there. Can I help at all?'

'Can you give him a message if he returns soon?'

'I can.'

He hesitated. 'You promise not to share it with anyone else, only I'm not sure I'm allowed to say anything to anyone.'

Louise smiled at his young innocence. 'Of course.'

'Only I wouldn't want to be the one caught spreading rumours.'

'Rumours spread pretty quickly around here, but I promise I won't say a word to anyone but the doctor.'

'Tell him to get to Liberton Tower as soon as he can. Or rather, Detective Inspector Aitchison needs him to get there immediately.'

'What has happened?'

'They've found a body. One of the missing children.'

Louise refused to let her face betray the shudder that went through her. 'How horrible. I'll be sure to pass the message on as soon as I see him.'

'Much obliged, madam.' The officer touched his hat and took off down the path. Louise watched him go down Kirkgate. She closed the door and stood in the hallway.

Don't panic. Don't let that life back in.

Louise picked up the telephone that Thomas had installed so patients with access to a telephone of their own could call in emergencies or arrange appointments. She got an operator to put her through to Craiglockhart. The telephone rang for a minute before the operator came back on to tell her no one was picking up at the other end. They must have finished for the day. Perhaps he was already at The Liberton Inn for his evening drink. She threw on her shawl and shoes and hurried across the road. She entered through the lounge door on the Kirkgate side, and went straight to the bar, where Rose was serving.

'Guid evenin', Louise. We dinnae often find ye here.'

'I'm looking for Thomas. Is he in the bar?'

'Ah havnae seen him, let me check fir ye.' Rose set a pint glass down on the bar to let it settle and walked to the other side of the u-shaped bar. 'Nae sign a' him,' she called back. 'Shall ah send him o'er tae ye if he comes in?'

'If you could, Rose, or give him a message to go to the tower as soon as he can.'

'The tower?' asked Rose as she came back, but Louise had already gone.

She returned home. There wasn't anything else she could do now except wait for Thomas to appear. Her mind swirled. She tried reading, but the book wasn't distracting enough. Dead child. Dead child. Dead child. Over and over. She couldn't slip back to that life. It had been so long ago; she had survived so much. She could never forget it; it was part of who she was, but she thought it would no longer be able to drag her down again. She was wrong. It would never leave her alone, it would always be there, waiting to pounce on her, waiting to punish her over and over again for what she had done in her past.

She went to bed and waited for Thomas to return. Now she heard Thomas shout out in his sleep. He was having a nightmare again. They never spoke about it. She knew the war had damaged him. *James Napier* was the name he always shouted, over and over again, but tonight he shouted something else. Muffled by the walls and doors between them, she tried to make it out. Then she heard it clearly and buried her head under her pillow to try and block out his cries. She was convinced it was her old mind playing tricks on her.

She was sure he was shouting *'it's only a baby.'*

7

WEDNESDAY, 17 NOVEMBER

1920

At some point she must have fallen asleep. She woke to the rain hitting off the roof and the glass pane in the bedroom window rattling in the wind. She heard Thomas moving about in the kitchen. She lay in bed, staring at the ceiling wishing she could stay there, sheltered against the swirling elements.

The telephone rang in the hallway. She heard his footsteps as he went along the hall to answer it.

'Doctor Stevenson speaking… Of course… Yes, I understand… Ten o'clock, yes. Good day.'

He placed the handset back in its cradle and went back to the kitchen. The telephone rang again. She followed his footsteps.

'Doctor Stevenson speaking… I'm afraid she hasn't woken yet… Yes, very troubling… That shouldn't be a problem, the practice will close this morning for the meeting… Goodbye, Mrs Henderson.'

The school had called asking for her.

His footsteps came back along the hallway and stopped outside her bedroom. He tapped on her door.

'Louise, are you awake?'

She didn't reply. He tapped again. 'Louise?'

'One moment,' she answered. His footsteps continued on to the kitchen.

She took one last moment, feeling the comfort and warmth of the bed. Then she could put it off no longer. She threw on the same dress she had worn the previous day and brushed and tied her hair into a loose bun. She took her time over her make-up, powdering over the blemishes and scars as usual, and added a spray of her jasmine and rose scent. Ten minutes later, she entered the kitchen. Thomas was at the table. She noticed his tea untouched in front of him. He was staring out of the window. He glanced towards her and gave her a weak smile. He looked tired, crumpled. He had drunk more than usual last night.

'The school called?' she asked, filling the kettle, keeping her back to him.

'They want you to help out this morning.'

'You don't need me in the surgery?'

'I'm cancelling the morning appointments.'

She placed the kettle on the stove, waiting for his explanation.

'There's been some terrible news. Mrs Henderson felt they might need extra support with the boys.'

'The child?' She stood at the stove, hiding her face from his gaze.

He answered matter-of-factly, hiding his own feelings from her. 'They found a dead girl at the tower last night. They think it is one of the children who disappeared from the poorhouses.'

Did he notice her flinch? The shudder that ran through her body? She shut her eyes tightly. 'How terrible.'

'The police have called a meeting at the church hall this morning. They're asking everyone who can attend to go along.'

'Shouldn't I go along to that?'

'I will go. You will be more use at the school. I imagine Mr

Russel and the other teachers will attend the meeting. They will need you to look after the boys while they are away.'

'Very well.'

The kettle boiled. She picked it up with the cloth in her hand and poured water into the pot, watching the clear water muddy as it mixed with the tea leaves.

'Would you like a fresh cup?'

Only then did he notice his untouched tea on the table in front of him. 'No, thank you.'

She sat opposite him. 'A police officer called at the door for you last night.'

'They needed a doctor at the crime scene. I met them on the way back from the hospital.'

'You saw the body?'

His eyes sank to the table. She knew not to ask anything more. He would tell her if he wanted to. That was how they had always been with each other, never pushing to find out more, accepting that they would share when they needed to. It was better if she didn't know more. She didn't want to know the details.

She placed her hand on top of his. She felt him flinch. It was not common for them to touch. Their eyes met. Their hands lingered together for a moment before he pulled his away.

'I had better reschedule the morning appointments.' He stood and left her alone in the kitchen.

Thomas watched her walk away, along the road to the school, from the living room window. He felt terrible, both from the effects of his excess the night before in the inn, and from the fractured sleep during the night. He was grateful that Plenderleith had been absent from the inn last night. Malachy and Joseph had been at their usual seats, and Arthur had been behind the bar. Word had spread about the police presence in the town. He had heard the ripple of shock when news of the body being found in the tower reached them.

Thomas listened but didn't allow himself to be drawn into the conversation. He let them speculate. He didn't correct them when the rumours started to spread. He saw Arthur looking at him at one point, but the landlord was a tactful reader of people and let him be.

He washed his face with cold water. He hoped he would not have to say anything at the meeting. The young officer who had called him this morning said Detective Inspector Aitchison requested he be there. Similar calls had gone out to those with telephones, while officers in the streets were rounding up as many residents as possible. From his living room, Thomas watched people begin to gather at the church across the road. There were many he didn't recognise. There were newspapermen and detectives and others who had the look of senior officials, drawn to this small corner of the city by the discovery last night. He saw faces from Liberton Dams and the surrounding villages of Greenend and Greenbank and Craiglockhart and Gilmerton. Soon the street was crowded as they descended on the church. At ten minutes to the hour, he pulled on his coat and crossed the road to join them.

He pushed his way through the doors into the hall, which was already crowded. In one corner, he saw the black servants from the big houses gathered together. It was unusual to see them all in the same place as the rest of the village. He wondered if they feared suspicion falling upon them, as it often could do, for no other reason than their skin colour. Among them, he saw Simon, the houseboy from Liberton House. He had been one of the appointments Thomas had cancelled that morning. His predecessor in the general practice had refused to see people of colour, even if they could pay him for any costs upfront, forcing them to travel into the city to find medical care. Thomas held no such prejudices. He had seen all men, black and white, fight and die together. He ensured they knew they could call on him for their care. For that reason alone, Thomas was considered a friend by the small group.

Fold out seats had been placed in the hall. At the far end, a table had been set up with chairs behind it, and Detective Inspector George Aitchison stood behind it with his fellow officers. They watched the people gathering. Did the Inspector have his eye on someone in particular? Thomas found it hard to believe anyone he knew in Liberton was capable of such cruelty.

He found a space to stand to the side. The remainder of the crowd squeezed in and the doors were closed. Aitchison cleared his throat to get the attention of the throng, then resorted to banging on the table until there was silence.

'If I could have your attention, please. Thank you all for coming at such short notice. I wanted to address as many of you as possible. There are no doubt stories already circulating among you about recent events. I want to present you with some facts, before any spurious rumours get out of control. I also want to appeal for your help in aiding our investigation.

'As you will know, over the last three weeks, three young children, babies, have disappeared from poorhouses around the city. Acting on information received, our search for these missing children brought us yesterday to Liberton and the surrounding area. At four o'clock yesterday afternoon, a child's body was found in the disused Liberton Tower. I'm sure you are all familiar with the tower. The body was found in the top room of the building. Subsequently, the body has been identified as that of Lily May Fitzpatrick, aged five months old, who was reported missing from the Craiglockhart City Poorhouse by her mother on Saturday 23 October. Our initial investigation of the crime scene has shown that Lily was the victim of a cruel and barbaric murder.'

There was a gasp in the hall as the rumours were confirmed. Neighbours turned to each other and voices rose. Aitchison raised his hands and his voice.

'I'm sure you will all have many questions, and you will have the chance to ask them in good time. I asked you here today for your help in our investigation. Anyone who thinks they have information that may help, no matter how small or trivial, come forward and speak to us. The sooner we establish a positive line of enquiry, the sooner we can catch the person who committed this evil act and make sure no one else comes to harm. There are two other missing children that have still to be traced, and their lives could depend on the information we receive from you today. Perhaps you have seen a stranger around the village in recent days, or someone acting suspiciously? We will follow up on all information received, even if it is to rule out any individual who is of interest to us.'

Aitchison pointed to the line of officers standing behind him. 'These gentlemen will listen to anything you have to say. Again, I urge you to help us get this vile murderer off our streets. If you would like to start forming an orderly queue, I will also be available to take any questions you may have. Just before we start, Reverend McIntosh would like to make an announcement.'

Aitchison stepped to the side and the local minister, who had been standing to the side, came forward to address the gathering. He invited everyone to a service at the church at midday to pray for poor Lily and her mother, who was in their thoughts and prayers. Thomas watched as the Inspector scanned the crowd. Thomas noted that he had said little about the crime scene other than the basic facts. He had left out the details of how the murder had been committed and the likely murder weapon. They would keep that information to themselves until they had a suspect to question. He was entrusted to keep what he knew to himself as well.

The Reverend finished his brief address. Uproar descended on the hall as people began discussing what had happened. The locals would have their own theories within minutes. He saw Simon and the group of black people slip out of the door. It was safer for them to be out of the way, and they would not want to be seen talking to the police. It was not their place. They would report anything they had to offer later, in private. He saw Plenderleith and Joseph and Malachy with Arthur. He nodded to Tompkinson, the newsagent. Grim looks were exchanged. Shock was expressed. A general consensus emerged that this was the sort of thing that happened in the cities, in the back streets of the Old Town in Edinburgh, or in the Gorbals of Glasgow, or in Whitechapel in London. Was this what being incorporated into the city meant for Liberton? Was this their own Jack the Ripper? Thomas heard *I told you so* or variations thereof, from the many who had opposed the expansion of the city boundaries. This was their future – crime and violence and denigration.

A few drifted towards the front of the hall and lined up in front of the waiting officers, who had now sat at a row of tables. The newspapermen gathered around Aitchison and were taking it in turns to question him. He was trying his best to deflect them and reveal nothing more. They were joined by Charles Murray, the local Member of Parliament for the south of Edinburgh. Thomas recognised him from his photograph that appeared in the local paper from time to time. As far as Thomas knew, Charles Murray had never visited Liberton before. This was what it took for a politician to take an interest in the lives of his constituents.

Thomas had nothing to offer to the police, and he wanted to escape before he had to deflect any questions from Arthur or Plenderleith. He had not revealed anything in the inn the previous evening.

He politely pushed his way to the door, which had been opened to allow people to spill out into the courtyard. They gathered in small groups. He took a last look back into the hall and stopped.

It was the limp that he noticed first. Then the brown hair being swept away from his forehead. When he reached the front of the hall, he turned and Thomas saw the unmistakable scar running down the side of his face. Duncan Watt sat down in front of one of the officers. The officer started scribbling notes down, occasionally looking up into the face of the former soldier and nodding. What could he have to say to the police? He wasn't local to the area. Perhaps he had seen something in Craiglockhart, something to do with the initial disappearance, but why was he in Liberton this morning? He could have gone to the police at any station in the city. He watched for a moment longer, trying to guess what was being said.

'Excuse me, doctor.'

'My apologies, Mr Rutherford,' Thomas replied, recognising the farmer who was trying to pass him in the doorway.

'Terrible business.'

'Indeed, it is. Shocking.' Thomas stepped to the side. When he looked back, the seat was empty. Duncan Watt had disappeared. Thomas scanned the room and found the officer Watt had spoken to. He had pulled Aitchison aside and was whispering in his ear. The Detective Inspector was listening intently. Thomas turned and left.

The school was calm. Morning assembly was taken by Mr Hastings. Louise was given the two youngest classes to look after and engaged the boys with writing practice and reading. The older boys were delighted to find maths lessons were postponed, to be replaced with a cross-country run around the neighbouring recreation park. Mr Tod was drafted in to look after those excused from the run and he put them to work sweeping up the leaves from the paths around the school.

Some of the boys wondered where Mr Russel and the other teachers were. Mr Hastings told them the truth. A body had been found, foul play was suspected, and the police had requested the community attend a meeting at the church hall. But by the lunch break, Louise heard salacious chatter in the corridors.

'It's the bogeyman come back from the war.'

'It's a serial killer on the loose, escaped from the loony bin.'

'I heard he likes to take small boys from their beds at night.'

Louise warned them to stop scaring the younger boys. After lunch was cleared away, the teachers had returned and afternoon lessons proceeded as normal, much to the dismay of the boys. While Betsy and Florence saw to their cleaning duties, Louise took her lunch with Mrs Henderson and Mr Tod.

'Just a baby, the police Inspector said.' Mrs Henderson had spoken with Mr Russel on his return and was relaying to them what had been said at the meeting.

'Horrible,' Mr Tod agreed.

'That's what'll happen now. It used to be such a safe place, but you bring the city folk in here and trouble follows. It'll only get worse. So many strange faces about the place now. Used to know everyone, and everyone looked after each other. Now we've got a child murderer among us.' Mrs Henderson threw up her arms and looked to the heavens.

'We don't know if it's someone who came from the city,' Louise tried to reason.

'How well dae we really ken anywan?' asked Mr Tod.

'You're not suggesting someone in the village had something to do with this?' Mrs Henderson was aghast at the thought.

'People kin be very different in public an' in private. Might be perfectly pleasant tae talk tae in the street, but behin' clased doors? Lot a' people ah ken in the village, but ah couldnae tell ye much aboot their past. An' after whit so many went through in the war, damaged a lot a' men, that did.' He looked to Louise, 'Yer doctor kens aboot that, doesn't he? Helpin' those that are mentally damaged.'

'I would know if I was talking to a bad one,' Mrs Henderson declared, before Louise could answer. 'Especially one capable of killing a child.'

Louise took a long sip from her tea.

'I wouldnae be so sure,' Mr Tod pressed his point. 'Take Miss Stuart here. She seems a perfectly normal person, but whit dae we ken aboot her outside a' this school? She lives wi' the doctor, an' before that she lived at the wummin's poorhouse. How did she end up there?'

'That's quite enough, Mr Tod,' Had Mrs Henderson detected Louise's discomfort? 'I think I'm safe in saying Miss Stuart is incapable of killing another soul, whatever her past situation.' She smiled at Louise.

'Ah meant nae offence, but some might see it a different way. Miss Stuart shares a hoose with a man but they are no' attached, an' she lived in a hoose a' disrepute.'

Louise stared at the school janitor. She had considered him a friend. He realised he had said too much, and mumbled an apology. 'No' that ah'm implyin' anythin' untoward, ye understand. Ye've never bin anythin' other than kind since startin' here.'

'Take no notice of him,' said Mrs Henderson, 'whatever has happened in your past, you've turned out a fine woman.'

If only they knew the truth. What would they think of her then? Would they suspect her of being capable of killing a child? If they knew she had once had a child of her own and had killed him. She needed to get out of the room. She could feel herself failing, fracturing along the fault lines of her past. She had to fight those emotions, keep them buried, or she would lose her mind to them again.

'I just hope they are able to find whoever would do such a thing quickly, before panic starts to spread around the village.'

Mr Tod, aware of the atmosphere he had created, took his leave of the women and returned to his duties. Louise was free to leave for the day, now that the teachers had returned. 'Or you can help out with more laundry if you wish. It will be waiting for you tomorrow in any case,' Mrs Henderson said. Manual labour gave her something to do and was preferable to sitting in the house alone. It was dinner time before she left the school. The chatter amongst the boys was filled with the most dramatic thing to happen in Liberton for many years. At home, she ate alone and left a plate of food for Thomas. She assumed he had gone to the inn again after his afternoon appointments. He needed a drink at the end of every day now. She felt like joining him, but would he welcome her company? He was dealing with his own demons; he would not want to hear about hers.

Under her blanket in the bed, she tried to sleep, but the shadows of her past chased her in her dreams.

8

THE RICH HOUSE

1911

Sir William Ferguson struggled up from his seat in the back of the red Argyll Flying Fifteen car, which had come straight from the factory just along the road in Alexandria. He hobbled from the running board to the ground, using Dunn's shoulder to steady himself.

'It might get us here quicker, Dunn,' he grumbled to his private secretary, 'but it's no more comfortable than the trap and horse I used to travel in when I was a child.'

'Perhaps when investment in the roads has been approved, the journey will be smoother,' John Dunn placated his master.

'I shall ensure the route from the office to my house is first on the list,' Sir William said. Dunn could only guess if the councillor was joking or being serious. It was well within his ability to have decisions on local matters bend to his will, such was the grip the mill owner held over local politics and politicians. The road from the centre of Glasgow to Clydebank to the north-west of the city could well be the first to be improved, if Sir William insisted upon it.

The houseboy emerged and Dunn left him to drive the motor car into the garage. Dunn's spirits dropped as he looked at the square façade of Dalmuir House. Built long before Sir William Ferguson had purchased it, the house nevertheless reflected its current owner's personality – sturdy and unappealing. Everything was built to have right-angles: the windows, the flat roof, the chimney stack, without an ornate curve in sight. Even the annex built onto the side was square. The front door was covered by a rectangular portico, held up by four plain columns. Sandstone steps ran up to the entrance. Like Sir William Ferguson himself, the building had no time for anything elaborate or fussy. It had always left John Dunn cold. To compensate, he turned away from the house and took in the view over the surrounding park. The situation of the house compensated for its character, with rolling slopes of grass surrounded by birch and yew trees. It was to the park that Dunn escaped on days when his overbearing master's behaviour became too much for him. He wished he could go there on this cool autumn evening, as the sun began to dip behind the tallest trees, but Councillor Ferguson had other plans.

Newman, the butler, was waiting for them at the door. 'Good evening, sir.' Ferguson grunted and carried on into the house, breathless from climbing the four steps. Dunn handed Newman the master's briefcase, coat, gloves and hat and followed him in to the hallway.

'Anyone called?' Sir William asked. Like the motor car, he was obsessed with the new home telephone he had installed in the house.

'No, sir,' Newman replied. 'The mail was delivered as usual though. I've left it on your desk.'

'Very well.' Ferguson waddled towards his office.

'Lady Ferguson hasn't travelled?' Newman asked Dunn.

'She's staying in London for another fortnight.' The butler raised his eyebrow and strode off to return to his duties. Dunn followed Sir William.

Newman entered the kitchen at the rear of the house. Mary Oakley was busy preparing the dinner. The smell of roasted chicken drifted around the room and the stove gave off a welcoming warmth.

'Only Sir William has returned. Lady Ferguson has stayed on in London.' Newman took a cigarette packet from the shelf above the side dresser and lit a rolled-up cigarette. He pulled out a chair from the dining table and sat down.

'Nae smokin' when ah'm preparin' the food, ye know that.'

Newman ignored her and took a long drag and blew a funnel of smoke out the side of his mouth. 'Where are the girls?' he asked.

'Makin' up the beds, though ah suppose they'll nae need tae bother wi' the Lady's noo.' She looked at him. 'Are ye goin' tae warn them?'

Newman shrugged. 'Maybe he'll behave himself with these two. After what happened.'

'Ah leopard disnae change its spots, Mr Newman. Ah think yer well aware a' that, an' ye kin firget yer wishful thinkin'. The lassies are fragile enough. Yer best tae warn them.'

'I should've told them two weeks ago, when they first got here.'

'Mibbe. They got two weeks a' pleasant livin' though, which they were due, ah reckon, after that place they came fae. A shame he's came hame an' ruined it.'

'And if it was to happen again?'

'Ah'm nae a fortune teller. That'll be dealt wi' if it wis tae happen.'

'Just send them back to the asylum, more damaged than when they left?'

Mary Oakley stopped chopping the cabbage and put the knife down. 'Wit else kin we dae? Yer predecessor tried tae tell the polis, an' where is he noo?'

Newman took another draw on his cigarette and squashed the stub into the table. 'It can't go on. He can't be allowed to act like this.' He stood up and left.

'Dinnae dae anythin' stupid, Mr Newman,' Mary Oakley shouted after him. She shook her head. 'This'll nae end well,' she muttered and carried on preparing dinner.

In the office, John Dunn opened the mail that had piled up during the last fortnight while they had been in London, siphoning out anything he thought Sir William needed to see. The rest he would deal with himself later on.

'Nothing from Gaberdine?' Sir William asked.

Dunn flicked through the pile, looking for the mark of the Gaberdine Real Estate Company on the front of the envelopes. 'Not that I can see.' The Gaberdine Company were acting as his agents in a deal to buy more land along the Union Canal, in the hope of establishing another mill.

'Bloody useless lot. I'm sure they'll still charge me even though I've nothing to show for their work.'

Dunn stopped at an envelope with distinctive writing on it. His stomach lurched.

'What is it?'

'A letter from Lady MacKendrick by the looks of it.'

Sir William's eyes widened. 'Probably wanting more money for that blasted asylum.'

Dunn opened the letter and read the neat, formal handwriting. To his relief there was no mention of the previous unpleasantness. 'You're right, sir. She wonders if you would be so kind as to provide them with an increased donation to help them over the festive period.' Dunn admired the nerve of Lady MacKendrick, the benefactor of Gartloch Hospital. She knew Sir William would acquiesce to any demand she made of him in order to keep the scandal hushed up. It wasn't quite blackmail, but it wasn't far off it. 'She also asks after the new girls and hopes they are settling in to your house staff.'

'Give her what she asks for.' For a moment only, he looked meek. 'No mention of the previous maid?'

'Lillian?' Dunn revelled in his master's discomfort at her mention. 'No, nothing. I hope she has settled back in to the hospital without further disruption.'

'Quite. You wouldn't mind pouring me a whisky, would you?'

'Is that wise, sir? Perhaps an early night is called for after our travels?'

'I don't need cosseting, Dunn. One drink to settle the nerves.'

He moved to the sideboard and filled a crystal tumbler with the opened bottle of Macallan, and placed it on the desk. Sir William drank the full measure in one go, throwing it down his throat and letting out a satisfied sigh.

'That hits the spot. No wonder the poor buggers like it so much.' Scotch whisky had for a long time been a drink of the working class. Only recently had the upper classes started adopting it. Sir William Ferguson had come from a working-class background, clawing his way up with a mixture of determination, hard work and ruthlessness. He was still rough around the edges, and tolerated by the gentry thanks to the business empire he had built. The upper class had no choice but to accept his uncouth habits now, including his over exuberance with alcohol. 'Another.' He held out the glass towards Dunn, who still had the uncapped bottle in his hand.

The second measure followed the first. Sir William wiped his mouth with his shirt sleeve. 'Just leave the bottle here.' He patted a spot on the desk. Dunn placed the whisky in front of him. There was no point in trying to argue with him once he had started. 'How are they settling in then, the new girls? What were their names again?'

'Anne and Jessie, sir. I'll enquire with Mrs Oakley as to their behaviour while we've been away.'

'Do that. Anne and Jessie. Charming.' A third measure disappeared down his portly gullet. 'I will talk to them later. Check they have settled in.'

His speech was already starting to slur and Dunn knew the rest of the bottle, which had been three-quarters full, would soon disappear. It was happening again, despite the shame, the unspoken reprimands from those who worked in his household, and the risk to everything he had worked so hard to achieve. He realised Sir William would never change. Lady Ferguson had seen it. That was why she had remained in London and refused to travel with her husband, and why she slept in a separate room, and why she was rumoured to seek comfort in the arms of other men.

Newman found Anne and Jessie in the master bedroom finishing making Sir William's bed. They stood when he entered and bowed their heads.

'Relax, I'm not the master of the house.' He inspected their work, checking the corners of the sheets had been tucked in and the pillows plumped just as Sir William liked them. They looked fragile and unsure. He knew where they had come from, though not exactly why they had been locked up in the asylum. The doctors said they were fit to work and serve, but looking at them now, standing in their black dress uniforms with the white aprons and hairbands, he wasn't sure he believed them. Anne, the taller of the two, looked healthier, her skin had more colour, her shoulders were rounder and her face fuller. The other, Jessie, looked pale and achingly thin. Her red hair was tied back in a bun. Her brown eyes watched him closely.

'That'll do very nicely,' he said, patting down the bedding. Anne's face broke into a broad smile of relief. Jessie remained unmoved. 'No need to sort the Lady's room, she's stayed down in London for another while. Just the master has returned.'

Did they know what had happened to Lillian? They must have seen her return to the hospital. Relapsed, the doctor had said when he was called to come and collect her from Dalmuir House. Something must have happened to trigger it; she had been progressing well. Could they think of anything that had happened at all? An upsetting incident? Newman had stood in the room, while Sir William had lied to the doctor. Dunn had looked ill, unable to look the doctor in the eye. Lillian lay sedated on the bed in front of them.

'Nothing that I'm aware of, Doctor,' Sir William had said, 'but then I don't see them much during the day. Newman, did anything happen in the staff rooms that I'm unaware of?'

That had been his moment. The gall of the man to bring him into the lie, to make him complicit in the cover up. He could have said something, he could have put a stop to it. But would anyone believe him? Word would spread. He would never find work on a house staff again. The butler before him had been dismissed when he had tried to speak out. So, he kept his mouth closed and shook his head.

'Most strange,' the doctor said, packing away his things in his bag and directing the orderlies to take Lillian to the waiting ambulance. 'Perhaps we pushed her too quickly. Psychiatry isn't an exact science.'

He looked at the two young women in front of him. He couldn't allow them to be subjected to the same ordeal. He would warn them.

'The Lady not being home might cause us some bother.' He was unsure how to broach the subject. They both looked innocent of the ways of the world, although both were in their mid-twenties, Mary Oakley had told him. Too old to be starting a career in service, too many bad habits already learned. 'The master may have a drink or two as he's on his own. I'm afraid when that happens he can get carried away, if ye catch my meaning.' They looked at him blankly. 'He might get a little aggressive.'

Anne still showed no sign of understanding what he was trying to hint at, but he saw a blush on the pale skin of Jessie.

'He sees it as his privilege, you see. Rich people, folk with power like he has, are used to taking what they want.' He took the plunge and hoped for the best. 'He might want to be alone with you, you understand?'

The penny finally dropped for Anne. 'Ye mean he'll dae inappropriate things?'

Before Newman could answer, the door opened and John Dunn came into the room.

'He's started,' he said to the butler.

'Bad?'

'Half a bottle of whisky already, and no sign of stopping.'

'Has he mentioned them?'

Dunn turned to Anne and Jessie. 'It's not safe for you to be here.'

'Wit d'ye mean by that?' answered Anne. 'We've only bin here a fortnight, we've nae even met him.'

'I'm very sorry but unless you want to come to some harm, then you have to get out.'

'An' go where? Back tae the asylum?'

'No, he would find you there. You have to leave and disappear.'

'Or whit? He wouldnae. He couldnae git away wi' it.'

'That's just the point, Anne,' Newman explained. 'He could get away with it. He already has.'

'He is rich, he has influence. He controls the police, the courts.'

'He cannae be that bad. Ah've had men leechin' o'er me plenty a' times afore. Ah'm sure ah can cope wi' an auld man lookin' fir a bit a' fun.'

'It's more than a bit of fun; once he starts, he gets … carried away.' Dunn hesitated trying to find the right words.

'Rape,' said Jessie. Her voice was calm. 'That's what he did to Lillian, wasn't it? I heard her talking at the hospital, but no one believed her.'

'Yes,' sighed Dunn.

'Did he beat her?'

'Yes.'

'I saw the bruises.'

'Then you understand.' Dunn looked at her. 'You must leave before he does the same to you.' He reached towards Jessie, trying to guide her by the shoulder. She stepped away from his reach.

'Why don't you stop him?'

'No one can, don't you see? He owns everyone and everything. It would be the word of a young woman just released from an insane asylum, against the richest businessman in Glasgow, a city councillor, a friend of the Prime Minister, a friend of the new king. It would be your word against the whole establishment of the United Kingdom. Who do you think they will believe if you try and tell them he assaulted you?'

'You would just let him do this? How many women has he done it to before?'

'We've no time for this,' Newman said. 'Mr Dunn is right. It's better if you disappear before he finds you. Get out while you can. Let us worry about how to deal with him.'

Anne stood her ground. 'Ye dinnae understand. We've naewhere tae go. We've nothin'. Nae family. Where wuld we stay? Where wuld we get somethin' tae eat? Ah'd rather take ma chances wi' the auld fool an' keep a roof o'er ma heid.'

John Dunn turned to the smaller of the two women and appealed to her. He stepped towards her and this time succeeded in holding her by the upper arm.

'You must go, you understand? If you stay, you will either be trapped here or end up back at the asylum.' Jessie nodded; her face set in grim determination. 'Gather your things quickly.' Dunn led her to the door. He could hear Sir William on the floor below, still in the office. He was shouting about the ills of the world that were lined up against him. Before long, he would come looking for someone to take out his anger on.

Dunn turned to Anne. 'I urge you one last time. Leave this place while you can, before it is too late.'

Anne folded her arms. 'Ah'm nae runnin' anywhere. Fir the first time in ma life, ah've got a' guid job, a place tae stay and ah'm nae beggin' oan the street worryin' where ah'll get ma next meal fae. Ah'll take ma chances in exchange fir that.'

Dunn looked from her to Newman, who only shrugged. There was nothing more he could say to try and change her mind. He could get the other woman away, though. 'Come with me, Jessie.'

Jessie looked at Anne, her eyes pleading.

Anne's arms uncrossed and fell to her sides; her defiant face dropped into a resigned look of pity. 'Ah cannae go back tae that.' She paused before adding, 'Any a' that.'

Jessie knew she meant more than the hospital. She meant the streets and the poorhouses and the hunger and the beatings. Jessie had got to know Anne's story in the two weeks they had spent in Dalmuir House, a brief, unexpected rest from the trials of their lives. They had known it was too good to last. Jessie knew it was over now. Anne, in her desperation, had to believe it could continue. It was this or nothing for her. Jessie understood.

'Come then,' John Dunn took Jessie by the elbow and pulled her away. Anne receded through the tall doorway, standing in the middle of the large bedroom. 'Hurry. Get your things. I'll meet you at the side door.' Jessie ran along the corridor to the staff quarters at the top of the house.

Night had descended by the time Dunn opened the side door of the annex. The cold air was a shock compared to the warmth of the house. He guided Jessie out. She had changed from her maid's uniform into a common threadbare cotton dress, the only garment she had brought with her from the hospital. Mary Oakley had given Dunn a shawl. He took it and wrapped it around Jessie's shoulders. In her hands, she held a small parcel.

'This is all you have?'

'I don't have much.'

'Perhaps it is better that way. You have to get far away from here, you understand? If you can, you should leave Glasgow. Start somewhere new. Change your name.'

'How will I get far enough away?'

'You could go to the canal. It is only a short walk. One of the barges would take you.' Dunn stopped as he saw the look of fear on the woman's face. 'What?'

'I can't go to the canal.'

Dunn saw the pain in her face. He had no time to ask about it now. 'Very well. Get to the main road into Glasgow and you will likely pick up a coachman or a rag-and-bone man who will give you a lift to the city, but don't stop there. You must keep going. If you disappear now, he may forget about you in time and you can live the rest of your life.'

'Very well.'

'Here.' Dunn took out a handful of coins. 'Take this. It will pay your way across the country and boarding and a meal for the next few days.'

'Thank you.' She took the money.

Then she was gone, running across the park in the direction of the road. Dunn watched until she reached the tree line and disappeared behind it into the shadows as an autumn mist began to form over the grass.

'Good luck,' he whispered after her.

'Dunn!' Sir William roared from inside the house. 'I thought I told you to bring those new girls! It's about time I was introduced to them if they're going to live under my roof.'

He took one last look into the darkness. Part of him wished it was him escaping into the night. He could no longer allow this to continue. He turned and went inside.

9

SATURDAY, 20 NOVEMBER

1920

Callum MacDougall, hand freshly dressed in a white bandage, left the doctor's house at eleven-thirty that morning. He hunched his shoulders against the wind and headed back along the road to Nether Liberton, where he would continue serving choice meat cuts to the people of Liberton despite the stitches in his hand. He was passed by a black motor car with the word 'POLICE' emblazoned across the front grill. He stopped and watched it go by. He had not seen one of the new police motor cars in Liberton before. Next to the driver, he recognised the Detective Inspector who had addressed them in the village hall two days ago. There had been little sighting of the police since then, although it was assumed they were still following up several lines of inquiry. Nothing further had appeared in the newspapers; the newspapermen had gone back to the city. There had been no further news about the other missing children. The car slowed and came to a stop outside the doctor's house. The Inspector and another officer stepped out of the vehicle and walked up the path to the front door. The driver stayed with the car and turned the engine off, restoring peace to the morning. The door to the house opened and the police officers moved inside. Callum MacDougall turned and continued on his way, armed with a bit of news that was sure to interest his customers over the counter that afternoon.

It was Thomas who answered the door to find Detective Inspector Aitchison standing outside.

'Doctor Stevenson,' Aitchison said, without waiting for any greeting. 'This is Inspector Fraser, part of my team. Might we trouble you for a moment?'

Thomas was surprised to find the police on his doorstep. 'Certainly, Inspector. I'm just tidying my surgery, but no more patients are due today.'

'It's not you we wish to talk to, Doctor.'

Thomas, about to show the officers into the hallway, paused. 'No?'

'The woman who lives here with you, a Miss Stuart. Is she home?'

'She's in the kitchen at the back preparing lunch. Can I ask why you wish to see her?'

'I'll let the lady explain that to you herself after we have spoken to her, if you don't mind, Doctor.'

'Of course, Inspector.' Thomas didn't like the tone the officer was taking with him. Whatever they wished to speak to Louise about, it appeared to be serious. 'Let me show you through.'

Since the events during the week, Thomas and Louise had returned to their normal routine. Louise had returned to the school on Thursday, Thomas had visited the sanatorium. On Friday, they had both worked at the general practice and had caught up on the appointments delayed from earlier in the week. After the spell of clear, crisp autumnal days, the weather had turned towards winter and the first signs of a storm were brewing. Rain was in the air and the wind had picked up, whipping in from the west round the Braid Hills and blowing through the main streets around the kirk. The officers followed him through the narrow hall. Thomas opened the door to the kitchen and Louise turned, her mouth open about to say something. She stopped when she saw the officers behind Thomas.

'The police would like a word with you, Louise.'

'With me?'

Aitchison stepped forward. 'Yes, Miss Stuart, if you don't mind.'

'Can Thomas stay with us?'

'I'd prefer to talk to you in private, Miss Stuart, as much for your own privacy as ours. Doctor Stevenson may not be aware of some of the things we would like to ask you about.'

She knew then that her past had caught up with her. It only remained to discover how much of it. 'Very well, we can talk in here. Shall I put the kettle on?'

'That won't be necessary, thank you.'

'I could insist on staying, Louise,' said Thomas.

'Thank you, but I'm sure I'll be fine.' She was lying to him. It would be good to have his support, but she did not want him to hear about her life from the police. She would tell him herself if she had to. She didn't want to lose his friendship before she had a chance to tell him her side of the story.

'I'll be next door.' Thomas backed out of the kitchen and closed the door. The three remaining people each pulled a seat out from under the dining table and sat, Aitchison facing Louise, and Inspector Fraser to the side.

Thomas made his way to the living room. The appearance of Aitchison brought the events of the last week back into his home. He wanted to know what the police could want to talk to Louise about. Some of the conversation would drift through the thin wall to him, but Louise had made it clear she did not want him to hear. It would be up to her to tell him. He should have gone for a walk and left them alone, but he had told Louise he would be there if she needed him, so he remained.

In the kitchen, Louise started the conversation. 'How can I help you, Detective Inspector?'

'How long have you lived here, Miss Stuart?' Inspector Fraser asked the question, while George Aitchison watched her intently.

Louise turned to face the questioner. 'Over a year now.'

'And the nature of your living here?'

'I'm sorry?'

'Your relationship with the doctor?'

'We are friends. I assist him in the surgery practice on occasion.'

'You don't think that a strange arrangement? He lets you live in his house rent-free and expects nothing in return?'

'I contribute money if I can and do my share to keep the house in order.'

'And before you moved in with the doctor, where did you stay?'

'At Alnwickhill House.'

'At the time it was called the...' Fraser stopped and checked his notebook on the table in front of him, 'Edinburgh Industrial Home for Fallen Women'?'

'That's right.'

'Would you like to explain what that was?'

'I think you know fine well what it was.'

'Prostitutes?'

Louise allowed herself to show a little disgust. 'It was a shelter for women who had been abandoned or needed refuge from abuse.'

'How long had you been at the Home before it closed down?'

'About six years.'

'And how did you come to arrive at the Home six years ago?'

'That's a very personal question.' Louise could tell they already knew the answer.

'Were you a prostitute?' Inspector Fraser asked in a blunt manner.

Louise took a moment to compose herself before answering, looking from Fraser to Aitchison, who remained impassive. 'I'm not sure I care for your tone or your question, Inspector. Perhaps you could tell me exactly what this is about. I had assumed it was about the poor child found at the tower.'

Now Aitchison spoke. 'Do you have anything to tell us about that, Miss Stuart?' He emphasised her name in a strange manner.

'I don't think I know anything that will help your investigation.' They looked at one another, neither willing to back down. Louise could sense the storm coming. They knew.

Fraser took up the questioning again. 'Perhaps you could help us with another case then.'

'Another case?' Louise looked back at Fraser in confusion.

'A murder. Quite an infamous one in fact, a few years ago. Did you ever reside at Dalmuir House in Clydebank, Dunbartonshire?'

Louise's heart sank, her stomach lurched, the world of safety she had built for herself crumbled. They had found her. She could think of nothing to say.

Aitchison followed up his colleague's question. 'If your memory needs refreshed, Miss Stuart, we could call you by a different name. How about 'Jessie'? Does that help? You see a woman called Jessie lived very briefly at Dalmuir House in 1911, before the war.'

She could do nothing to stop them. She could only sit there and let them tell her what they knew. They were playing with her, toying with their prey before pouncing.

'Not long after this Jessie left Dalmuir House, the owner of that house, a prominent businessman and politician, Sir William Ferguson, was murdered. His private secretary, a man called John Dunn, and his butler confessed to the crime before any investigation could begin, but there was a suspicion they were protecting a young maid who worked at the house. A scandal involving young women in the employ of Sir William was covered up in the aftermath of his death. No need to besmirch the reputation of the wealthy and the dead. A proper investigation would have wanted to speak to this Jessie, as a person of significant interest, but Jessie had disappeared, never to be seen again, and there was little appetite to find her, with a war looming and a scandal buried. The case was closed and everyone walked away, except for the private secretary and the butler, of course. They ended up in prison.

'We did a little digging in the old case files kept by our colleagues in Dunbartonshire. Could you read the description of Jessie that was taken at the time, Inspector Fraser?'

'Certainly, sir.' Fraser flipped to another page in his notebook. 'Age around mid-twenties, height between five foot five and seven inches, hair copper red with grey streaks, pale skin marked with small scars and blemishes, eyes brown.'

'Sound familiar?' Aitchison asked her.

'My hair isn't copper red.'

'You wouldn't be the first woman to dye her hair. Should we go and see if there is a bottle amongst your possessions?'

'There was one other distinctive mark which would identify Jessie conclusively,' Fraser continued. 'She had a deep scar across her upper chest, just below her neck, that ran from one shoulder to the other. A self-inflicted wound.'

'You are known around here to always wear dresses and blouses with a high neckline, Miss Stuart. Would you care to unbutton the top of your dress just now?'

They had spoken to people around the village. They had been back through old records. She knew now that they knew it all.

'I would not.'

'Shall we stop pretending then?' Aitchison pressed her. 'You are this woman 'Jessie', isn't that the case?'

She hesitated. The confession, after all this time, was small and silent. No weight lifted now that her secret was known. Instead, the truth bore down upon her. 'Louise' disappeared in that moment.

The persona she had inhabited for the last seven years disappeared in the blink of a tearful eye.

'You fled Dalmuir House because Sir William Ferguson threatened you? Did he harm you?'

Jessie looked at the table and said nothing.

'It doesn't matter. We can imagine what may have happened behind closed doors. Let us assume that the rumours about Sir William Ferguson were correct. We are more interested in how you came to be staying at Dalmuir House.'

Her past was tumbling from the Detective Inspector's mouth, and there was nothing Jessie could do to prevent it.

'At the time, he donated money to an asylum, the City of Glasgow District Asylum for Pauper Lunatics in Gartcosh. In return for his money, the asylum would provide him with staff for his house and office, those deemed well enough recovered from their mental maladies. I suppose it was seen as some sort of social charity. There are records of a 'Jessie' at the asylum from 1905 until 1911, when she was taken into the care of Sir William. This was you, Miss Bruce? Bruce is your family name?'

Jessie nodded.

'You were at the asylum?'

'Yes.' Her voice was nothing more than a whisper.

'This morning, records for this Jessie arrived at the police station, sent from the asylum by a Doctor Andrews. I've spoken to this Doctor Andrews. He treated you. He thinks he would be able to identify Jessie if he saw her again. A memorable case. One that he was proud to call a success until he learned of her sudden disappearance from Dalmuir House.'

A vision of the young doctor flashed before her; his eyes framed in the rectangular gap of the white metal door that had imprisoned her.

'The medical notes reveal little personal details. The woman arrived as a seventeen- or eighteen-year-old at the institution, brought there by the police. No one ever identified her beyond her first name. No concerned family ever came searching for her. No effort was made to trace any family. She had been rescued from a canal. The police thought she had made an attempt to take her own life.'

'No,' she managed a feeble resistance, but Aitchison would not be stopped. Tears rolled down her face.

'In the asylum, in her treatment, Jessie made an upsetting claim. She said she had killed her own child at the canal.'

The words hung in the air between them.

'No.'

'The police searched a canal lock near Castlecary. Remains were found of an infant, a boy only one year old. The police believed this to be Jessie's child. Your child.'

As the painful memories flooded over her, she began to sob. Her tears fell onto the table.

'Nothing could be proven. The only evidence was the confession of a mad woman in an asylum. It was not the first time remains of an unwanted child had been found at the bottom of a canal.' He paused. She looked up, into his face. Aitchison leaned forward, bringing him close to her. She could feel his breath as he spoke, tainted with the scent of cigarette smoke.

'But this story leaves me with a problem. Five days ago, I started investigating the murder of six-month-old girl in Liberton. And now I find there is a self-confessed child killer with a history of mental illness, hiding under an assumed name, within a mile of where the body was found.'

Shock replaced fear, her eyes wide in disbelief. 'You think I did it?'

'It's my job to think anyone could have done it. To look for evidence, to follow leads, to look for patterns. This is a pattern I would be foolish to ignore.'

'I didn't do it. I couldn't do it.'

'Couldn't do it? You'll forgive me for taking that with a pinch of salt, Jessie. You've admitted to having done it before. If you could kill your own child, why not someone else's? You have a history of mental illness and self-harm. You're fragile, still traumatised by the guilt of killing your own son. Something snapped. You wanted your child back. You wanted another chance to be a better mother, was that it?'

'No.'

'You took these children. You know the poorhouses of the city. You used to live in them yourself. You knew you could find a child there. But when you had these children again, these innocent babies, you couldn't cope. Just like you couldn't cope with your own child. It reminded you of your failure as a mother. That made you angry. It made you lose your mind again. Doctor Andrews told us you were likely to suffer relapses of mania brought on by guilt.' Aitchison had raised his voice. Now he dropped it to a whisper and leaned forward. 'So, you killed them, just like you had done before.'

'No.'

'Where are the other two children, Jessie? Are they dead already?'

'I don't know!'

'If they are still alive, you need to tell us. We could still save them.'

'It wasn't me!' Jessie shouted.

Aitchison raised his voice to match hers, 'Where are they, Jessie?'

The kitchen door flew open.

'Enough!' Thomas shouted. He saw Louise in her chair, her head bowed, her cheeks streaked with tears. Aitchison was out of his chair, leaning across the table, standing over her.

At the interruption, Aitchison backed away.

'Forgive me, Doctor Stevenson. Tempers became rather heated.

We have all we came for just now. Inspector Fraser.' Fraser stood and stepped round Thomas. As Aitchison passed, he leaned over her once more. 'We will be back. One bit of concrete evidence is all I need. You had better pray those two children are still alive.' He passed Thomas in the doorway. 'We'll see ourselves out.'

10

SATURDAY, 20 NOVEMBER

1920

Thomas waited until the front door had closed before he turned back into the kitchen. Louise remained at the table; her head bowed.

The shouting had forced him to interrupt. He had come to the kitchen door when he first heard raised voices. Now he had so many questions. Aitchison had called Louise 'Jessie' just before he had stopped them. Other words made no sense to him. A canal at Castlecary, an insane asylum, Dalmuir House. What could any of this have to do with Aitchison's investigation of a murdered child? He needed Louise to tell him what had happened.

He placed his hand lightly on her shoulder. 'I'll put the kettle on.'

He wanted to support her. He put the mug of tea in front of her and sat at the table beside her.

Her hand came from under the table and clasped his own.

'What happened?'

She shook her head, holding back further tears. She had to tell him. If he could not forgive her, the man who had taken her in when she was in need, then she would know all was lost.

'There's so much you don't know.'

She looked up. His look encouraged her to tell him more.

'My name isn't Louise Stuart.'

He kept hold of her hand.

'Keep going.'

'My real name is Jessie Bruce. I had just turned seventeen when I found out I was pregnant. My parents wanted nothing to do with me when they found out. They refused to help me have an abortion. I was a disgrace to them. They were appalled that I had been with a man. It would cause a scandal. They sent me away until I gave birth. They wanted me to put the child up for adoption. I wouldn't let them, so they kicked me out. I didn't want to stay with them by then anyway, so I left. I've never seen them since.

'I loved my beautiful boy. I named him Alexander. I survived for a year on my own with him, but it wasn't easy. I had never had to cope on my own before. We were a well-to-do family. I was not used to the harsh life I was exposed to. My parents made sure friends and families closed their doors to me. The boy's father wanted nothing to do with him or me. I ended up on the streets. I found shelter in poorhouses. I wasn't equipped to survive on the streets. Up until then I had lived a sheltered life. My family were well off. I couldn't take care of myself, but with Alexander it was worse. I thought of giving him away, of leaving him with a family or finding someone who would pay for him, but I couldn't bear to part from him. I loved him. You have to believe that I loved him.'

Thomas let her talk. He hid his own emotions as he realised he had no idea who this woman really was. What he thought he knew of her, her motivations, her life, her worries, was changing as she told him her story. He wanted to hold her.

'Then the colder weather arrived. When I couldn't find a bed for the night, I was forced to spend the night in doorways, or under trees, or on park benches. Because I had a child with me, some places refused to take me in. The police sometimes found me and took sympathy on me and put me in a cell for the night. Alexander grew weak. He couldn't cope in the cold. I couldn't give him up, but I couldn't look after him either.

'One evening, I found myself at the canal near Castlecary village. I thought I might find a barge we could sleep in for the night. The owners left them unlocked while they stayed at the inn. But there were no barges at the lock. I was tired, I sat down to rest with Alexander on my chest, wrapped in a shawl. I fell asleep. Something stirred me. I knew something was wrong. It was too still, too quiet. Alexander had stopped moving. He was still. He had stopped breathing. At least, that's what I think happened. I was numb, like I was in a trance. And I knew I didn't want to live without him. I was tired, I had lost everything. I found myself standing over the lock, on the edge of the wall, looking down into the water. I didn't jump, I just fell, wanting the darkness to swallow me up. I don't remember anything after I hit the water.

'Someone pulled me out. I was put on a horse and taken to a doctor. I woke up during the night screaming. Where was Alexander? Where was my baby? I was hysterical. The doctor took me to the police the next day. I don't know how long I stayed in the police cells. I started to have nightmares about Alexander. I was falling into the canal again, but he wasn't dead, he hadn't stopped breathing. He was alive and I jumped into the water with him. I held him down, under the surface, drowning him.'

She was getting agitated again. Thomas had only ever seen her be composed, her emotions always kept in check. He recognised some of the same behaviour in the veterans he had treated. Her mind was in turmoil. The trauma of losing her child had never gone away. It had been locked deep within her, unhealed, waiting for a chance to resurface. Her eyes were wide and unfocused. He still held her hand on the table. He tried to hold it tightly, to reassure her she was safe with him. She didn't notice. She was back there, at the canal.

'You didn't drown him,' he told her.

She snapped and stared at him. 'I killed him. He hadn't stopped breathing. That was just my imagination. He was alive, looking at me. He trusted me. He thought I would protect him no matter what. I killed him. I drowned him. I held him down.

'They took me to the asylum. I told them what I had done. I wanted them to punish me. I deserved to die, but they did nothing. They just talked to me all the time, telling me everything was okay. The other women there hated me. I was a child killer. They beat me, scratched me, drugged me. I let them. I deserved it. I deserved worse. No one would kill me, so I tried to kill myself.'

She withdrew her hands from his and undid the top buttons of her dress. She revealed the top of her chest. For the first time, Thomas saw the deep, raw scar, raised against the pale skin.

'They wouldn't let me die. They said I was getting better. They said I was good enough to leave and sent me to the rich man's house to be his servant. Dalmuir House. There were stories about him. Another girl from the asylum had gone there and came back because he had abused her. They told me to run, so I did. Soon after, the rich man was dead. They covered up any scandal. By then I was in Edinburgh. I thought they would come looking for me, so I changed my name.'

She finally stopped.

'And that was how you ended up at Alnwickhill House?'

She nodded. 'And then you took me in and were so kind to me. I couldn't tell you the truth. You would hate me. You would have kicked me back out onto the streets. How could you not? I killed my own child.'

In the back of his mind, Thomas saw Plenderleith, pointing at the newspaper report in The Liberton Inn and telling him *'It'll be another Jessie King'*. Sharing her name with the notorious child killer was surely just a coincidence.

'No, you didn't. You loved Alexander.'

Tears fell from her face again. 'I did, but I couldn't be a good mother. I failed him. I killed him.'

'You did all you could. You were let down by other people, by everyone you knew. There should have been somewhere for you to go. You shouldn't have been left on your own. What about the father? Did he not offer to help?'

'He was only a boy, just like I was only a girl. It was his idea to do it, to have intercourse.' She whispered the word. 'It would have ruined his life too if I had forced him to marry me or be with me. I avoided him at first. When he found out, he said he wanted to help, but he could never admit to being the father. When I left to have the baby, I left him too. I sent him a note when Alexander was born. I told him he was a father and he had a son and when we got settled somewhere I would send word for him to come and visit, but I never did. We never got settled anywhere.'

'And now the police think you have something to do with the child found at the tower?'

'I didn't do anything. Not this time.'

'Of course you didn't. No one could think that.'

'They do, the police. Maybe they're right. Even if I had nothing to do with this child's death. I should be punished for killing Alexander. I always knew this day would come. I couldn't run forever.'

'You haven't done anything. You didn't kill your son.'

'How can you know that for sure?' She dared him to challenge her.

'I know you. I know you couldn't do something like that. You are kind and considerate.'

'Ha,' she laughed at him. For the first time he sensed a delirium in her. 'You don't know what I had to do to survive. If you knew everything that I have done, you would believe them. You would believe I could be the murderer of that girl.'

'I would never believe that.'

'You are too trusting.'

She stood up, knocking her chair backwards. It clattered onto the hard floor. Before he could stop her, she left the room, the door swinging closed behind her. He followed her, but by the time he got to the hallway she was opening the front door. He ran after her, into the street. He saw her running down the hill, past the kirk and the graveyard and towards the recreation ground. Across the road, Plenderleith and Arthur stood, looking from her back towards him.

'Gentlemen,' Thomas said. He couldn't run after her. They would already be speculating. She was in tears, her dress undone, running from his house. He turned and went back inside. He knew she hadn't done anything, not then, and not now. He knew her, but the more he thought about it, the less sure he became. Did he really? He had known none of this until this morning. She had kept it all locked away from him. He had known nothing about her lost child. What else did he not know? What else had she been through?

11

THE STREETS

1912

The newspaper board announced the disaster in bold: 'TITANIC DISASTER GREAT LOSS OF LIFE'. The boys were out selling the special edition, crying out among the pedestrians on Princes Street. *'Unsinkable Titanic sinks! Collides with iceberg on maiden voyage! Rich and famous among the missing and dead!'* Many stopped to pick up a copy. Some stood on the spot and read. Bystanders gathered round, peering over shoulders. There were gasps of shock.

Crowds of people are what Lucy liked. The sinking of a cruise liner in the middle of the Atlantic was of no interest to her, but it would ensure she had a dinner tonight. While the people clustered together, craning to read the small print, she was able to dip into pockets that presented themselves invitingly.

'It's awmost tae easy,' Lucy said as she walked away, coins in hand. Walking away was the key. Act natural and don't draw attention to yourself. Don't give them a reason to pat their pockets and feel the lightness where there should have been weight. She would have walked fifty yards or more before they realised. They would look round, but all they would see was a busy street and a thousand suspects, and Lucy would be walking in the opposite direction, just another vagrant of the city.

Outside the shops on Princes Street was always a good starting point. As the housewives exited the Jenners store on the corner of St David Street, she watched for potential targets. Tourists, new to the city, distracted by the grand buildings and the pointed Walter Scott Monument, were easy prey. She followed them along the pavement, waiting for the right moment, the open pocket, the unattended handbag, or, like today, a crowd that will provide cover.

Isla was with her today. Lucy had come to think of her as a younger sister, although they were around the same age, somewhere in their mid-twenties. She had taught her how to survive on the streets. Six months ago, at the start of winter, she found her, lost and hungry and in need of a friend. Isla was not the girl's real name, but Lucy was not one to question. If she had something to hide, or someone to hide from, Lucy was not going to betray her. 'Ye look like an Isla, wi' that red hair,' she had told her. On the streets, it was unwise to become close to anyone, but Lucy had taken to the girl. Isla was painfully thin and pale. She had gone weeks without a proper meal. In comparison to Lucy, she was an innocent. Lucy had grown up on the streets of Edinburgh, hustling and stealing since she was five or six years old. They bonded through adversity. Isla relied on Lucy to survive, and Lucy enjoyed having someone to look after. It was nice to have someone she knew would not betray her.

The night she found Isla, huddled on a bench in Princes Gardens, she asked Lucy how she had ended up on the streets. 'My ma left her family fir a man, but he wisnae leavin' his family fir her, nae even when ah turned up a few months later. She went back hame eventually, back tae her man, but ah wisnae welcome in his hoose. She stuck me in the orphanage an' ne'er looked back.'

'You never saw her again?' Lucy delighted in the girl's posh accent. She had come from a well-off home and had been educated. You didn't meet many living on the streets with educated speech.

Lucy shook her head. 'Nae idea where she is, or her name, or whit she looked like even. Ah wisnae desperate tae find her after she abandoned me. Ended up wi' a foster family, but that wisnae sae guid, either. Ran away when ah wis auld enough.'

'Do you ever see them?'

'Ah go back when ah have tae. When there's nae other option. But they dinnae want me there, an' ah dinnae want tae be there. After a couple a' days ah always leave again, an' they're glad tae see the back a' me, ken.'

'It must be better than this, though.'

'Whit d'ya mean, Isla? Why, don't you know ah am a queen in this fair city?' She put on her best posh accent and lifted her tattered skirt and twirled, dancing through the open air of the park.

In return, Lucy asked Isla how she had ended up on the streets, but her answers were always vague. She saw the scars and scratch marks on her face and arms and drew her own conclusions. She saw an ugly red scar hidden under her top. Whatever the reason, she had been through some tough times.

They had become inseparable, apart from those times when Lucy went with a client for the night. She had taught Isla her secrets. Not just pickpocketing, but places to go to seek shelter – the poorhouses, the churches, the charities – and when they had money, the best cheap hotels where you could get a warm bed for a night. She had shown her the places to avoid, where the men were rough and took what they wished. Lucy had resisted selling herself for a long time, until there had been no alternative. On nights when she had a customer, as she called them, Isla would wait for her outside the hotel, or stand lookout at the top of the side street while the man had a *quick one*.

Isla asked her how she could do it. 'Ach, it's no' that bad maist a' the time. They're usually sad an' feelin' guilty afore they've even started, ken? Ye get the few that like tae be a bit rough, force themsel' oantae ye, but it's o'er quickly enough an' the bruises are nae worse than ma foster da used tae gie me at hame. The oanly wans ah cannae stand are the bastarts that ha' their way an' then dinnae pay. After a couple a' them, ah got masel' this.' She showed Isla the switchblade concealed in her brassiere. 'They dinnae pay, ah'll slice the bastart and let him explain that tae his missus when they git hame.' She laughed.

When Lucy had been with a man, they had money. Those nights, they could afford a warm meal from a café in the city, or a drink at a bar. Lucy always paid for Isla's share with her earnings, even though Isla refused to entertain men. They shared their rewards from begging, stealing and selling. Occasionally they made an honest living doing deliveries or selling cotton for the stall owners in the Lawnmarket. They also stole clothes from the market, which they would wear until they were falling apart at the seams. Some nights they had been cold and hungry, but in the main they got by well enough.

Not long after Lucy had found Isla, when there was snow on the ground and the pickings were rich among the busy festive shoppers, Isla had stopped and stared at a headline on a newsagent's stall. Lucy kept walking until she realised Isla was no longer beside her. She turned and saw her reading the newspaper.

'Isla, whit are ye dain? Time's a wastin'.' Lucy joined her and read the headline herself:

SIR WILLIAM FERGUSON MURDER

TWO HOUSE STAFF ARRESTED

'Who's that? D'ye ken him?'
'I lived at his house.'
'Oh, git ye. Mixin' wi' the rich an' famous, were ye? He wisnae

yer man, wis he?'

'No, I worked for him. Only for a few days. I hardly met him.'

'Wit did ye leave a nice hoose like that fir? Ye didnae murder him, did ye?'

'No. I didn't know he was dead.'

Lucy read a bit more. Her reading was slow, her lips moved, mouthing the words as she went. 'His butler, Newman, an' his private secretary John Dunn ha' bin arrested. Musta' bin a richt horrible bastart fir his ain servants tae dae him in. Reckon they'll hang fir that, the rich folk'll nae tak' nicely tae the underclass risin' up against them like that.'

Isla didn't respond. She wasn't listening, and Lucy suspected she knew more about it than she was letting on. Not that she cared, maybe Isla did know something about it. Maybe she murdered the rich bastard. More power to her if she did. He probably deserved it. She wondered if Isla would have it in her, this innocent girl who wouldn't even go with a man. Maybe that was it. Maybe the rich man had tried it on with Isla and she had killed him. 'Come oan, Isla,' Lucy tugged her arm, 'standin' gawpin' in the street'll no' get us a hot meal, ken?'

Spring was in the air. The icy waters of the Atlantic may have claimed the *Titanic*, but Edinburgh was thawing out after the cold winter. They crossed Princes Street and turned up The Mound. Two engines thundered along the tracks that led to Waverley Station, sending steam clouds into the air around them. Lucy kept a lookout, glancing behind to ensure they weren't being followed. They followed the steep curve of the road onto St Giles Street and, once safely hidden amongst the buildings of the Old Town, inspected what riches they had managed to purloin.

'Ach.' Lucy spat in disgust. 'Bloody cheapskate. Aw ah've got is a few coins.' She showed her palm to Isla. 'No' even a shillin'. Looked like a richt well-tae-dae an' awe. Bloody poser. Whit aboot ye?'

'Not much better,' shrugged Isla. She had lifted a purse from an unsuspecting housewife. 'Must be her man that holds her money for her.'

They added up their meagre earnings. 'Nae even tae shillings, lass. Ah'll hae tae git us somethin' else fir tonight if we're gonnae git a feed, ken?'

Lucy made light of it in front of Isla. The thought of having to go with a man again did not fill her with joy, but it was the only option they had. She would have to bear the pain. Better that than no food for another night.

'We could try again,' said Isla.

'Dinnae ye worry, wee Isla. Ah'll be grand.'

They turned away from the looming St Giles Cathedral and headed towards the castle along the cobbled Lawnmarket. They turned and headed to the Grassmarket and the White Hart Inn. Lucy was known there, and tolerated, so long as she was discreet. She wasn't the only woman who touted for business around the Grassmarket and the inn, which had stood there in the shadow of the castle for 400 years. It would be full of regulars on a Tuesday evening, men who went there after a day's work. But there were always new faces: travellers just arrived in the city with money to spend and naivety to spare. Tourists could always be relied upon as well, wandering in to experience a traditional pub atmosphere. It would be a rare night if she was unable to find a client. With her tall stature, long brunette hair and an enticing figure, Lucy could be hard to resist, even if they had gone a few days without the chance to bathe and her clothes were shabby.

Lucy went in while Isla stayed outside. It was easier to pick up a man alone. When Lucy emerged with a man, Isla would follow at a discreet distance. It was their routine. She watched the girl cross the Grassmarket and lean against a wall on the far side. The sun was starting to dip behind the castle on the rocky promenade above. Lucy entered the smoke and noise. It was busy, which made her task easier. After eyeing up the clientele, she latched onto a group of men she hadn't seen before. She got talking to them, they bought her a drink. They were from the north, Aberdeen, and were in the city for the Farmer's Market, looking to purchase livestock. It only took Lucy an hour before she propositioned one of them, a broad-shouldered and bearded burly lad in his early twenties. He was eager to take her up on her offer.

They emerged together. Lucy glanced in Isla's direction. She was still there, leaning against the wall. Lucy laughed as her partner made a joke and they walked towards the High Street. Lucy led the way. She looked back and saw Isla following. The man was likely married. Lucy had flirted with him and offered herself. He had told her he didn't have anywhere to take her. He was looking for a quick bit of fun before returning home the next day. Lucy would take him to one of the narrow closes off High Street, where the steep walls and dark shadows would give them privacy from prying eyes.

They passed St Giles Cathedral and headed down the sloping street. They crossed the bridge and passed Blackfriars Street. The man moaned about how far they were walking as they passed several suitable closes. Lucy reassured him, 'Ah always go tae this wan, it gie's us a wee bit a' privacy.' She gave him an enticing look. Isla was still there, keeping them in sight. She would know where they were going, Lucy always took them to the same place. At Chalmers Close, Lucy turned. It was a narrow and dark alleyway, enclosed by steep-sided buildings, and covered with a roof provided by the second floor of the buildings continuing overhead, creating a short tunnel over the entrance. Beyond that, the steep sides kept going until steps further on marked a steep descent and led to an adjoining street.

It was dark now. Isla would wait for her just inside the Close entrance. Lucy let him kiss her and touch her and she touched him and did what she had to do, hoping it would be over quickly and without pain. Isla would know what was happening. She would be able to hear them. It didn't take him long. After a rough, drunken coupling, it was over.

'That was a quick wan, richt enough,' Lucy couldn't resist.

'Hush, ye cheeky tart.'

'Ye seemed tae enjoy it guid enough.'

'Ah've had better.'

'Charmin'. Ye'll still pay the rest a' the money, though.'

'Like hell ah will. Ye should've asked fir it aw up front, ya daft whore.'

'Ah come oan, dinnae be like that. Ah gave ye whit ye wanted, richt enough.'

'Yer nae worth mare than the four shillings ye've got awready.'

The slap echoed around the steep walls when his hand hit her cheek.

She recovered and picked herself up. She had the switchblade drawn in her hand. 'Hand o'er the money an' we kin part wi' ae fond kiss.'

'Put that blade away, ye stupid wee lassie. Ye'll git yersel' hurt playin' wi' that.'

He lunged at her, reaching for the blade. She bit his arm as he smothered her. He cried out and lashed out and Lucy fell and her head hit the stone ground with a thud.

A dark fog smothered her. 'Ah'll beat ye 'til nae man would ever come near ye again, ye dirty whore.' He was on her now, kneeling over her body as his fists punched her face.

Her head rolled from side to side. She tried to yell, but she was weak and disorientated. She begged him to stop, crying out in pain, but he kept going. She had been with men who had hit her before. She was used to that, but this was different. He kept going. She could see her own blood spraying from her face and clouding her eyes. She heard the crack of her skull as he slammed her head into the ground again. She saw a glint on the ground. The switchblade, lying where she had dropped it. She waited for the final, fatal blow to come. Then he paused. He was unsure, suddenly wakening from his rage and discovering what he had done in his fit of temper. He looked to the side. Lucy rolled her head over and saw Isla. She tried to warn her, to tell her to get away.

She could only watch as Isla darted forward and picked up the switchblade. The man was too slow to react. Isla slashed at him with wild anger. She aimed for his arms, his shoulders, his neck and face. Isla knew how to slash the jugular, Lucy thought, she had done it to herself once.

He was too big and powerful. He fought her off. He threw her aside. Isla hit the wall. She had slashed him and drawn blood from several cuts. Lucy prayed he would leave her alone. Please don't kill her too. Then there were other voices, people at the top of the close. He looked towards them, then to Isla, then at her, lying in a pool of blood, and then he ran. He carried on down the close until it reached the other street and he disappeared around the corner. He left a trail of blood behind him. With luck, he would die from his injuries, Lucy thought. It would serve him right.

Isla scrambled over and knelt by her. She was in tears. She placed Lucy's head on her lap. Lucy's face was a pulp of blood and bones and twisted cartilage. Isla tried to wipe the blood away. She opened her eyes, white orbs in a sea of red. She tried to speak. She managed to get out a single word. 'Bastart.'

The voices from the High Street drew closer. Someone was coming. Isla had to go. If she was found with Lucy beaten and half-dead, they would take her to the police. The police would want to know who she was, where she had come from. Lucy knew Isla was hiding from her past. Everyone on the streets was in some way. Their eyes met and she willed Isla to leave her and run.

Isla cradled her and put her mouth next to her bloodied ear and whispered, 'Forgive me,' and then she let her friend go. Lucy saw her feet receding. She got to the street at the end of the close and then she was gone.

She turned her head and looked up at the stars in the night sky and knew she was dying. She had finally run out of luck. She had survived longer than most on the streets. She hoped Isla would find a way to get back on her feet, to get off the streets and make something of herself. Her final thoughts were of her friend, as she felt the blood gurgling in her throat and she coughed and spluttered and closed her eyes for the last time.

12

TUESDAY, 23 NOVEMBER

1920

Two days had passed. Since he had last walked along the path round the Braid Hills to Craiglockhart, so much had changed. Had it really been a week since Constable Inch had stopped him and sent him into the tower?

Jessie had come home after she had calmed down. She went straight to her room and shut herself away. He had been unable to ask her anymore about her past. He knew not to push her if she did not wish to talk. She appeared for breakfast on the Sunday morning, but remained in her room for the rest of the time. She helped out at the surgery on Monday, but hid herself from the patients, staying in the back room. When Thomas asked her if she was okay, she responded with everyday pleasantries. He could tell she was putting on a brave face, determined to pretend that nothing had changed between them. She wanted things to go back to the way they had been before, but she must have known that wasn't possible. Her behaviour confused him. He was sure they had made a crucial breakthrough in their reserved friendship. They could now trust each other to share more of their lives. At the same time, he acknowledged he had not shared anything of his war experience with her. Was he ready to open up? He had to get used to her new identity, not just her name, but the woman he now knew. She wanted to close down again and retreat; he was determined not to allow this to happen. He knew from his work with the soldiers at the hospital and the *talking cure* that shutting her emotions away was not the answer. Locking feelings inside only let them eat away at you. That was his own experience. They both needed to open up to the other, he as much as she. When he returned home after his day at the hospital, he would sit her down and persuade her to talk.

The police had not returned. In fact, they had been conspicuous in their absence from Liberton. The newspaper that morning had revealed why. The investigation had taken a twist elsewhere.

MISSING CHILD FOUND SAFE AND WELL

SENSATION AS BABY FOUND LIVING WITH WEALTHY COUPLE

MOTHER UNDER POLICE ARREST

A child reported missing from a city poorhouse in Edinburgh was last night found alive and well.

Miss Abigail MacPherson, known as Abi, reported her six-month-old son, Roddy, missing to police on 8 November, claiming he had been abducted from her care while staying at the Craigleith Poorhouse on Crewe Road.

A nationwide police investigation was launched to find the missing child and two others who had disappeared in similar circumstances in recent weeks. One child, a six-month-old girl, was found brutally slain in the Liberton area last week. In a sensational turn of events, Roddy MacPherson has been traced and found alive and well, being cared for by a married couple in Morningside.

Detective Inspector McHarg, from the city police force, is leading the investigation into the disappearances. He told the gathered reporters that Miss MacPherson was now under arrest, charged with falsely reporting a crime and wasting police time. 'It appears Miss MacPherson decided to give her child up after becoming unable to care for him. She sold her child to a wealthy couple who were looking to begin a family. Sometime later, Miss MacPherson changed her mind about wanting to give up her child. After hearing reports of two babies being taken from poorhouses elsewhere in the city, she contacted police to report her own child missing in an attempt to have the police trace and return her child to her.'

The officer added there would be criminal charges for those involved in the incident.

'It is illegal to buy a child off the street. There are correct and lawful channels to follow for those wishing to take on a child for whatever reason. It is also illegal to sell a child for money. Miss MacPherson has been charged with this offence, alongside wasting police time. She has been remanded at this time ahead of a trial. Her actions have caused much distress, not only to her own child and the family whom she engaged in her unlawful practice, but she has also harmed our ongoing investigation into the other disappearance and the murder of Lily Fitzpatrick last week in Liberton.'

He declined to name the couple involved, suggesting they were entitled to anonymity at this troubling time. Meanwhile, Roddy MacPherson is being cared for in the city orphanage.

The body of Lily May Fitzpatrick was found in the village of Liberton, in the south of the city last Tuesday night. She had been the subject of a brutal attack. Investigations to find the murderer are ongoing. Detective Inspector McHarg refused to give any update on the current investigation, saying only that he was confident the perpetrator would be brought to justice.

A third child, Adam Symons, was reported missing from the Queensberry House of Refuge by his mother.

'The safe discovery of Roddy MacPherson gives us hope that Adam Symons will still be found safe and well and we are committed to using every resource to accomplish this. I again urge anyone who may have any information as to his whereabouts to get in touch with the police as soon as possible.'

Thomas read the article to Jessie over the breakfast table that morning. She gave no reaction to the news that a child had been found alive and well. Thomas thought it may have reminded her of her own experience, but she showed no emotion. She commented that it was good news, then left the table and returned to her room. Thomas left before she emerged. She was due at the school as usual. He wondered if she was in denial. He was glad one of the children had been found, however unsavoury the circumstances of the boy's disappearance.

Constance MacKay could talk of nothing else when he got to the hospital. She knew of the discovery in Liberton the previous week, and her eyes widened when Thomas told her of his own involvement. He did not tell her the woman who lived under his roof had been questioned by the police.

He had a full day of appointments once more. Doctor MacMyn found him during a mid-morning break and delivered bad news. The remaining services at the hospital were to be wound down completely by the end of the year.

'They have agreed to open a small unit at the Corstorphine Hospital where I will be able to continue to see patients. I'm afraid the travel might make it impossible for you to continue your service, Doctor Stevenson, but I implore you nonetheless to consider it.'

Thomas replied he would have to think about it. Corstorphine was further to the west, at the opposite side of the city from Liberton, and the journey there and back, even if he had access to a horse or a motor car, would make for a long day. He assured his patients that Doctor MacMyn would take them on and he was a more than capable doctor. Nurse MacKay would make the move with MacMyn and treatment would continue. Thomas couldn't help but feel he was letting his fellow soldiers down, a fresh abandonment by a brother officer.

By the end of the day, the prospect of the walk through the dark back to Liberton filled him with trepidation after what had happened the previous week. As he was about to leave, his coat half-pulled on, Nurse MacKay knocked.

'I'm very sorry, Doctor, a patient has just arrived unannounced.'

'Are they upset?' he asked, pulling his arms out of his coat with reluctance.

'No, he seems perfectly fine. It's Private Watt, the man who came last week.'

The mention of his name made Thomas stop. 'I'm not due to see him again until next week. Did he say what he wanted?' He tried to hide his annoyance.

'No, only he insisted he had to see you and he couldn't wait another week.'

'Very well, send him through, but make it clear to him that I have only fifteen minutes and then I must be on my way.'

Nurse MacKay left the room. Thomas returned to his seat behind his desk. He was not going to allow Private Watt to get comfortable in the armchairs he normally used when consulting a patient. More than the inconvenience of Duncan Watt's visit irritated Thomas. His appearance brought back the discomfort of Watt's threats about Thomas's drinking, and his insinuations about Jessie's character, not to mention his appearance at the church hall. This unexpected appointment presented an opportunity to ask him exactly what he had been doing there.

The tall man entered, the scar on his face creased by the wide smile on his face. Without waiting to be invited, he pulled a chair out from the desk and sat opposite Thomas, crossing his long legs and leaning backwards. 'Thank you for seeing me, Doctor. I'm sure you've had a busy day.'

Thomas was in no mood to be polite. 'I am weary, Mr Watt, and ready to see the lights of home, but as you have made the effort to come, it would be remiss of me to deny you a moment of my time. How can I help?'

'Call me Duncan. I think we can be on less formal terms now.' Thomas couldn't have disagreed more. 'I understand you've been helping the police with their investigation into the missing children.'

Thomas was taken aback by the unexpected question. 'That's not something I can discuss with a patient. I'm sure you understand.'

'Must have been a terrible sight, though.'

'As I understand it, the police have not divulged what the crime scene looked like.'

'Well, I'm guessing a dead child is not a pleasant thing to see.'

'Private Watt,' Thomas failed to hide his irritation, 'was there something about your condition you wished to talk about?'

'Alright, calm down, Doctor,' Duncan Watt held his palms up in mock alarm. Thomas had an uneasy feeling. 'It's just with your troubles, from the war and with the drink, I thought you would have been struggling with something as traumatic as that.'

'Of course, it was upsetting to see such a thing. I leave it to the police to find the person responsible and my involvement in the matter is at an end. Can I help you with something, Mr Watt?'

'Duncan,' he again corrected Thomas. 'I hope you're not angry with me, Doctor. You see, that dead child is what I wanted to talk to you about. You see, it's brought back some nasty memories for me.'

Thomas was taken aback again. He looked closely into Watt's eyes, studying him. He searched for the telltale look that would give him the truth. He had seen it in every war veteran he had helped care for at the hospital and at his practice. He could not see it in this man's eyes. He did not carry the haunted, tortured look that stayed with all those who had seen the true horror of the trenches.

'In what way?' he asked.

'From before the war. Long before it.'

'What happened?'

'I was a father, but the wee soul didn't survive. The doctors said it was an illness in the lungs. Not strong enough.'

'I'm sorry to hear that.'

'I was only young. It didn't hit me too bad at the time. I thought I would have had plenty of time to start a family. When I was a bit older and ready to settle down. But the mother, she took it badly and wouldn't have anything to do with me after that. Even then, I didn't mind. She was entitled to go and live her life, and I thought I would find another to marry.' He stopped and took a pack of cigarettes from his pocket. 'You mind?' Thomas shook his head. 'Then I never did settle down after that. I was a jack-the-lad, enjoying myself through my days as a young man. I had no idea there was a war round the corner.'

Lives interrupted, families not started or torn apart. The chance of a normal family life destroyed. There were many stories like his.

'And look at me now.' Watt waved the cigarette at his scarred face and with his other hand slapped his left leg. 'No nice woman is going to want to take up with a disfigured cripple like me. I'd just be a burden to them and a useless father. You see, Doctor, what I'm getting at is the war took away my chance of ever being a father, and then I saw this story about the missing children and then one of them turning up dead. It triggered something in me, Doctor.'

Thomas's antagonism faded as the man told his story. 'I understand. I'm afraid there is little I can offer to take away those painful memories. I can only imagine what it must have felt like as a young man to lose a child.'

'Yes, I wouldn't wish it on my worst enemy.'

'However, aren't you being a little pessimistic about your

future? You're still a healthy young man, you have employment. There are many young women out there for you. Women capable of looking beyond a scar or a limp, able to see the man beyond them. Women who understand the sacrifice you made for their country and who would love you for that.'

'That's not the reaction I get when I try talking to any women in the pub.'

'You have just not spoken to the right woman yet. I don't wish to belittle your experiences, but I have seen men return from war in much worse condition than you, with missing limbs and burnt flesh, deaf and blind, and many have returned into the arms of a loving family or have met a wife and made a fresh start. You mustn't be so pessimistic.'

'You're right, Doctor. It's just when I see the stories about the missing children and think how my life could've turned out, I get very depressed about it, and angry.'

'That's perfectly understandable, Duncan.' Thomas softened his approach. He clearly was upset and had issues that needed to be discussed further. 'I'm afraid you may not have heard, but the practice here is to be closed down completely by the end of the year. I would be happy to refer you to Doctor MacMyn, who will carry on his work at the hospital in Corstorphine.'

'No. I wouldn't want to trouble him. I guess I'll just soldier on.'

'I have one or two more days here before the end of the year. Keep your appointment for next week and book a further one with Nurse MacKay. I would like to explore this more with you.' Thomas couldn't leave him in this troubled state, despite his earlier misgivings.

'I might just do that, aye.' Watt ground his cigarette into the ashtray on the desk. It had burned down to the butt while being held in his hand. He stood to leave and offered his hand to Thomas, who rose to meet him.

'Do you stay nearby?' Thomas asked.

'Not far away from here, Doctor. Gorgie.'

'I saw you the other day. In Liberton at the church hall.'

'Yes, like I said, I took an interest in the dead child they found.'

'I saw you speaking to one of the detectives.'

Without missing a beat, Watt replied. 'I was curious to know more about what they had found.'

It made sense, given what the man had confessed to about his past. There was more to it though, something he was hiding from Thomas. 'And did they tell you anything more?'

Watt smiled, the scar creasing up again as he did so. 'No, of course they didn't. Playing their cards close to their chests.'

They were still holding hands over the desk. Thomas released his first. 'Well, I must be off home, and so must you. I'll see you next week, and make that further appointment with the nurse.'

'I will, Doctor.' Watt limped over to the door and opened it. As he was about to step out of the office he turned back to Thomas. 'Of course, if you're in Liberton, perhaps I could carry on seeing you at your own house?'

Thomas looked up. 'There would be a cost to see me as a private patient.'

'You'd not be generous enough to do it for free? One soldier to another? I reckon I'd like to visit you, Doctor.'

The grin turned into a sneer once more, the same look that had perturbed Thomas the previous week. 'I also heard the police turned up at your house, Doctor, to question that woman you have living with you. Why would they be talking to her, exactly?'

Thomas was caught off guard again. 'You would have to ask the police that question, Private Watt. I wasn't there for the conversation they had.'

'I heard it was more than a conversation. I heard that she's a prime suspect.'

'That's quite enough, Mr Watt. I would ask you to kindly leave now.'

'Don't get upset, Doctor.' The scar was bright red and threatening. 'I'll see you next week and you can confess all to me.' He let out a loud mocking laugh. 'I'd like to meet this woman of yours.' He walked out of the door.

Thomas was left on his own. He didn't know what to think about the mysterious Private. His manner was more threatening than someone looking to stir up trouble or to find out the latest gossip. Had he been sent by a newspaperman to dig up some information? Thomas had heard about the underhand tactics being used by the press, but that did not explain the hostility Thomas felt from him. He picked up his coat and locked the office door behind him.

Nurse MacKay was putting on her coat.

'Did Duncan Watt make an appointment?'

'No, he has one for next week already. He walked straight out without so much as a goodbye. A little rude I thought, but then I suspected you had a difficult talk with him. I hope everything is okay.'

'Fine,' Thomas lied.

'Was he supposed to make another appointment?'

'I recommended he did.' He paused. 'Do we have contact details for him?'

'He filled in an address last week. Do you want me to look it out?'

'No, never mind. What about his papers from the War Office, have they arrived?'

'Still no sign of them. I'm sure they'll turn up eventually, but we might not be here by the time they do arrive.'

'Very well. I suppose we have to hope he brings himself back next week. If he doesn't, I'm afraid there's nothing more we can do for him.'

'Such a shame.' Nurse MacKay shook her head, showing her pity for the poor souls damaged by the war.

'Goodnight, Constance.' Thomas waved her goodbye as he set off down the corridor, 'I'll let you lock up as usual.'

When he stepped out into the dark November evening, Thomas feared Duncan Watt might be waiting for him. There was no one there, yet he could not shake the feeling that he had not seen the last of him. He thought back to what he had seen in the man's eyes. The haunted torture of war had been absent, but in its place was something more disturbing. A look Thomas was unsure upon whom it was directed and one he did not know how to deal with. Watt's eyes had the look of malevolent hatred burning through them.

13

TUESDAY, 23 NOVEMBER

1920

Since the policemen had visited her on Saturday, she had hidden away. When she had stopped running, she found herself in the playing fields behind Kirk Brae. The Industrial School was sheltered behind the line of large trees. She looked towards it. Had anyone seen her? The mad woman flying across the grass, her hair in disarray, her dress flailing behind her. She breathed in shallow sobs until she regained control of herself, bent double, her hands on her knees. She could not go back. Not to the madhouse where they had trapped her, not to the streets of the city, not to the poorhouse. And not to the canal, not to that night. It had broken her once; she would not let it happen again. She must stay in control this time.

Deep breaths. Calm. The cold air stung her warm, flushed cheeks. She had done nothing wrong. Not this time. She had hurt people before. Alexander, Lucy, Anne. Not this time. She would be strong, no matter what it took. Truth was on her side. The police had no evidence. She would face up to them. But how had they found her? Regaining her composure, she began to think. Who had the detectives been speaking to? No one in Liberton knew of her past life or her past identity, yet someone had tipped them off about her. Someone who knew her fifteen years ago and recognised her now. Someone who knew she had been in the asylum and had been at Dalmuir House. She had revealed this past to no one until that Saturday morning when the police arrived.

They couldn't think she could kill a child. They must know she did not mean to kill her own child. She hadn't killed him; it was not her fault. Or had she? No, she must not think like that again. She must keep herself together. She must be strong. She walked back to the house. News of the police visit would already have started to spread around the surrounding houses and the inn and the local shop and the church hall. She would face them all; she had nothing to hide from them. These people would judge her, they already did because she had stayed at Alnwickhill House with the other women. She got home and went to her room.

Thomas called on her through the door, asking if she was okay. She replied, but remained locked away, letting her mind settle, her thoughts collect. After a disturbed night, she got up and dressed. She stayed in her room, only leaving to take her meals. They made small talk and avoided her past, though she sensed Thomas wanted to talk to her about it. She knew he would be kind to her. She took advantage of his kindness, telling him she would be fine and they could talk more when she felt able. Sitting in her room, looking at herself in her mirror, wondering what had happened to that young girl who had fallen into the canal all those years ago, she made one decision. She would no longer dye her hair black. She had no reason to any longer. She would let her red hair grow through.

Thomas was busy the next day with patients, and Jessie helped, though she stayed out of view of the patients. Her fear was that the police visit would cause Thomas's reputation to suffer. He had put a lot on the line already by having her in the house with him. She did not wish to bring disrepute upon him.

This morning at breakfast, she had appeared dressed for school. He made her tea. It was like any other Tuesday morning. It was an illusion that would not last.

'Perhaps we could talk this evening, if you feel strong enough,' Thomas said.

Jessie looked down and hid her face behind her cup as she took a sip of the warm tea. 'Perhaps.'

Thomas said no more about it. He left for Craiglockhart and the hospital. Half an hour later, Jessie put on her cloak and left the house for the first time since that weekend. She kept her head down as she walked to the school. She could feel them looking at her. She noticed it as soon as she had left the house. She glanced up and saw them watching her. What were they saying about her? Thomas had shown her the newspaper that morning. One of the missing children had been found. They knew she had nothing to do with that. Did they believe she had something to do with the dead child found in the tower? Deep breaths. Calm. She had to keep control of her emotions. She had to remain collected. She could not let paranoia overwhelm her. She had done nothing wrong. None of these people knew anything about her, or her past.

She paused at the entrance to the school. One of them did know about her past. One of them had told the police about her. If they had told the police, who else had they told? Had the police told others the story of the fallen woman who lived among them, pretending to be respectable? Voices sprang into her mind as her thoughts spiralled out of control.

'She killed her own child.'

'Drowned him because she couldn't look after him.'

'What mother would do that to their own?'

'Only a monster could do such a thing.'

'She stabbed an innocent man in the city.'

'Typical of women like that. They start young and get an appetite for it.'

'If she's done it before, who's to say she didn't do it again?'

'Maybe she snapped again. Been in the loony bin, I heard.'

'Maybe she has a taste for it. A serial killer.'

'Stop it!' she whispered under her breath. She had to stop them. She could not let them in again, the voices that convinced her she had killed Alexander. The voices that drove her out of her mind. The voices she had defeated. She had not banished them after all.

Mrs Henderson failed to hide her alarm when Jessie entered the hall. Betsy and Florence stopped gathering plates and cutlery and stared from her to Jessie, unsure what to do.

Mrs Henderson recovered herself. 'Chop, chop, you two. Get those plates into the kitchen and cleaned up. Lots to do today.' The young girls set about their work, stealing glances at Jessie as they went.

'Good morning, Mrs Henderson.'

'Louise, I wasn't sure if we would see you today.'

'And why would that be, Mrs Henderson?'

The school matron was caught off guard. 'I had just heard... well, that is, the police.' She tailed off. 'Would you prefer to be called Louise or Jessie?'

'Jessie is my real name.' There was no point in denying anything; word had clearly reached the school. She was convinced Mrs Henderson would see through her brave face and notice her trembling hands. 'What about the police?'

'I heard they came to visit you.'

'I imagine the police visit many people while conducting enquiries in a local area.'

'I heard they questioned you about the dead boy.'

'Who did you hear that from, Mrs Henderson? I do hope the police have not been gossiping with members of the public.'

'No, quite right. It's just, you know, around the village.'

'Well, let me put your mind at ease. I spoke to the police as part of their enquiries and have tried to assist them in their investigation, as I'm sure any decent member of the public would do. Beyond that, there is nothing more I can tell you. Now, does the usual laundry need done this morning?'

Mrs Henderson could only nod as Jessie walked past her to the laundry room. It was a small moment of triumph, but it showed she could do it. She could face up to the gossips of the village. She was strong enough.

This conviction lasted until mid-morning, when Florence found her in a dormitory. 'Mr Russel would like to see you.'

Jessie's heart sank. She knew what he would say before she had even knocked on the door to his office.

'Come in.' The Superintendent was sitting behind his desk and didn't look up as Jessie entered. 'Take a seat, Jessie.' He had obviously spoken with Mrs Henderson.

Jessie sat in the chair opposite him and placed her hands on her lap. Mr Russel finished writing in a notebook and closed it and tidied away his pen and ink. He cleared his throat.

Jessie broke the silence as he looked at her. 'You wished to see me, Mr Russel?'

'Indeed, I did, Louise, or, I mean…' He cleared his throat again and shifted in his chair. He leaned forward and clasped his hands in front of him on the desk. 'I'm afraid this isn't an easy thing to discuss. You will remember when you started here with us I made it quite clear that we were willing to forgive any past indiscretions. I believe in giving people a second chance in life, you understand, so despite whatever misfortune had befallen you, despite whatever led you to Alnwickhill House, I was convinced you deserved the opportunity to rebuild your circumstances.'

'I'm very grateful for the opportunity, Mr Russel,' Jessie cut in.

'We took a risk on the understanding that the reputation of the school must come first in these decisions.'

'Of course. I hope I haven't let you down in my time here.'

'Not at all. You have become invaluable, not just to Mrs Henderson, but to the teaching staff, and to the boys as well.'

'I'm pleased to hear so.' Jessie waited for the conversation to turn against her.

'Which makes it all the more difficult to have to relieve you of your position at the school.' He paused, expecting Jessie to object or react in some way. When he saw that she didn't, he proceeded to explain his decision. 'It has come to my attention that the police visited you last Saturday in connection with the child found in the tower. I do not wish to know what was discussed between you and the police, that is a private matter, but I understand you have lied about your real name and certain events from your past. In light of these matters, I think it better if you cease to be involved with the school for the time being.'

'I see.'

'You understand, if it was just up to me alone… I don't for a second think that you would be involved with anything like this.'

'Yes?'

'I have to think about those who donate money that we need to fund the school, our benefactors. There are people talking now. Saying that you once had a child of your own…' He left the rest of the sentence hanging, not wishing to recount what was being said about her.

Jessie felt the anger rising inside her. The injustice of it, the determination to fight, the fear, the regret. All were simmering now, ready to explode. She could not let that happen in front of Mr Russel.

'Are there any truth to these rumours?' he asked.

What use was it to deny it any further? The truth was out there now, circulating among the people of Liberton, among those who knew her and those who did not. All were judging her, wondering if she had something to do with the dead child. Was she a murderer? A prostitute? A lunatic? A danger to them?

She hid her pain from the superintendent. She would not break down in front of him. 'I can see that I have put you in quite a difficult situation, Mr Russel,' she said, ignoring his question about her past. 'I would not want to see the school suffer, or the boys. Thank you for the opportunity you have given me. It is unfortunate that you wish to end our arrangement in this manner, though I quite understand your reasoning.'

'Jessie, I...'

'It is quite alright, Mr Russel. Neither of us wishes to make this more uncomfortable than it already is.' She stood up from her chair.

'Perhaps in the future, once this matter has been settled...' But they both understood that Jessie would never be able to return to her position at the school. The damage to her character was set in stone among the community, whatever the outcome of the police investigation. Even if she was to be exonerated of this crime, her past had been revealed to all. She was no longer a fit and proper person to be educating the young boys.

'You are very kind, Mr Russel. I thank you for the opportunity once again. Good day.' She left the room before Mr Russel could rise from his chair.

She ran. She didn't care who saw her. All the composure that she had mustered in Mr Russel's office was gone. She left by the main door, not stopping to say goodbye to anyone. Once outside, under the branches of the tree-lined avenue, she started sobbing. She could feel her mind slipping, giving in to the turmoil. They all knew. She hadn't imagined it. They stared and pointed. They looked at her with disgust. She heard the voices. 'Whore', 'child killer', 'murderer', 'lunatic'. She was all of these things. She pulled the pins out that held her hair in place, letting long, dyed-black strands flow out behind her as she fled. She felt trapped. She clawed the top buttons of her dress open, exposing the angry red scar, letting the cold air get to her skin. Tears ran down her face, she wiped them with her sleeve, smearing her make-up, revealing the patchwork of scars and marks from her years of hardship. They all knew the truth about her. They could see her for what she really was. Let there be no doubt. They were right to accuse her, to believe she could murder a child. She had done it before. She was fallen, out of her mind, out of control. She had been with men. She had killed poor Alexander. She had stabbed a man. She had allowed Lucy to be murdered while she stood and did nothing.

Her dress billowed behind her as she ran down Kirk Brae. Thomas would be out. She had brought shame onto him as well. Now he would look at her with disgust, too. The police would be back for her. The girl who had killed her baby. She could not go back to the asylum. She would rather die than be locked up again.

She would escape. Get out of Liberton and start again somewhere else. She would go to London, a new country, a new city. She had the skills she needed to keep going, to keep running. Thomas would be harmed no further by his association with her. Liberton would be free of her stain. The police would come after her, but she had outrun them before. What did they care about a common whore? It would be better for everyone if she disappeared. They might want her dead, but she would not give them that satisfaction.

Back in her bedroom, she packed what little she would need. She had to shed the skin of her Liberton life. She filled a small bag with a blouse, a dress and a hairbrush. She collected the few coins she had from the dresser. There was nothing else she needed. She would pick up what food she could on her way, as she used to do on the streets.

She took one last look around the house that had sheltered her, the place she had allowed herself to think of as home. She had dared to picture herself living here when she was old, with Thomas. She caught sight of herself in the mirror. Louise was gone. She saw the real Jessie now. Smeared make-up ran down her tear-strewn face, her dress was ripped open, her hair tangled. A mad woman. She laughed at herself. That was what she was. A poor lunatic. She was what they said she was. She tore down the mirror from its stand, smashing it onto the wooden top of the dresser. Shards of shattered glass spilled onto the floor.

She ran down the path, the front door of the house left open behind her. She had only a vague idea of where she was going. She took the road north towards the city. The important thing was to head away from there, leaving her past behind once more.

14

THE POORHOUSE

1913

Agnes Nelson took the steaming mugs of hot tea and sat them on the dining table in the middle of the small kitchen. Sitting on a chair, she removed her shoes and rubbed her aching feet. The rain battered the window and the wind gusted round the gables of the house. She was glad to be indoors, but nights such as this made her think of all the women who had no place to shelter from the elements.

She started as the door flew open and Pete Boyd was blown into the room. He pushed the door closed, locking it with the heavy steel bolt, before removing his soaked mackintosh and boots.

'Tea's brewed.' She pointed to the mug on the table.

'Much obliged.' He nodded. 'That's it aw locked up fir the night, bit the gutters 'roun' the back are overflowin' agin. Ah'll need tae git the ladders an' clear them in the mornin'.' Pete pulled out the seat opposite her and took the mug between his hands, letting the warm steam encircle his face.

'Nae need fir ye tae stay the nicht,' Agnes said. 'They're aw settled doon awready.'

'Sure? Nae expectin' any late callers?'

'They were telt last week an' ah've nae foun' any mare trouble since. Ah think they git the message.'

'They're a fine bunch.' Pete took a welcome sip of the hot tea, feeling it warm his insides as it slid down his neck. 'Ah wonder why ye bother wi' it aw, Agnes. Yer tae kind tae them an' they dinnae deserve ye lookin' after them.'

'Somewan has tae, Pete, ye ken that. Ye cannae leave these poor wummin abandoned. Ah wish somewan else wud dae it, richt enough. It shouldnae be left tae the likes a' me and places like this. The cooncil and the government should be helpin' them.'

'Helpin' them? How are they goin' tae pay fir that? Mare taxes? Most a' them git themselves intae this state by themselves anyway. Why should others bail them oot?'

'Peter Boyd,' exclaimed Agnes. 'Y'er a mare worldly man than that, if ye think these wummin became fallen oan their own.'

'Ach, ye ken whit ah mean.'

Agnes did know what he meant. It was the way that most of the people around Liberton thought. It was the way most of the people around the whole country thought. That the women who needed to seek refuge in the Edinburgh Industrial House for Fallen Women did so by choice. No one was interested in their stories. No one cared to hear what had driven them into a life on the streets of the city. They were prostitutes, whores, criminals. They deserved little sympathy and certainly not any help from the good society. They deserved to be forgotten. Agnes was one of the few who saw these women as victims. Some were victims of tragic circumstances or bad luck, some were victims of poor choices, some were victims of abusive men. They were all victims of the society they lived in. A society that turned its back on those in need. A society run by men, where men made the laws and held the power in public office, in the courts and in the family home. It was these men who ensured these women became victims. Half of the twenty women she was sheltering in the refuge were there as a direct result of a man's action. The bastard children they carried with them were testament to that. Others suffered through the male-dominated institutions that held the power over them – the judges, the priests and the ministers, the managers, the husbands – who abused them, or failed to sympathise with them. Agnes had never cared for men. Her father had brought her up well, but she soon realised he was an exception and she had never desired the company of a man in her life. It irritated her now, in her advancing years, that she had to rely on Pete Boyd to help with the manual tasks around Alnwickhill House. Built only twenty years ago, the house seemed to have developed a worrying amount of maintenance issues in recent years, from the rattling tall windows to the leaks in the tiled roof and the unstable chimney stacks. At least the sandstone walls were solid enough against the onslaught of the wind and rain and kept the home warm.

'Weel, ah'll be aff then, if yer sure yer settled fir the nicht. Ah'll pop back in the mornin' tae look at they gutters, if the rain has stopped by then.' He took his empty mug to the sink and sat back down to pull his boots on. Agnes took a sip from her tea and watched him. He wasn't a bad sort really. He helped around the place for very little pay, accepting only what Agnes could afford to give him, which never amounted to much. Despite what he said in their moments alone, she knew he cared for the women of the house. He was always kind to them, even happy to enter into some of the coarser chatter with them that Agnes tried to discourage. She liked to try and set an example, even to those who had not experienced that before in their lives. She could have ended up with someone a lot worse than Pete to help her around the place.

'Thank ye. Git hame quick an' dinnae be stoppin' at the inn oan the way. Better tae be hame by the fire oan a nicht like this.'

'Dinnae worry aboot me, Agnes. Ye concentrate oan lookin' after they wummin a' yers. Ah kin look after masel.'

She decided not to get into an argument about his drinking again. Pete was well known around Liberton for being much too fond of whisky of an evening and was often found wandering the streets in a drunken state. Agnes wished he would get himself some help, but he was right. She had too much on her hands tending to her fallen women to take on an alcoholic, too.

He pulled his damp mackintosh back on and turned the hood up. Just as he unlocked the bolt, they heard the faint knock from the other side of the door. Pete turned and looked at Agnes, who shrugged. She was not expecting anyone, and doubted anyone would choose to come calling on such a foul night as this. Pete pulled the door open and stepped back as a bundle of rags collapsed on the doormat in a soaking heap. Agnes jumped to her feet, her chair scraping across the tiled floor.

'Good God,' Pete exclaimed.

'Help her up,' Agnes shouted. It was a woman who had landed in front of them. She was soaked through. Her clothes were tattered rags. Her hair was a tangled, damp mess that obscured her pale white face. Her eyes were closed. Pete pulled her up and dragged her into a chair at the table. Agnes closed the door behind them. The pitiful creature slumped forward, her head on the table. Her breathing was shallow and weak. A pool of water began to form around the base of the chair, dripping from her clothes. She shivered uncontrollably.

'Git some towels fae the cupboard in the hallway,' Agnes instructed. She had been in this situation before. 'An' go tae the laundry room an' fetch some dry clathes.' Pete left the room. Agnes poured water into the kettle and set it on the stove to boil again. While she waited for Pete to return, she sat next to the woman and whispered a few calming words into her ear. She pushed the damp, matted hair away from her face. On closer inspection, Agnes saw it was copper red. A stillness settled over the kitchen. The small details of the moment were heightened. Agnes heard the drip of the rainwater on the floor, the wind gusting outside, the bubbling water in the kettle and the tick of the clock in the hallway echo around them. She took the woman's limp hand in hers and rubbed it.

'There, there, yer safe noo, dear,' she whispered. The woman's breathing settled into a steadier rhythm.

The silence was broken by the harsh whistle of the kettle on the stove and Pete returning with a handful of towels and an assortment of clothes he had grabbed from the laundry. Agnes poured the hot water into a fresh mug of tea. She took the bottle of scotch from the cupboard and poured a double measure into a glass tumbler. She brought the drinks over to the table, where Pete stood with his bundle of clothes.

'Leave those oan the table an' gie us some privacy while we git her changed oot a' these wet things.'

'Ah'll wait in the drawin' room,' he looked conspicuously at the woman. 'Shout me if ye need help.'

'Ah'm sure we'll be jist fine, Pete, but thank you.'

She waited until Pete had closed the door behind him and they were alone again.

'Richt, let's git ye sorted, young lady.' She lifted her head from the table, sitting her upright in the chair. She brought the glass of scotch to the mouth of the woman. Her lips were cracked and colourless. Agnes saw scratches on her face and the pink droplets of rainwater mixed with blood that ran down her cheeks. Her cheekbones stuck out from her undernourished face. She held the scotch under her nose, letting the fumes linger in the hope it would help revive her. The woman's eyes flickered.

'There we go, dear. Git some a' this doon ye.' She tipped the scotch into the narrow parting between her lips, a little at first and then the rest of the measure. It elicited a sudden, hacking cough as the warm liquid disappeared down her throat. 'There we go, that's brought ye back tae life noo, hasn't it?' The woman's eyes opened and for the first time she took in her surroundings. Her body became rigid. Agnes could sense the reactions of a woman who was used to being in danger. She was on guard.

'Let's dry ye aff.' Agnes started with the woman's hair, standing behind her and placing a towel over her head. The woman didn't react, she seemed numb. Agnes helped her stand. 'Let's git these wet rags aff ye.' She lifted the tattered dress, made of rough hemp, and the woman raised her arms and allowed the sodden garment to be removed. She folded her arms across her bare chest and glanced at Agnes from under downcast eyes. Agnes had seen women in many states of distress over her time running the House for Fallen Women, she had seen the bruises and the scars and the cuts, the damage inflicted upon them by men, but she couldn't fail to gasp when she saw the marks on the woman's body. She was painfully thin. Agnes could see her ribs sticking through the translucent pale skin. She was covered in dirt and grime, but the raw pink and red scars stood out. Above her arms, running from one shoulder to the other across the base of her neck, was an ugly, raised scar. Agnes wondered how the wound had not killed her outright. There were puncture marks and slashes down her arms and torso, right to the top of her drawers, which were torn and dirty. Agnes knew her thighs would be covered in similar marks. She gathered herself and dried her without commenting. Her questions could wait until later.

Agnes picked clean drawers and an underskirt and blouse and a cotton nightdress from the bundle Pete had brought from the laundry. She had no idea who they belonged to, but they could worry about rewashing and replacing them in the morning. 'Ah'll turn roun' an' let ye change.' She turned to face the wall. There was a pause before she heard the woman pulling on the new clothes.

'Dae ye ha' a name?' Agnes asked.

'Lu-' There was a hesitation. 'Louise.' The voice was small and uncertain.

Agnes was sure she was lying, but it was not the first time an arrival at her door had wanted to keep their real identity secret. Many of the women under her roof had a history they were trying to escape from. 'Ah'm Agnes. Ye kin ha' that hot tea when yer ready.'

Agnes waited until she heard the woman sit at the table. When she turned, the woman calling herself Louise had her hands wrapped around the mug and sat hunched over it.

'Thank you.'

'Dinnae be daft.' Agnes gave her a reassuring smile and picked up another of the towels. She set about drying up the pools of rainwater on the floor and table.

Louise watched her and after a couple of small sips from the mug asked her in the same small voice, 'Is this the House for Fallen Women?'

'Aye, it is.' Agnes picked up the wet rags the woman had arrived in and dumped them into the sink along with the towels. She would deal with them in the morning. 'Ye were lookin' fir us?'

'I was.'

Agnes noted that, despite appearances, the woman was well spoken. 'Where ha' ye came fae?'

'The city.'

Her accent was not from Edinburgh. Agnes recognised a hint of west coast in her voice. 'Ye walked oan yer own? In this weather?' Although the city was creeping up to the boundaries of Liberton, it was still a good three miles from the centre to the village.

'I was hoping to find somewhere to stay.'

'There's plenty poorhouses in the city that wud take in a wummin in yer circumstances.'

'Please. I was hoping to find somewhere different.'

'Different?'

'Safer.'

'An' whit makes ye think this hoose will be any better than those in the city?'

She only looked at Agnes and repeated, 'Please?'

There was no point in pressing the issue at the moment. The poor woman needed a bed and a long sleep and a good meal. No doubt she had her reasons. Probably a man, a customer who had threatened her, or an angry wife who had found out about her husband's dalliance. Agnes looked closer as she sipped the last of her tea. Her copper red hair was streaked with grey; her eyes were a pale brown. She looked to be in her mid- to late twenties, though the hard life she had clearly lived had left her pale skin calloused and pockmarked and lined with premature wrinkles.

'Ah've nae spare beds at the moment. We're full up.'

'I don't need a bed, or a room to myself. Just a roof. I can be useful. I can cook and clean,' she pleaded.

'Ah expect aw the wummin who stay here tae dae aw that. They work in the laundry an' aw take their turn doin' the chores a' the hoose.'

Her head dropped and tears began to form. 'Please, I don't think I can go on any longer.'

Agnes had seen plenty of women who had reached the end of what they could take. When they reached that point, they preferred it all to end. Death was preferable to a life being beaten and left in the gutter again and again.

'Ye kin sleep oan the sofa tonight. Ah'll git Pete tae put some sheets oan it fir ye. We'll decide whit tae dae in the mornin' after ye've had a proper meal.'

'Thank you, Agnes.' There was no smile, but Agnes could tell she was grateful. There was something about the woman that she liked, although she knew her real name wasn't Louise and she wasn't from Edinburgh.

'Awright. Wait here while ah git ye some sheets sorted.' Agnes left the kitchen and went off to reassure Pete that everything was okay and he could head home for the night after all, once he'd helped her make up the temporary bed in the living room.

The woman now calling herself Louise waited until the kind woman had left before letting her shoulders sag and her head drop. She had made it. A nurse in the city had told her about this place to the south, a place that only women lived in and that rewarded hard work with the chance to stay for longer than one or two nights. Agnes did not know it yet, but she had saved Jessie's life with her simple offer of a bed for the night. Tomorrow, Jessie would prove to her that she was worth keeping on. She would make herself useful. She would have to, because finally, after the years in the asylum and on the streets, Jessie knew she could no longer go on.

15

TUESDAY, 23 NOVEMBER

1920

Thomas did not notice the open front door as he passed his house, heading to the inn at the crossroads. A feeling of impending disaster refused to disappear. The image of Watt's scar pulled up by the leering smile and the threatening implication of their conversation about Jessie played on his mind. Watt had been gloating over her unfortunate past. Did others in the village feel the same? Tolerating her presence while secretly hoping for her downfall? Guilty or not, no one seemed to care, suspicion was enough to convict Jessie for past crimes.

He had seen no one on the path from Craiglockhart back to Liberton, as the night had descended. He had spoken to no one. At the bar, he ordered a drink from Rose and took his usual seat. Joseph and Malachy, perched in their window seat as always, gave him a cautious greeting, but talked in low whispers and cast fleeting glances in his direction. Plenderleith burst through the door with customary bluster. He greeted Joseph and Malachy with a loud 'good evening', but gave only a brief nod as he passed Thomas. His drink ordered, he took his place at the bar and drew the newspaper from under his arm. The story of the found child in Morningside was plastered prominently across the front page.

Thomas ordered his second drink. The atmosphere was subdued. No one attempted to engage him in conversation. The door opened again and Hershel Fiszer, the Polish Jew who had emigrated at the end of the war, entered. He had met a Scottish nurse on the battlefield in Kaniv in 1918 and had come to trace the angel who had saved his life. He had only her first name, Laura, and his memory of her appearance to go on. No one mocked him for his futile search. The men who had been saved by the doctors and nurses on the battlefield understood his obsession. Despite a distrust of foreigners, particularly those from Eastern Europe, Hershel had been accepted by the majority in Liberton, liked by some more and pitied by others. Thomas was on good terms with him and had treated him for the minor ailments that affected workers in the fields.

Hershel only glanced at Thomas before turning away to join Malachy and Joseph. There were further glances in Thomas's direction. Thomas tried to ignore them and avoided their stares. After five minutes, Hershel rose from his seat and went to the bar, where Rose poured him a drink. Hershel spoke across the bar to her in hushed tones and both glanced in his direction. Hershel took his drink and returned to his seat.

Thomas sensed he was not welcome. He finished his beer quickly. He knew it was not his presence that was causing a stir, rather it was his association with Jessie. Looks followed him as he rose and took his empty glass to the bar. He placed it on the bar top. Plenderleith looked up and turned away, swivelling his vast bulk on the creaking stool and lifting the newspaper to avoid making eye contact.

'I won't have another tonight, thank you, Rose.'

The barmaid leaned forward. 'Ye might want tae git hame

quick, Doctor.' She looked at the three men sitting at the window, who were watching what was happening at the bar. 'Hershel wis sayin' yer front door wis lyin' open when he went past an' he says Mrs MacPatrick is tellin' everywan she saw Jessie runnin' fae the hoose late this mornin'.'

'Running from the house? But she was at the school today.'

Rose shrugged. 'Ah'm oanly lettin' ye ken whit's bein' said.'

Thomas headed for the door, trying to walk at a normal pace while his mind told him to run. As soon as he crossed the threshold into the cold evening air, he broke into a run, dashing round the corner and across the road, ignoring the horse and cart that almost knocked him over as he sprinted towards his house.

He reached the gate, which was swinging unlatched in the cold wind. Hershel had been right. The front door lay wide open. There were no lights in the house. The living room and Jessie's bedroom were in total darkness. Perhaps she was sitting in the kitchen, getting a heat from the stove? It was not uncommon for Jessie to do that after she had eaten dinner. Maybe she had forgotten to shut the door behind her when she got home. She had been distracted in recent days. But as he entered the house and moved down the hallway, he could sense there was no one in the house. He threw open the door to the kitchen. It was empty and cold. No one had used the stove since the morning.

'Jessie!' he shouted. He looked out of the window into the small back garden. 'Jessie!' he called again. He ran out the back door and opened the door to the outdoor toilet. There was no one there. Maybe she had gone to bed early. She had been left exhausted by the ordeal with the police. He came back into the house and lit a lamp and carried it back into the hallway. Her bedroom door was closed. Of course, she was in her bed. He had been stupid to think otherwise. He knocked on the door and called her name. He rapped his knuckles against the wooden panels. There was no other option but to enter. He pushed the door open and held the lamp up.

The bed was empty, the sheets were in disarray, and clothing had been pulled out of drawers and thrown around the room. He moved the lamp around the room, the flickering light shimmered across fragments of glass that lay on the floor. Thomas stepped forward and glass crunched under his shoe. He saw the remains of the smashed mirror on the dressing table. He reached out and picked up a large shard. It sliced through his finger and he drew back in pain, looking at the red blood droplet that ran down his finger. Jessie had gone.

The next morning, sunlight broke through the living room window. Thomas sat in the armchair where he had remained all night. He had no memory of sleeping, though he must have dropped off at some point. The lamp had died. He could not decide what to do. He should go out and find her, but he had no idea where to start looking for her. Where would she go? She had no friends or family that he knew of where she would seek shelter. She had no other home or place to stay. He knew she was scared, and that she had run from her past before. She was doing the same again. At no point did he take her fleeing to be a sign of any guilt in the case of the murdered child, yet he knew that the locals in Liberton would leap to that conclusion. What would Detective Inspector Aitchison believe? Would he see it as a sign of her guilt? He should report her missing to the police. They were best placed to search for her. But what would they do when they found her?

Paralysed by doubt, Thomas sat in the living room and waited. He tipped the hip flask to his mouth, but it was empty. He had finished it during the night. There was a chance she would come to her senses after a while and realise that running away was not the answer to her problems. She could come back to him. He should have realised that she could not. He should have realised their lives could never be the same again.

With the coming of daybreak, his mind cleared. The police were reasonable men. They would not think she was a killer just because she had run. They would need evidence even if they thought it could be true. They were the best people to find her and return her safely. He went to the telephone in the hallway. The operator put him through to the police station at Abbeyhill and after a few moments he heard the voice of Aitchison on the other end of the line.

It was mid-morning when Detective Inspector Aitchison and Inspector Fraser arrived. The police cart drew up and Thomas, watching through his living room window, saw the men and women in the street turn and watch as the two officers walked down the path to his front door. Thomas greeted them and repeated what he had told Aitchison over the telephone. He showed them Jessie's room. Aitchison inspected a shard of broken glass in his hand. Fraser circled the bedroom, picking up various items of clothing and putting them down again.

'Is anything missing?' the senior detective asked Thomas, placing the glass back onto the top of the dressing table. 'Clothes, valuables?'

'It's hard to tell. Some clothes, perhaps. A bag.'

'Did she have money?'

'Yes, she kept it in the drawer.' Thomas pointed to the dressing table.

Fraser opened the drawer and looked inside. He pulled out some make-up, brushes, hair pins. Then shook his head at his colleague.

'Seems she's taken off with her money and some clothes then.'

Thomas felt the need to defend her. 'She was unsettled after your visit. It brought back painful memories.'

'Was she afraid that we might suspect her?'

'Don't you?'

'I rule nothing out. We have to follow up on any leads we have. Running away doesn't help her case.'

'How did you come to know about her past?' Aitchison only raised an eyebrow in response. 'I'm worried she might do something drastic.'

'I'm not sure there is much we can do.'

'Aren't you going to look for her? Isn't she a suspect?'

'She's a grown woman. It would've have been helpful if she had stayed while we carried on with our investigation, but there is very little we can do if she has chosen to leave.'

'She left because of you. You have to find her. You said yourself she has questions to answer about her past.'

Aitchison stepped across the room and stood in front of Thomas. 'I have to find a child who has been missing from their mother for the last three weeks. I have to find the person who murdered another child not a mile away from here. Those are my priorities. Do you think I should take men away from those investigations to help find your woman?'

'No, of course not.' Thomas stepped away. 'You have to do something, though. You can't just let her disappear.'

'I had been prepared to end our investigation into Jessie Bruce. Apart from her history, there is no evidence to link her to the missing children, and only geography links her to the crime scene at the tower. Her running off will reignite suspicion. The locals will jump to their own conclusions. I doubt anyone in Liberton will be sorry to see her leave.

'If she hasn't returned by the end of the month, you can report her missing to the police. You are not married or engaged therefore you have no legal hold over her. She is a woman of individual means and legal age and can go wherever she pleases.'

Thomas had nothing left to say.

Aitchison signalled to Fraser and they left the room. At the door he stopped and turned back. 'I will put out her description.

We will keep our eyes open. I can alert the ports and train stations. That's all we can do. Even if they spot her, they can't detain her, unless I make her a suspect or person of interest in our ongoing investigation. There's really not much else I can do, unless evidence arises that links her to the case. I'm not sure you want that to happen.'

Thomas said nothing as the officer followed his partner out of the door. Through the bedroom window, Thomas watched the cart pull away and disappear along the road. He stood alone in the room, Jessie's belongings strewn around him. He caught his shattered reflection in the broken mirror, his face split into an abstract mosaic. He had only himself to blame. He should have spoken to her. He could have shared his own past, he could have been open with her. He tried to help others with the *talking cure* and refused to open himself up to the same scrutiny. If they had been closer, if he had made more effort, then she would not have run away. She would have come to him for help. She would have known he would have kept her safe. Now it was too late. He had no idea where she could be. He knew of no family or friends. He knew she had come from the west side of the country, like him, but he was certain she would not return there now. She was running away from her past, as she had been for the last fifteen years. Where was left for her to go?

He gave a dispirited sigh. If the police weren't going to help him, then he would have to do it himself. He could not give in, sitting here doing nothing while she was out there alone. There must be something he could do. She had told him she had come from the city, that she had spent time living on the streets and moving around the poorhouses. Perhaps she would go back there. The poorhouses from where the children had disappeared. The poorhouses were at the centre of all of this. They were where he might find Jessie and bring her home. He didn't know anyone in the poorhouses who could help him, but he knew where they were.

It was almost midday now. If he left straightaway, he could catch the omnibus and be in the city by mid-afternoon. He picked up his coat and pulled on his boots.

The knock at the door stopped him. He threw it open, hoping it was her.

It took him a moment to recognise Constance MacKay without her white nursing cap on. Her blonde curls fell around her shoulders and she wore everyday clothes: a long brown coat with a chequered scarf wrapped around her neck. Her arms were folded across her chest holding a manila folder.

'I'm sorry to bother you at home, Doctor.'

Thomas collected himself. 'Thomas, please, when we're off duty.'

'Of course, Thomas.' She took in his coat and boots. 'Have I come at a bad time?'

'Not at all, but I do have to be getting on in a hurry.'

'It's just I thought you should see this right away, so I came over in my lunch break to give it to you.' She held out the manila file.

'What is it?' he asked, taking it from her.

'Private Watt's War Office records. They finally arrived this morning. I didn't think you should wait until next week before seeing them. I hope you don't mind, but I couldn't help but notice after Private Watt's visits, you looked distracted. And if you'll forgive me, I've overheard a little of what had been said between the two of you.'

He knew Nurse MacKay would think it unprofessional to listen in on a conversation between doctor and patient, and would certainly not spread anything that she heard around the wards. It meant something that she was willing to admit to it at all. Of course, she was right. The visits of Private Watt had unnerved him, but that did not explain why she felt the need to hand deliver his War Office records to him in person.

'You needn't have walked all the way over from the hospital just to deliver this to me.'

'I wouldn't normally, only I thought you should know sooner rather than later.'

'Know what?'

'That he's been lying, Thomas. Or at least misleading you. You see, it says he never actually served in the trenches at all.'

'Pardon?'

'I just thought, how could he be suffering from shell shock if he was sent home before ever reaching the frontline?'

Thomas looked from her to the file. It was thin, holding only two or three pages. His own handwritten notes from their meetings, and the form Watt had filled in were clipped to the front. He flipped it open. A sepia-tinged photograph was clipped inside the front cover. It was Private Duncan Watt, younger and without the scar running down the side of his face. It was the standard photograph that was taken when new recruits were enlisted into the army. Watt smiled at the camera. His hair was shorter and tidier, his jawline softer. The collar was of the uniform of a private in the army. Thomas scanned the first page of personal details, all of which matched those Watt had provided Nurse MacKay and had told Thomas. He turned to the next page. 'Discharged' was stamped across the top of it. Next to it was a description of a court-martial judgement. He read the basic information. Constance was right. He had been lied to.

Private Duncan Watt had not volunteered in 1914. He had been conscripted from prison, where it stated he was serving a sentence for assault. It gave no details beyond that. He had shipped to France in 1915 with the Thirteenth Battalion, that much was true. Everything he had told Thomas after that had been a lie. He could not have fought at the Battle of Loos at the end of 1915 because, according to the file, Private Watt had been court-martialled in August 1915, charged with affray and assault against a Frenchman. The brief report of the crime described a drunken Watt getting into a brawl with the local man over a woman. Watt had tried to force himself on the woman and she had beaten him off. Her husband had sought Watt out and attacked him with a knife. Watt had suffered a deep slash wound down the side of his face and a fracture of his left leg. When he had recovered enough to stand trial, he had been found guilty, discharged and only avoided a penal sentence in a military jail due to a sympathetic judge advocate who deemed his lifelong injuries punishment enough. He was sent home without pay or a pension.

Thomas turned the page but there was nothing else in the file. Private Duncan Watt's entire military career had lasted no longer than a few months training. He had never fought in the war. He thought back to their first interview, when Watt had spoken of a shrapnel wound obtained at Bullecourt. He had got the place name wrong because he had not been there. He had made up his military career and his post-war trauma.

His head swam. He dropped the file and held onto the door frame to steady himself.

'Thomas?' Constance asked, as she bent down and picked up the folder. The photograph of the younger Watt had fallen loose from its clip. She gathered it up.

Why had he lied to him? Why had he wanted to see him? This man had suddenly come into his life at the most inconvenient of times. Somehow it was wrapped up with the missing children, a brutal murder and Jessie. Watt had shown an unhealthy interest in her. He had called her a whore. He had made veiled threats about exposing Thomas's drinking habit. He had been at the police meeting. What else had he told him? That he had lost a child when he was younger. Was that true or another lie?

'I must be getting along I'm afraid, Constance.'

'Are you sure you're okay, Thomas. You should have a seat.'

'There's no time I'm afraid, and you must be due back at the hospital.'

'You're right, I had better be on my way. You will be careful, won't you?'

'Of course, don't worry about me. It's just tiredness.'

Constance did not look convinced, but there was nothing she could do, and she did have to get back to the hospital where the afternoon appointments would begin within the next hour.

'Very well. What about Private Watt?'

'Do you mind if I hold on to the file? I will keep it locked in my surgery. I'd like to study it further and perhaps make some calls.'

Constance looked unsure. It was irregular enough that she had taken the file out of the hospital. It was her responsibility to make sure it was returned. Thomas sensed her hesitancy. 'I will return it as soon as I can. Next Tuesday, if not before.'

'Should we inform the police, or the army?'

'That's what I will make some calls about, what steps to take next.'

She bade him a reluctant goodbye and hurried off along the street in the direction of the path that would take her back to the hospital.

Thomas gathered himself and his thoughts returned to finding Jessie. He had wasted enough time already. He needed to get to Edinburgh and start trying to track her down. He put the folder down on the side table in the hallway. The photograph lay on top of the cover, staring at him. He picked it up and put it in his coat pocket, then went back into the house and picked up the photograph of Jessie from the sideboard in the living room. It was the only one he had of her, taken at the Liberton fete the previous summer. Jessie did not like to have her photograph taken. Thomas had always thought she looked radiant and had never understood her reluctance. The revelations of the last few days explained it. In the photograph, she was smiling. It had been a happy day with warm sunshine and a clear sky. His war was forgotten for an afternoon. The worst of the Spanish Flu pandemic was over. There was a sense that the world was ready to move on at last from the horror of the last decade. He had paid the travelling photographer for the picture and insisted Jessie stand for her portrait. Now he was glad he had insisted. He could show her likeness around the poorhouses and perhaps someone would recognise her.

16

WEDNESDAY MORNING, 24 NOVEMBER
1920

The streets had not changed in the years since Jessie had last seen them. There were more automobiles on the roads, roaring along Princes Street alongside the trams, while horses and carts were less common. The buildings were the same; the castle still stood looking down on the bustling streets that came alive with the sunrise. Commuters hopped on and off the trams and omnibuses; pedestrians hurried along the pavements, desperate to get out of the cold and into heated offices and shops. After living among the gentler surrounds of Liberton, the bustle came as a shock to Jessie.

She had arrived in the middle of the night. She had left the house and walked along Liberton Road, the main route into the city. She was unwilling to hitch a ride with any cart or car that passed, determined not to leave any trail that could be followed. She kept to the shadows, pulling a shawl over her head to protect her from the night chill and to hide her appearance. As the night grew colder, she added layers of clothing to keep warm. Electric street lights ran along the road through Craigmillar, past the dark expanse of The Meadows and over the South Bridge, which brought her back into the Old Town. Memories of her last time in the city flooded back. She found a bench in Princes Gardens and sat waiting for the sun to come up. Early walkers had stared at her. She did not care what they thought of her – a woman of the night, a homeless beggar, a drunk – they could think what they liked. After years of worrying about her reputation among the folk of Liberton, it was a relief to cast off any pretension. She could be honest now, this is what she was, her true self – a woman cast aside and abandoned, left to fight and fend for herself.

She was sure no one would recognise her. It had been seven years since she had last been on these streets. No one here would be looking for her, unless the police were still looking for someone in connection with the murder of a whore in Chalmers Close in 1912. She had remained in the city for a time afterwards, though she steered clear of the places Lucy and she had used to haunt. There had never been any investigation that she knew about at the time. The paper had mentioned the discovery of a woman's body and the police had made a plea for any witnesses or information. That was all she had ever heard.

The park got busier. More people passed her and stared. A man stopped and asked if she was okay. She couldn't remember what she answered, but he shrugged and carried on, his good deed done and his conscience clear.

During her walk in the night, she had decided what she would do. There was nowhere left for her to hide in this country that would allow her to escape her past. She had to go further away to leave it all behind. She needed to disappear again, somewhere she couldn't be found among the masses, where she would be just another poor, lost woman that no one would notice or care for. Her thoughts turned south, to the big industrial cities of England. Manchester and Birmingham were teeming with poor people and workhouses. She could find shelter there. Or why not go beyond them, to London? No one would find her there and no one would care about another woman struggling to survive on the streets. She would be anonymous, and there were plenty of opportunities for a woman in need. Shelter, poorhouses and the chance of a low-paying job that could earn her enough money to feed and clothe herself. What more could she hope for from this life?

Her mind was made up. The money she had taken from her bedroom would buy her a train ticket and a meal or two. She would go to Waverley Station and find the first train heading across the border. As if to confirm her resolve, a sharp blow of a train's whistle pierced the morning air in the park. She stood and, taking her bag of meagre belongings with her, made her way towards Princes Street. She joined the throng of pedestrians hurrying along the pavement. She kept her head down, not wanting to make eye contact or see the disapproving pity in the looks of those passing her. She got to the Waverley Steps and clung to the central handrail that took her down the three flights, taking her to the platforms below. The world seemed to be travelling in the opposite direction to her, as workers spilled upwards, ascending to the light, while Jessie plunged into the underworld. On the bottom step, she was bumped roughly and lost her footing and found herself on her hands and knees on the grey concrete ground. A strong hand hooked itself under her armpit and pulled her up. 'Best watch yourself, little lady,' said a gruff voice in her ear. She shook herself free of the hand that held her and hurried away without looking back. Something about the voice unnerved her. He did not sound kind. His warning had sounded like a threat.

The station concourse was grey and covered in a thick acrid cloud, spilling from funnels that came and went and added to by smoke from the pipes and cigarettes of the men striding backwards and forwards. The platforms were a hive of commuters, barrelling in all directions as trains arrived and departed. She found herself in front of the departure board for the North British Railway.

The Special Scotch Express left at 10am, stopping at York before carrying on to London. She would make that. The large clock had only just tripped past 9am.

Jessie looked round and saw the ticket office. She fought her way across the concourse to reach it and joined a queue. When she got to the front, she faced a man in a railway uniform with a broad moustache sat behind a glass panel.

'London, please.'

'Today, madam?'

'Yes.'

'The Special Scotch Express leaves at 10am from platform one. Arriving at London King's Cross at 6.30pm this evening.'

'Very good.'

'That'll be—' he stopped as the distressed woman spilled a handful of coins and notes onto the counter and slid them towards him through the gap under the glass panel. He looked at her and she averted her eyes, casting them downwards. 'Begging your pardon, madam, but is everything quite alright?'

Jessie pulled herself together. She put a smile on her face and looked at him, brushing a bedraggled fringe of hair away from her eyes. 'Yes, quite. In a bit of a rush this morning, thought I'd miss the train. Didn't have time to do my hair and make-up.'

He took at the dishevelled clothing which had been clearly thrown on without any care, and looked like it had been slept in. Her make-up was a day old and smeared, her hair unkempt and unbrushed. Jessie willed him to give her the ticket.

'Very well.' He picked out the correct money required for the ticket and pushed the rest back to her. As she reached for the ticket, he kept a hold of it, causing her to look at him once more. He saw the anxiety in her eyes. 'You're quite sure you don't require any help, madam?'

He said it so softly, with a look of genuine concern, that Jessie was tempted to tell him everything. But how could he ever understand? His first reaction would be to call to the nearest police officer and point her out. She was on the run. She was the child killer suspect. The one who had killed her own child and slashed a man and had run from the asylum. They would put her back where she belonged, away from society, no longer a threat to them all.

'I'm fine, thank you.' She pulled the ticket free. The ticket officer watched her go. If he had not been faced with a queue of impatient travellers in front of his kiosk, he would have followed her, or alerted a colleague to the distressed woman who was now fighting her way through the crowded station. As it was, he turned to the next woman who appeared in front of him, similarly dishevelled as she tried to contain three young children and various items of luggage while maintaining her calm.

Jessie had time before going to the platform to buy a cup of tea from the café on the station concourse. She collapsed into a seat at the back of the room, hiding herself as far back in the shadows as she could. Once she made it onto the train, the worst of her worries would be over.

A waitress brought over her tea in a cup on a saucer with a teaspoon. She sipped it, letting the hot liquid warm her insides after the cold night spent outdoors. She would have to remember she was no longer a young girl, that her body had become soft after years of comfort. She would have to prepare herself for life on the street once more. At least London was a few degrees warmer than the central belt of Scotland. She contemplated using her real name once she had arrived in London. She would be safe to call herself Jessie for the first time in years. Louise Stuart was dead; Jessie Bruce could finally re-emerge. This made Jessie smile as she took another sip of tea. A reclamation of her identity. That was something, at least.

The station clock bell rang out three chimes. It was 9.45am. She had allowed time to drift by and the train would be leaving in fifteen minutes. She picked up her bag and left the café. She did not notice the man who had been sitting on the bench outside. He rose as she left and followed her towards platform one.

The platform was crowded. Porters with trolleys piled with suitcases, hatboxes and parcels blazed a trail through passengers engaged in final farewells with loved ones. The air was thick and claustrophobic. Jessie pushed her way through to get to a carriage door. A conductor, who had been aiding an elderly woman up the step, turned and looked her up and down and asked to see her ticket. Jessie had it in her hand, crumpled from the tight grasp with which she had been clinging to it.

'As I thought, madam.' He addressed her with polite words while his tone made it sound like an insult. 'Third-class carriages are to the rear.' He handed the ticket back to her and pointed back along the platform.

'Can't I get on here and go through the carriages?'

'I think it best if you entered the correct carriage door, madam.' The conductor stood in front of the step and Jessie knew she had no option but to retrace her way back along the platform. 'You have time before the train departs.'

She turned and stepped straight into the broad back of a gentleman and muttered an apology. The man, in an expensive tailor-made suit and bowler hat, had the courtesy to offer a reciprocal apology, before the conductor greeted him and waved him into the first-class carriage. Jessie noticed the gentleman was not asked to produce his ticket for inspection.

She began to work her way back. The crowd had grown even thicker as the departure time approached. At the third-class carriage, there was a mob of people clamouring to gain access. Their efforts were hampered by a portly man who had managed to get his oversized luggage case trapped in the narrow door. The station conductor had begun to close and lock the other doors, resulting in a bottleneck as all the latecomers tried to push their way aboard. Jessie found herself swamped between those already trying to embark and those arriving behind her. A scrum was now taking place. The station master and assistants arrived to try and restore order. 'Please calm down everyone, there's plenty of room for you all onboard. Have patience!' There were many shouts at the portly man, who was red-faced and puffing, encouraging him to give up and climb down in order to let everyone else on.

The scrum swayed to and fro like a sea, waves pushing forward and being repelled and falling backward, but making little progress in either direction. Jessie was pressed up against the backs of those in front of her. She had no way to escape the melee and could only fight to stay upright.

In her tight prison, she felt a body press against her. He was so close that she picked up the scent of his aftershave or cologne. She recognised the strong smell from the steps, the same man who had picked her up when she had stumbled. If she had been more observant, she would have recognised him as the man who had followed her from the café. Jessie knew it could not be a coincidence that the same man who had rescued her earlier was now next to her again. A feeling of dread crept over her. She was scared to turn round and look. She remembered his threatening voice and a shudder ran down her spine. Any cry for help would be swallowed by the noise of the angry passengers and impatient staff. It did not matter; she did not get the chance to cry out. His arm was around her, and she felt his hand upon her face. It held a cloth that covered her mouth and nose. She gasped for breath as the sweet-smelling odour rushed through her nose and mouth. She felt tired and drowsy and wished only to lie down as her legs gave way and she crumpled forward. Her eyes closed and the frantic scene at the train carriage disappeared in blackness.

The man caught her as she went limp. He took her weight and held her upright. He was a tall man and was able to make his voice heard over the chaos around him. 'Make way! Make way!' he bellowed, 'the lady has been overcome in the crush!'

Those around him realised what had happened and joined his shouts and an exit from the crowd materialised. 'A lady has fainted! Stand back!' Others joined in his plea for calm and soon he was able to drag her free into open space on the platform, which was now clear apart from the fracas around the third-class carriage. No one spotted the wet cloth he slipped into his coat pocket.

A man in railway uniform came to offer his assistance.

'It's quite alright,' he insisted. 'She's my sister. I will take her home. You can be sure I will be complaining to the North British Railway about this intolerable situation.'

He ignored the profuse apologies and the promise of complimentary tickets for the following day's Scotch Express. He propped up the unconscious woman, putting one arm over his shoulders and dragging her away with him.

The portly man and his oversized luggage having been removed from the doorway, the remaining passengers were free to alight the train and, with some relief, the station conductor was able to blow his whistle and signal the departure to the driver of the steam engine. The Scotch Express departed at 10am exactly, as the North British Railway proudly declared it always did.

No one missed the woman who had expected to be heading towards her new life in the capital city of the empire, but who had become overcome in the last-minute crush.

17

WEDNESDAY AFTERNOON, 24 NOVEMBER

1920

Thomas stepped down from the omnibus onto the cobbles of High Street. He checked his pocket watch. It was a quarter to three. He had cursed every delay along the way, giving impatient looks to those instructing the driver to stop so they could alight or embark.

From High Street, he was within walking distance of several places in the city centre where Jessie may have been seen. One was the train station, only seventy yards away if he turned north and followed the bridge that ran across the tracks. If Jessie wanted to escape the city the train was the fastest way to head south to England or north to Fife or the Highlands beyond. She would go somewhere she would be completely unknown, somewhere she could hide. It was most likely she would run to another country. If that was the case, then he was already too late. The daily service south left in the morning. Jessie could have been on that train this morning. If he made no progress today, then tomorrow he would look for her on the platform.

His best option for this afternoon was to carry on east along High Street, following the route of the Royal Mile, to Canongate. At 64 Canongate was the Queensberry Poorhouse. It was from there that the third missing child, Adam Symons, had disappeared. He couldn't imagine Jessie was involved in the abduction of an infant, but he could not escape her link to the events of the last week. Would she visit the poorhouse herself and try to find out what had happened to Adam Symons? It was a tenuous link, but he had to start somewhere. The poorhouse was also the closest place to the train station where she could seek shelter for the night if she was thinking of catching the train the following morning. She would not have money for a hotel or inn. He started walking.

Where High Street merged into Canongate, the street widened slightly and sloped downwards. He passed under the tollbooth clock and carried on. It had been a long time since he had walked through the city. Since he had settled in Liberton, he had avoided the noisy and busy streets. It did his shattered nerves no good and there were too many temptations for a drink in the hostelries and pubs of the Old Town. Jessie had never shown any inclination to come to the city for an evening's entertainment or to visit the large department stores on Princes Street. Thomas understood her reluctance now.

The tightly packed houses and shops began to give way to larger buildings as Canongate continued to wind its way down to the end of the Royal Mile. He could just make out the front of the Palace of Holyroodhouse, the residence of the King when in Scotland, with its white conical turrets reaching into the sky. He arrived at number 64 and stopped outside the brick building. How incongruous to be about to enter a building set up to shelter the poor and the needy, while, fifty yards away, the riches of the monarchy were on full display, taunting the less fortunate subjects of the crown.

Queensberry House had a distinctive dark colour which stood out from the sandstone of the other buildings on Canongate. Rectangular windows with white borders and sills punctuated its grey façade. At each corner, a column of white decorative bricks climbed like a ladder to the roof of black slate. It was built in a U-shape, with two wings extending forward from a central section, in the middle of which was the main doorway. A low wall ran along the perimeter, separating the grounds of the house from the street. Thomas stepped through the gate and walked across the cobbled forecourt to the entrance. The door was closed. Thomas lifted the large door knocker and thudded it against the black metal. Compared to the poorhouse in Liberton, Queensberry House of Refuge was an altogether bigger and sterner institution. Thomas had no idea what reception he would receive.

The door opened. A man younger than Thomas, with black skin and a pleasant manner, looked at him through wire-rimmed spectacles. He took in Thomas's clothing and demeanour and knew he was not looking for a room for the night. 'Good day. How may we help you?'

'Good day.' Thomas noticed the white dog collar, topping a black shirt covered by a V-necked sweater. 'I wonder if you could help me. I'm looking for a missing person.'

This was a request that had been made of the young minister before. He held the door open and beckoned Thomas to enter. 'Of course, please come in and we can talk in my office.'

The interior of the house was as stern and uniformed as the exterior. Thomas had expected squalor and chided himself for making that assumption. The floors were clean and swept, the walls covered in a whitewash and wooden doors to individual rooms were freshly varnished. He saw no sign of anyone else, either staff or residents.

'Our upper floors are used to house those that require to stay with us for longer periods,' the minister explained. 'These rooms are kept free for those that require an urgent refuge for a night or two only.'

His office was at the end of the corridor. The room was more like a drawing room than an office. A window faced out onto Canongate. There was no desk, only a low coffee table in the centre of the room with a small sofa and two armchairs surrounding it. Along the walls were bookcases and a sideboard. The minister beckoned Thomas into one of the chairs.

'Tea, Mr...?'

'Doctor Stevenson, and yes, please.'

'Very good. I'm afraid I will have to brew it myself. No money in the budget for a maid, I'm afraid.'

The minister went to the far corner of the room and disappeared through a narrow door. Thomas heard the clatter of cutlery as a cup and saucer were located and soon he heard a kettle coming to the boil. The minister returned carrying two cups. 'Milk or sugar?'

'No, thank you.'

He placed one cup on the table in front of Thomas and took the other seat, crossing his legs and holding his own cup on his lap.

'Now then, Doctor Stevenson, I should introduce myself. I'm Samuel Drysdale. I run this house on behalf of the local council, in conjunction with my church. You say you are looking for someone? It won't surprise you to learn we receive many people looking for lost loved ones, and the police often visit looking for people for various reasons. How can we help you?'

'I'm looking for a woman,' Thomas began. 'Her name is Jessie Bruce, but also goes by the name Louise Stuart.' He gave a brief summary of Jessie's disappearance from Liberton the previous day, omitting the details of her past and the police interview that had triggered her flight.

Drysdale listened as Thomas described Jessie's appearance, including the clothes she had been wearing. He looked at the photograph Thomas showed him.

'I'm afraid no one of that name or appearance stayed with us last night. However, I can assure you I will keep an eye out for her over the coming days. Do you have a telephone number where you can be contacted?'

It had been a slim chance that she would have come here, but nonetheless Thomas was disappointed. Drysdale stood and picked up a notepad and pencil from the sideboard and handed them to Thomas. He scribbled down the number for the telephone at the surgery and handed it back.

'I'm sure there is nothing to worry about, Doctor Stevenson. From what you say, she is a capable and bright woman. I'm sure there will be a perfectly innocent explanation for her absence.'

'I'm afraid I haven't been entirely honest with you, Mr Drysdale. There are further circumstances that may have a bearing on her disappearance.'

The smile on Samuel Drysdale's face faded for the first time since he had opened the door to Thomas.

'You will have heard of the missing children in the city recently, who disappeared from the poorhouses.'

'I suspect you are fully aware that one of those children disappeared from Queensberry. A most upsetting occurrence.' The smile turned to annoyance. 'You're not from the press, are you? Making up this story about a missing friend in order to work your way in?'

'I assure you, I'm not,' Thomas answered. 'I think Jessie's disappearance is somehow linked to the missing children.'

'On what basis do you think this?'

'The police came to interview her after the body of the child was found in Liberton.'

'The police? Is she a suspect?'

'You would have to ask the police that question, but it brought up painful memories from her past. She lost a child too, when she was younger. She has had a hard life since then, she spent some time in a mental institution. She lived in the poorhouses and on the street. I think she may have come back here to revisit what she knows, before trying to disappear again.'

'Running from her past, that sort of thing?'

Thomas nodded. 'I thought perhaps she might come here, with the link to the missing boy. She's unstable, you see, she's suffered a great shock.' He paused as a thought occurred to him. 'Is the mother of the missing boy still here?'

'I don't think that's an appropriate question for me to answer, Doctor.'

'Could I talk to her? You see, I think Jessie feels linked to her, having been through the same loss. She may have tried to contact her, to sympathise with her.'

Drysdale looked at him, then stared at the ceiling, apparently deciding what to do.

'Very well, Doctor Stevenson. Miss Symons is still staying here. As I'm sure you understand, she is in a very fragile state. I am reluctant to put her through anything that she may find upsetting, but I think she would never forgive me if I let you walk away without letting you talk to her. She would do anything in order to get her baby back. For that reason alone, I will take you to see her.'

'Thank you.'

'But,' Drysdale raised a warning finger, 'I will stay in the room with you and if I see that you are causing her any distress, I will ask you to leave. Do you agree?'

'Of course.'

Drysdale waited for another moment, measuring Thomas up, convincing himself he wasn't making a mistake. 'Very well, follow me.'

They left the office and retraced their steps along the corridor to the central part of the house and the main staircase.

The second floor mirrored the layout of the first, and was maintained to the same high standard of cleanliness. They turned at the top of the stairs and followed the corridor to the east wing once more. They came to a closed door that was directly above the office below. Drysdale knocked on the wooden door and waited. Thomas stood at his shoulder.

'If she does not wish to see you, I will not force her.'

'Of course.'

The door opened and the face of a small woman peered through the gap.

'Minister.' Her voice was weak and tired.

'Please forgive the intrusion, Miss Symons.'

'It's quite awright, ah wis awake, jist...' she trailed off.

'There is a gentleman who wishes to see you. He is looking for a missing woman. He thinks her disappearance may be somehow linked to Adam's disappearance. She lived in Liberton and once lost a child of her own. Would you be willing to see him for a moment? I have told him he must leave if you refuse. Do not feel pressured into anything.'

Miss Symons opened the door a fraction wider and looked over the minister's shoulder. Thomas stood awkwardly, unsure how to present himself.

'Dae ye think it'll help find Adam?' she asked the minister, while staring at Thomas.

'I can't promise anything, Sarah.'

'Bit it cannae hurt tae try, kin it?'

'I will stay with you and if I sense Doctor Stevenson is making you uncomfortable, I will escort him out of the room.'

'Very well.' Sarah Symons retreated into the room. Drysdale and Thomas followed her. Her room was sparsely furnished with just a single bed and a small table. There was a bucket of water for washing in the corner and a chamber pot. The floor was bare wooden floorboards. The window let in a small modicum of light. On the table was an unlit candle and a few small trinkets: a necklace, a brooch and a photograph card of a small baby. There was no sign of any other possessions, no clothes hung anywhere, there was no wardrobe or dresser.

'Ah'm afraid ah cannae offer ye a seat.' She perched on the end of the bed, placing her hands on her lap after tucking her straw-like hair behind her ears. She looked at the floor, afraid of how she was being judged.

'That's quite alright.' Thomas stood in the middle of the room. Samuel Drysdale positioned himself by the door, his arms folded, watching Thomas closely.

Thomas pointed at the small picture. 'This is Adam?'

Sarah nodded. 'Taken jist after he wis born in the hospital. The nurse gie me it tae keep. Noo it's aw ah have a' him.'

'I hope he will be found safely.'

'The polis think there's still a chance he's alive. They found that other child alive and they havnae found a body so far.' The weight of what she was saying sunk in. They both knew it was unlikely that Adam would be found alive now.

'There is always hope,' Thomas offered.

'Ye ken somethin' that might help find him?'

'I'm not sure. A woman, a close friend, is also missing. She ran away from Liberton after they found the missing child there. She lost her son when she was younger. I thought she might have come here to visit you.'

Sarah Symons looked at him sceptically. 'Why wud she visit me?'

'It's difficult to explain, but I have realised recently that I didn't know her as well as I thought I did.'

'Has she somethin' tae dae wi' Adam?'

'Not directly, no,' Thomas admitted. 'I just have a feeling she thinks she is linked to these missing children, or is somehow at fault.'

'Ah'm afraid ah dinnae understand.'

Thomas wiped his brow. He saw Drysdale take a step towards him from the door.

'Wait.' He stepped towards the bed, and reached inside his coat. 'Could I show you her picture? I just want to know if you have seen her.'

Sarah cowered back as he approached. Drysdale moved to cut Thomas off, grabbing at Thomas's arm to hold him back.

'Please just take a look.'

'Ah havnae seen anybody. Ah havnae left this room fir days.'

Drysdale had a hold of him now. Thomas's hand was caught inside his coat pocket, he had a hold of the photograph. He managed to free his arm and pull the picture out. As the minister held him back, he threw it towards Sarah. The photograph landed on the floor at her feet. He gave up resisting Drysdale's attempts to restrain him and the minister pulled him back and pinned him to the door.

'I warned you, Doctor. Now I must insist that you leave at once.'

'I'm sorry, I just want her to look at the picture, that's all. Perhaps she has seen her.'

'She has told you she has seen and spoken to no one.'

'Wait!' Her voice was loud and urgent and brought both men to an immediate stop. The minister turned to look at her. Sarah was kneeling on the floor. She had the photograph in her hand. 'Who is this?' She turned it round to show Thomas.

It was not the photograph of Jessie. That was still on the floor next to the kneeling mother. It was the sepia portrait of a young Private Duncan Watt that she held.

'Do you know this man?' Thomas asked.

'Ah think ah've seen him afore, but he wis older an' different somehow. Changed.'

'Did he have a scar on his face? Down the left side?'

She thought for a moment. 'Aye, that's it. He hid a scar an' his hair wis different, longer, an' he wis older. He had a limp.'

Thomas fought to contain his emotions. 'Did he tell you his name?'

'No, ah dinnae ken his name.'

'Where did you see him?' Thomas pushed past the minister, who no longer tried to stop him, and knelt next to the woman.

'It wis here, ah'm sure. Before.'

'Before Adam went missing? Was he here on the night that Adam disappeared?' Thomas was excited now. He had suspected Watt of something. He was mixed up in this somehow, appearing in Liberton at the same time as the dead child, attending the police meeting, lying about his military history and faking his need for a psychiatric doctor. This was evidence that linked him to the missing children. Somehow Jessie was linked to him too. He had asked questions about her, called her offensive names, insinuated threats about her.

'Ah cannae be sure. It wis around then, ah'm sure, but ah cannae remember if it wis that night. D'ye ken him?'

'Not well. He is a patient at the military hospital.'

'Dis he ha' somethin' tae dae wi' yer missin' friend?'

'Perhaps.'

'An' wi' Adam?'

'I don't know. Perhaps.'

Sarah Symons looked again at the photograph. 'Ye ha' tae find him. Ye ha' tae tell the polis.'

18

WEDNESDAY AFTERNOON, 24 NOVEMBER

1920

He left Sarah with Samuel Drysdale in her room after taking the photographs of Jessie and Duncan Watt from her. She was right, he had to tell the police what he knew about Watt straight away. Abbeyhill Police Station, where the investigation led by Detective Inspector McHarg was based, was only a short walk from Canongate. Thomas ran down the cobbles, ignoring looks from pedestrians as he veered around them. At the junction at the end of the road he turned left, away from the royal residence in front of him, and found the single-storey, squat, red brick building with pointed turrets at either end on Abbeyhill. He burst through the main entrance. No one was in the reception area apart from the sergeant behind the desk. Thomas gathered his breath after his exertion.

'I need to see Detective Inspector McHarg right away.'

The sergeant looked down at him. 'Indeed. And what do you need to see him about?'

'I have information about the missing boy, Adam Symons.'

The sergeant took marginally more interest. 'Very well. Your name?'

'Doctor Thomas Stevenson.'

'Take a seat, Doctor, and I'll see if someone is available.' Thomas nodded his thanks and sat on the wooden bench which ran along the wall. The sergeant disappeared through a door at the back of the room.

Everything in the reception room was the same colour. The floor, the doors, the panelling on the walls, the desk behind which the sergeant stood, all were made of the same dark-stained, heavily varnished wood. Only the green baize of the noticeboard stood out against the bleak uniformity; a rectangle covered with pieces of paper giving public service information. In the centre of the board, with 'MISSING' in bold type, was a poster asking for information into the disappearance of Adam Symons.

The sergeant returned after five minutes and resumed his station behind the desk, only telling Thomas that Detective Inspector McHarg was not at the station at the present time, but someone would be out to talk to him shortly.

And then nothing happened. The only sound was the ticking of the clock on the wall above Thomas's head, and the occasional shuffling of paper by the sergeant. After fifteen minutes, Thomas dared to ask why no one had been to speak to him. 'It's urgent. I have important information about the case.'

'Someone will be out presently, sir.'

The adrenaline was still running through him from the shock of Sarah Symons's revelation. Her sighting tied Duncan Watt to Queensberry House and the disappearance of Adam Symons. His appointments with Thomas at Craiglockhart Hospital, across the street from the poorhouse, tied him to the location of the disappearance of Lily Fitzpatrick. His appearance at the police meeting in the church hall tied him to Liberton. He had lied about his military service and how he had got his injuries. He had made lurid remarks about Jessie that hinted at something devilish. They were connected somehow. Both Jessie and Duncan had lost a child, unless Watt was lying about that. He was willing to wager that it had been Duncan Watt who had tipped off the police about Jessie's past, which meant somehow their paths had crossed before.

After another ten minutes of silence, Thomas began to sigh and tap his foot on the hard floor to remind the sergeant he was still there. The sergeant looked up and gave him a withering look. The reason for his attitude became apparent soon afterwards.

Thomas stood and approached the desk. 'It really is most important that I see someone right away. I have vital information.'

'Please take a seat, sir. Someone will be out. As I'm sure you can imagine, they are very busy.'

'But I must see them. I think I know who might have taken the children.'

'If you could sit back down, sir—'

The officer was interrupted as the door behind him swung open. 'It's alright, sergeant,' said Detective Inspector Aitchison. 'I'll see Doctor Stevenson now.' He lifted a panel in the desk and came round to stand next to Thomas. It was only that morning that they had been together in Jessie's bedroom.

'I apologise for the wait, Doctor. I can assure you I have passed on a description of Miss Bruce to my colleagues. I'm afraid there has been no further word about her whereabouts so far, but it has only been a few hours. Perhaps we will hear something tomorrow.'

'This isn't about that,' blurted out Thomas. 'Well, it is about Jessie, but this is something else. I think I know who took the children.'

Aitchison stared at him, deciding how seriously to take this new development. He didn't like members of the public interfering with his investigations, especially those who thought they were amateur detectives. He had wasted enough time with the Doctor and his errant woman.

'You told me you would need evidence that linked Jessie to your ongoing investigation before you would do anything more. Evidence that shows she is linked to these children somehow. I think I've found that evidence.'

Aitchison could not ignore him. Though he would never admit it to the doctor, they had few leads despite all their efforts to find Adam Symons or the murderer of Lily Fitzpatrick.

'Very well, follow me.'

He led the doctor through to a corridor, off which were meeting rooms used to interview members of the public. Aitchison showed Thomas into one of the rooms. In the middle of the room was a bare wooden table with a seat on either side. They sat down across the desk from each other.

'Well, what do you have to share with me?'

'I went to visit Sarah Symons—'

'You did what?'

'Let me explain. I came to the city to look for Jessie after you left Liberton. You left me with no option but to try to find her myself. You know yourself that she used to live in the poorhouses of the city.'

'You just happened to choose the poorhouse from where Adam Symons disappeared.'

'It seemed as good a reason as any to start there. I think she is linked to the missing children somehow.'

'What makes you think she is? You were adamant she could have nothing to do with it when we questioned her.'

'Because of this.' Thomas slid the file photograph of Duncan Watt across the table.

Aitchison stared at it. 'Who's this supposed to be?'

'His name is Private Duncan Watt.' The detective took a closer look at the picture, lifting it from the table. 'You know that name from your investigation, don't you? He was the man who first tipped you off about Jessie's real identity and past.'

Aitchison placed the photograph back on the table. 'I can't reveal sources.'

'I saw him talking to your officers at the public meeting the day after the body was found. He told you there was a woman in Liberton who had a history of psychiatric problems and who had lost her own child under suspicious circumstances.' Aitchison remained tight-lipped. 'This photograph was taken in 1914, when Duncan Watt volunteered to join the army. Before he got the scar on his face. I took it from his War Office records.'

'How on earth did you get access to his War Office records?'

'Because he is a patient at the Craiglockhart War Hospital. He came to see me for the first time a couple of weeks ago. I volunteer there, helping veterans struggling with mental trauma from the war. Duncan Watt told me he had been injured while fighting in the trenches, but his war record tells a different story. He was discharged before he even made it to the front line. He lied to me about his injuries.' Aitchison was a veteran of the trenches. A man lying about his war record did not sit well with him. 'He also asked questions about the woman I lived with and made threats to expose my own issues to my general practice patients.'

'Why would he do that?'

'That's what I didn't understand until today, when I visited Sarah Symons. She saw the picture of Duncan Watt and recognised him.'

'From where?'

'From Queensberry House. She had seen him at the poorhouse around the time that her son was taken.'

Aitchison sat in thought. 'There are plenty of veterans who have fallen on hard times and make use of the city poorhouses.'

'Yes, there are,' Thomas agreed, 'but he's not really a veteran. And he has a criminal record for assault. He was conscripted into the army from prison.'

Aitchison paled at that revelation. 'It could just be coincidence.'

'It could.'

'You say you treated him at Craiglockhart Hospital?'

'Next to the poorhouse where Lily Fitzpatrick went missing.'

Thomas waited as the detective made the connection. A man who had tipped off his investigation to a potential suspect had also been present at both poorhouses where the children had been abducted and had a history of violent assault.

'You think he chose to tell us about Jessie Bruce to deflect the investigation away from himself?'

'Yes, but more than that.' Thomas grew excited as he saw Aitchison finally start to think along the same lines as he was. 'The only way he could have tipped you off about Jessie Bruce is if he knew her from her past. He didn't just want to protect himself. He wants her to take the blame for a child's murder. He wants to punish her for some reason.'

'It would need to be a serious reason in order to justify murdering a child. Good God, man. He would have to be insane.'

'I think he may well be. I don't know what Jessie may have done to him in the past. He told me he had lost a young child, just like Jessie did, but he may have made that up along with everything else he told me. I can tell you he is not from Liberton; it's still a small enough place that his face would have been known, so he didn't meet Jessie there. He must have known her before, maybe at the asylum, or in the poorhouses before the war.'

'Very well. You've convinced me to take a closer look at Duncan Watt. I'll send a team to track him down. Do you know where he lives?'

Under normal circumstances, Thomas may have had reservations about sharing a patient's details with the police, but in this instance, he had no such qualms. 'He gave his address on the hospital form as 2 Regent Road.'

'2 Regent Road in Edinburgh?' Aitchison repeated the address with a resigned smile on his face.

'Yes. What?' asked Thomas.

'Regent Road is in Calton, Doctor Stevenson. It's the address of the city jail.'

Thomas emerged from the police station. It was dark and rain had started to fall on the grey city streets. The street lamps were defeated by the surrounding gloom, casting only weak shadows on the ground. The false address given by Watt had left Detective Aitchison at an impasse. He agreed with Thomas that they needed to question him, but they would have to track him down. With no known address, it was not clear how long that could take. The worst case, Aitchison had gravely told him, was that the boy was already dead and Duncan Watt had already fled. His men were already spread far and wide, trying to track down Adam Symons, whose safe return remained the priority. Detective Inspector McHarg would be reluctant to pull men from the search for Adam to go after Watt, unless there was more concrete evidence that he was the man who had taken the boy and murdered Lily. Everything that pointed towards Watt so far was circumstantial evidence, no matter how strongly Thomas believed it to be the case.

'And Jessie?' Thomas asked before leaving the meeting room.

'Nothing has changed from this morning.' They would not devote any more time to finding her. At least the detective's tone was more sympathetic now. Perhaps he felt some guilt about having not looked closer at the man who had come forward and tipped them off about Jessie.

Standing at the bottom of the Royal Mile, Thomas felt the size of the city around him, the hopelessness of locating a single person among the half million people who lived here, especially if she did not want to be found. His only slight remaining hope was that Jessie might be at the train station in the morning, boarding a train to get her out of the country. It was all he had to cling to in the desolate night. Rather than make the trip back home to Liberton and risk returning too late the next morning, he decided to stay in the city. It would mean appointments at his surgery would be missed and he imagined angry patients turning up to find the door locked and the surgery empty. For now, his priority was doing what little he could to find Jessie.

He didn't have enough money to stay at the big railway hotels on Princes Street – the Caledonian at one end and the North British next to the station. He walked back along Canongate and contemplated imposing himself upon Drysdale at Queensberry House, but the thought of coming face-to-face with Sarah Symons didn't appeal to him. He had no comforting news he could give her. He continued along the Royal Mile, up High Street and then the Lawnmarket. The small inns along the old street were full. He turned and followed the road down to Princes Gardens until it met the wide shopping thoroughfare. From there, he crossed into the New Town and onto Rose Street, and then up the slope until he reached George Street. A number of hotels mixed with shops, banks and private housing and, as he approached Charlotte Square, he found a small hotel that had a room available.

The cost of the room was more than he had expected, but by now he was weary after a long day, which had followed a sleepless night. He was shown to a small room on the second floor. He had not eaten a meal all day, so he went down to the cosy dining room and when the dish of steak and potatoes and vegetables was placed in front of him, he devoured the food. There was also a small bar in the hotel which stayed open for residents until midnight. Thomas bought a pint of beer and sat in a quiet corner, watching the other residents gathering for the evening. The accents were English or from the Highlands, visitors to the city for business or pleasure. Thomas spoke to no one and after a second pint, he had used up most of the money he had brought with him. He retired to his room after requesting an early morning wake-up call from the night porter behind the reception desk.

He had not brought any clothes to sleep in, so had no choice but to sleep in his undergarments. He had no razor for shaving with, nor a comb or brush for his hair. His clothes would last another day, but if he wished to stay in the city longer, he would have to return home to pick up these things. He hoped it would be academic, though. When he got to the train station in the morning, perhaps he would find Jessie on the platform, waiting for the train to London or Manchester or York, and he would convince her she had nothing to be afraid of. This time tomorrow he could be back in Liberton with Jessie.

He drifted off into an unsettled sleep, haunted as always by the blood-soaked pleas of James Napier, mingled with the mutilated body of Lily Fitzpatrick and the strange addition of Jessie Bruce, deranged and running through the rain-soaked streets of Edinburgh, chased by the menacing figure of Duncan Watt.

19

THURSDAY MORNING, 25 NOVEMBER

1920

She came round to see only blackness. Her head ached, her hearing was muffled, like cloth was covering her ears. Gradually, her senses awoke. She was lying on her back, still wearing her dress. She felt with her hands, groping into the unknown that surrounded her. The floor was cold, smooth stone. She tried to sit up, but as she raised her head, she felt dizziness and nausea swell up inside her stomach and gut. She lay back down and stared up into the dark. Her hearing cleared. She tried to make out the slightest sound in the silence. Somewhere in the distance she heard a faint scuffling, a mouse or a rat scurrying across the floor. There was nothing else within or without the room. Nothing to tell her where she was, no horse's hooves on cobbled streets, or engines roaring past, no shouts from street sellers, or the loud whistle of a steam engine.

The last thing she remembered was the platform at the train station and the crowd as she tried to get onto the carriage. She felt the crush of the scrum and then, nothing. Her mind was blank.

The air was damp, a stale smell pervaded. Shadows and shades of grey emerged from the blackness. She could make out a ceiling above her. She turned her head to the side and could see a wall and the join where it met the ground. There was no window in the room, no light could enter. She pulled herself up into a sitting position, one hand supporting her weight while the other held her head. She managed to pull herself up onto her feet. The room swayed around her like she was on the deck of a ship. She reached out a hand to steady herself. She groped in the dark and lost her balance and fell forward and her hands found a wall in front of her, which stopped her from crashing back to the floor. With her back to the wall, she used her hands to feel her way around the room. It was a square, four walls of equal length. Along the fourth side, she found a door. She tried to turn the handle. It didn't move. She gripped it and pushed and pulled, but the door was firmly shut. She banged on the wood.

'Hello?' she yelled, making her head pulse with the sound of her own voice. 'Is anybody there?'

No one answered. She hit the door again and gave the handle another futile pull. Nothing moved, no one answered, no one came. She slid down the wall and sat with her back against it, the cool stone against her back, countering the burning flush of her skin.

She urged herself to try and remember what had happened to her. She remembered buying her ticket; she remembered the café and the cup of tea. She had got to the platform and gone to the wrong carriage. She remembered the conductor who looked at her with disdain and directed her to the third-class carriage. There was a man with a suitcase blocking the door. She had been crushed up against other bodies.

Then she remembered the strong smell. A man's cologne. Right before she had blacked out. She had felt faint and he had grabbed her; the man wearing strong cologne. The same strong cologne had belonged to the man who had picked her up when she had fallen at the bottom of the steps; the man who had spoken to her. Alone in the room, in the pitch dark, a feeling of dread crept over her. His voice had seemed familiar, a west coast accent. She grasped at the memory that was just on the edge of her consciousness, but in her drugged state, she could not make the connection.

His hand had clamped itself over her mouth. The sweet taste that she had inhaled was still there, in her mouth. Chloroform. She had come across it in Thomas's medicine cabinet. He had drugged her and carried her away from the train before she could get onboard. She could still be in Edinburgh then, locked in a cellar or some storeroom. He had abducted her.

More returned through the haze. She had felt a rocking motion. She had felt the sensation of movement. He had taken her somewhere. She could be anywhere. Had he put her on the London train after all, or on a completely different route?

A wave of nausea came over her again. She put both hands on her pounding head and pressed and rubbed and felt the room spinning and she fell to the side and her head hit the cold stone floor and the darkness swallowed her once more.

She had no idea how long she had been sleeping for when she opened her eyes. It could have been minutes or hours or days. She was propped up against the wall. When she raised her hand to rub her aching head, she felt the trickle of blood down the side of her face. Had she sat up again on her own or had someone moved her? She stood again, taking her time to get her balance, and found the door. Again, she tried turning and pulling the handle. It refused to move. She turned away in frustration and her foot kicked a bowl on the ground, sending it spinning across the floor with a metallic scrape that echoed through the stillness. She was sure it had not been there before.

On her hands and knees, she found it in the middle of the floor. It was wet. Water had splashed over the side when she had disturbed it. There was still some left in the bowl. She felt the thirst in her throat and raised the bowl to her lips and gulped the water down.

Someone had been in the room. Someone had left a bowl of water next to her and propped her up against the wall. She was not alone. She got up and went back to the locked door and thumped it with her fists.

'Hello! I'm awake. Let me out!' She stood and waited and was answered only by eerie silence.

There was nothing more she could do except wait for the person who had brought the water to return. She paced the square room, feeling steadier on her feet as the effects of the drug wore off. She measured the room. It was only five paces from corner to corner. A coal room for a townhouse in the city, or a cellar for a store or an inn? But it was empty. Nothing was being stored in the room, nothing gave her a clue as to where she was being held.

She gave up her aimless pacing and lay down on her back. She had to rest, to conserve her energy. She thought about the last time she had been confined in an empty room this size. It was in the asylum at Gartloch. When she had misbehaved, or had an episode, she would be taken to an empty room like this, without a light or a window, with a metal door with a grate in it so that the doctors could check on her. When she had banged her head against the stone bricks, they had moved her to another room, with padded walls and an orderly who sat at the window in the door and watched her all the time. Maybe she was back there now. Back in the asylum, where she belonged, away from the public and the children that she could harm. She would not have the strength to survive an institution like that again. She had barely survived the last time. Her fingers ran across her chest and felt the raised scar under her dress, the reminder of how close she had been to death.

She was defeated. After all this time and all she had been through, they had finally broken her. She had nothing left with which to fight them. Those people that judged her and were determined to punish her for what she had done. She felt tears well up inside her, a sob rising in her chest and throat, a sting in her eyes.

Then she stopped. She heard something. She held her breath and listened. It had been faint. There it was again. She let out her breath and pulled herself up onto her knees.

She turned her head towards the noise. It was coming through the wall. She crawled over the floor until she found the wall and she put her ear to the cold surface and listened.

It was crying. Not crying, wailing. It was the scream of a child, a baby. She remembered Alexander's cry, when he was hungry, or tired, or cold. She would never forget that sound. This sounded like him. Was she imagining it? A nightmare in the cold, empty room.

'Alexander, is that you?' she whispered against the wall. Was this her purgatory? She imagined her afterlife would be like this, if not a straight spiral into Hell for what she had done to her own child. But Alexander couldn't be in Hell, not an innocent baby. Had he been here this whole time, since that night at the canal, when he had drowned, waiting for her all these years, begging and wailing for his mother to come to him, and never being answered because she had abandoned him in death?

'I meant to come with you,' she shouted to her son. 'I wanted to come with you, but they wouldn't let me. The men, they pulled me away from you, and they kept pulling me away every time I tried to come for you.'

She had tried at the canal, she had tried in the asylum, but then she had stopped. She had lived on the edge, but she had stopped trying to join him. Why had she left him alone for so long?

She would do anything to break down the wall in front of her to be with him. She clawed at the bricks, ripping her fingernails and breaking the skin on her hands and fingers in a frenzied effort to get to him. The screaming continued. 'Somebody help him!' she cried. She fell to the ground and put her hands over her ears. The screaming got louder, it went through her body, sinking inside her, terrorising her, bringing the guilt onto her, entering her soul. 'Make it stop!' she screamed. It got louder. It wasn't coming through the wall anymore, it was inside her, hammering in her head, overwhelming her. She clawed at her face and ears and tried to dig the screaming out of her as it invaded her mind.

Time passed. Her tears ran dry and she grew calmer. When she tried to hear the noise again, it was gone. She pressed her ear against the wall. Had Alexander gone? Had he left her?

She heard another noise, the low murmur of a deep voice. It was soothing. It was a man talking to the baby. She couldn't hear what was being said, but the baby had stopped crying.

Thank goodness. Someone was looking after him.

Her mind cleared and she gathered the fragments together and willed herself to take back control from the nightmares. It couldn't be Alexander. That was a trick of the dark and of her mind. She had heard the cries of a baby that was still alive. One that was being kept in a room next to her, in a dark, empty cellar. Her rational mind suddenly gave her the answer that made sense. One that was a logical explanation for all that had happened in the last few days.

It was the missing boy, the baby who had been kidnapped from the poorhouse. He was here, through the wall from her. The man who had drugged her and taken her from the train station and brought her here was the same man who had taken the boy from his mother. The same man who had taken Lily May, the girl who had been found dead, from her mother..

A new nightmare emerged, one that was not the product of her imagination. This one was real. This one was terrifying.

She had been taken by the same man who had murdered the baby girl and left her dead in Liberton Tower.

20

THURSDAY MORNING, 25 NOVEMBER

1920

After a sleepless night in the hotel, he had risen early, while it was still dark outside and before the housekeeping staff had left fresh warm water in the communal bathroom. He splashed his face with the cold water leftover from the evening before and used the hotel soap to scrub his face and under his arms. He was shocked by his reflection in the mirror, lit by the flickering gaslight on the wall. He looked gaunt and haggard with a layer of stubble adding to the deep shadow cast by the light. His eyes were sunken and sharp cheekbones stuck out. He had the haunted look of an unwell man who had not eaten properly in days. His skin looked jaundiced and unhealthy. With a comb found next to the sink, he dampened down his unruly hair. His clothes were rumpled and creased.

Leaving his room, he went downstairs and passed the reception as the night porter was finishing his shift. The receptionist who had checked him in the previous evening was anxious that he was not leaving early because the accommodation was unsatisfactory. Thomas assured him the room had been perfectly adequate and he had to be somewhere early. Asked if he would like his room kept for another night, Thomas demurred. He would not be in the city for another night. He settled his bill and stepped out into the Edinburgh dawn; the sun beginning to rise over Arthur's Seat, standing watch to the east side of the city. There was a crisp frost on the ground; his footsteps crunched as he made his way down Princes Street. Already horses and carts filled the cobbled main street, delivering fresh goods to the shops and hotels along the thoroughfare. Street sweepers and lamplighters went about their business, preparing the city for another day.

He arrived at Waverley Station as the metal gate was being unlocked and pushed aside at the bottom of the steps. He went to the departure boards and studied the routes and tried to imagine which one Jessie would most likely take. On the tracks, carriages were shunted into position and engines puffed up and down. The first arrivals appeared with screeching brakes, steam clouds and whistles. The concourse began to fill and Thomas began to panic. There was no good vantage point that would allow him to see over the full run of platforms, and the increasing flow of people coming and going made it impossible to keep track of everyone who passed by. He could only do his best. He made a mental list of the trains Jessie might possibly take and went first to platform five, where the Caledonia line had a service due to depart for Inverness. Departures to Glasgow, Dundee and St Andrews, and the Borders had followed. He was certain he had not seen Jessie leave on any of those trains. He pictured the dark dress she had been wearing the last time he had seen her, her dark hair and her pale complexion. His heart leapt when he saw a woman dressed in the same way. She had the right build and carried herself as Jessie did. He saw her from a distance, from behind, heading towards the platform for the 8.45am service to Glasgow. As he grew closer, he was sure it was her – her hair was dark and the right length. He chased after her, apologising as he bumped into those in his way, pushing his way through the crowd. He reached out and grabbed her by the upper arm, spinning her round mid-step to face him. It was not Jessie. She was younger, her skin was sallow, her eyes were green. He apologised to the shocked woman as she cursed him and turned on her heel, leaving him standing alone in the middle of the bustling platform.

As the morning rush began to die down, the departure time of the Scotch Express drew closer. This was the most likely train she would be on. The platform filled until it seemed no more people could fit onto the concourse. It was impossible to see over the top of the bowler hats and bonnets that crowded around him. He resorted to jumping repeatedly, turning as he did so to take in each direction. All he could see was a uniform mass of black and grey heads, broken occasionally by a splash of colour from a hat feather or bow.

Finally, the crowd began to thin as final farewells were made and passengers embarked. Loved ones gave a final wave and made their way out of the station. Thomas found a foothold at the base of one of the iron pillars that supported the station roof and raised himself up off the ground. He took in the train from one end to the other, peering through the clouds of steam billowing from the engine, casting everything in a white-grey pallor. Through the mist, he thought he glimpsed her several times, but every time the head turned the face was not hers, or the woman picked up a child and hugged them goodbye as only a mother could, or she embraced a gentleman in a loving farewell. None of them were Jessie. There was a last flurry of latecomers with hurried walks and comic trots and lastly a man sprinting at full tilt as the whistle sounded and the last doors were closed. The cloud grew thicker as the engine was stoked and the brakes were released. The wheels began to turn; the carriages clanked against each other as the couplings tensed and expanded and the huge iron horse began to crawl away from the platform. The last man leapt and grabbed the handle of the last door of the final carriage and balanced on the foot step, ignoring the furious station conductor berating him from the platform. He managed to get the handle, turned and opened the door and manoeuvred his way inside, shutting the door behind him. He gave the official on the platform an apologetic smile and wave.

Thomas stayed on his perch until the end of the last carriage disappeared into the distance. Those that had stayed to have a last farewell on the platform walked away. He had not seen her, but he couldn't be sure she had not got on the train without slipping past him.

There was a lull now. Services were more sporadic until the afternoon rush hour began and commuters would make their return journeys home. He hadn't thought beyond this moment. What more could he do now? There were the other poorhouses in the city. He could spend the rest of the day going round them and showing Jessie's picture in the hope she was still here or that someone would recognise her. If she did not want to be found, it was a slim hope. She knew how to lose herself in the city; how to hide and remain undetected. She had done it before. He was not a detective. He did not possess the skills needed to locate a missing person, but he knew he had to try. This was not like James Napier. There was still a chance he could do something.

His spirits rose when he thought that Jessie could have come to her senses and returned to Liberton by herself. It was perfectly plausible. Why hadn't he thought of it until now? After running away in fright, after a day of reflection, she would realise the futility of her actions and would come back. She knew his house was always a safe place for her. He had passed a new public telephone at the entrance to the station, next to the ticket office. He made his way towards it and stepped inside the red booth. He had a few remaining coins in his pocket. He took one and inserted it into the slot and picked up the receiver. An operator connected him to the telephone at his house. After a minute or two, the operator came back on the line.

'I'm afraid there's no answer at that number, sir. Would you like me to keep trying or try another connection?'

'No, thank you.' He placed the receiver back in its cradle. What now? Either she was still in the city or she had already left. If she had already gone, he might never find her. She could have taken a train the previous morning, and be hundreds of miles away already. It was hopeless. He had to concede there was little more he could do. He pulled her photograph from the inside pocket of his coat and stared at it. Jessie smiled at him, a look of joy spread across her face, despite her reluctance to have the picture taken. He would take the photograph and show it around the other poorhouses in the city. Before giving up on the train station altogether, he had one last idea.

He joined the queue at the ticket office. There were only three people in the line and he was soon at the front, facing the ticket officer behind the counter.

'Yes, sir?'

'I wonder if you could help me, I'm looking for someone.'

'Do you want to buy a ticket, sir?'

'I wonder if you have seen a woman.'

'I see hundreds of women every day, sir.'

'I have a photograph of her, if you would take a look at it for me?'

'Sir, you're holding up the line.'

Thomas looked behind him and saw another four people had joined the queue after him. They were all staring at him with a look of impatience as they heard the conversation unfold. 'I'm very sorry, if you could just take a moment to look at this photograph and I'll get out of the way.' He slid the photograph of Jessie under the glass.

'Sir, I must ask you to step aside and let these customers get their tickets.'

'It would have been yesterday morning or this morning that I think she would have been here.'

A woman in the queue shouted out, 'Excuse me, my train is about to depart.'

'One moment, madam,' the ticket officer replied. 'Sir, please move out of the way.'

'Were you working here yesterday morning?'

'Yes, sir, but so were plenty of other ticket officers.' He picked up the photograph to hand it back to Thomas. As he did so, he stopped and stared, and then slid it back towards him. 'I need to serve these people, sir. I get my lunch break in half an hour. Wait for me over there.' He pointed to the waiting room.

'You recognise her?' Thomas's heart leapt with the first hint of hope he had experienced since he had arrived in the city.

'Wait for me over there,' the ticket officer repeated.

Thomas stepped aside, apologising to those in the queue behind him.

Half an hour later, Thomas saw the ticket officer leave the counter and his place was taken by another man in identical uniform. He walked over to the waiting room and joined Thomas sitting on the wooden bench.

'Show me the photograph.' Thomas handed it over. He looked at it again, as if inspecting a train ticket. He held it up towards the light. After a moment, he handed it back. 'That's her, I'm fairly sure.'

'You saw her?'

'Is she your wife?'

'A friend.'

'Yesterday morning,' he nodded. 'She bought a ticket for the Scotch Express. I have to tell you, sir, that she looked in some distress.' He paused. 'You wouldn't be looking to cause her any trouble, would you?' Thomas assured him that he was not. The ticket officer continued. 'She kept looking about her as if she was being followed. And she was in some disarray, in her appearance,

I mean. Make-up smeared, clothes crumpled, hair disorderly. I remember her because I was alarmed at the time and asked her if she was okay? She said she was fine and hurried away. I was too busy to pursue it.'

Thomas felt mixed emotions. He was elated that he had been right. As he suspected, Jessie was trying to get away, out of the country, and had gone south. But he had missed her. If she had taken the train yesterday, she was already in London by now. The ticket officer's description of her appearance worried him further. With her history of mental illness, the strain of her present situation was clearly troubling her.

'Did you see her get on the train?' he asked, seeking final confirmation.

'She bought a ticket. I can't tell you if she got on the train or not. Would seem odd if she bought a ticket and didn't. You could try asking the station manager. He supervises the platform for the Scotch Express, it always being busy, and makes sure those in first class are treated properly.'

'Where can I find him?'

'Follow me, I'll take you to him.'

The station manager was having his lunch in his office. He didn't take too kindly to being interrupted when the ticket officer knocked on the door and introduced Thomas. The ticket officer left them, wishing Thomas good luck in tracking down his friend.

It was a small room, with space only for a small desk in the corner and one chair. Thomas waited while the manager put his sandwich down and wiped his mouth and fingers.

'Now then, who is this woman you're looking for?'

Thomas again handed over the photograph. The station manager shrugged. 'I could have seen her, but then she looks like a hundred or more women that come through the station every day. What's happened to her? Run off with another man, has she?'

'She bought a ticket for the Scotch Express yesterday morning. Your ticket officer remembered seeing her.'

'Yesterday morning?' The manager looked at the photograph again. 'Now that you mention it, I think I might have seen her. Wearing that same dress.'

'Did she get on the train?'

'As a matter of fact, she didn't, that's why I remember her.'

Thomas's heart fluttered again with a moment of hope. She had not left. He might still be able to find her in the city.

The manager continued, 'Bit of a rammy yesterday morning, usually is with the third-class coaches. Daft man blocking the door, everyone trying to push past him. Got a bit heated. I remember her because she was caught in the crush and fainted. A man pulled her out and carried her away to recover.'

'She couldn't have made it back to the train before it left?'

'Didn't see her again. The train pulled away just after that, once I sorted out getting the bloody passengers aboard in an orderly manner. I assumed the man knew her and was looking after her alright. They must have left the station. I didn't see them again. Hope she was okay.' He handed the photograph back to Thomas. 'Sorry I can't help you any more than that.'

'That's quite alright. You've been very helpful. At least now I know she didn't make it onto the train. The man that carried her away, what did he look like?'

'Big fellow. I didn't see his face, but he walked with a bit of a limp. Of course, he was carrying this woman, so it may have been just that.'

Thomas knew who it was. It had to be. It couldn't just be a coincidence. The man with the limp was Duncan Watt. He had followed her and taken her. He took out the picture of Watt. 'Was this the man who carried her away?'

The manager looked. 'Like I say, I didn't see his face. He had a cap pulled down low. I couldn't say.'

Thomas thanked him for his help again and left him to eat the rest of his sandwich. He returned to the station concourse. He had made progress at last. He had a firm sighting of Jessie. She had meant to get the train to London, but had been stopped and taken away by Watt. He was sure it must have been Duncan Watt. He had known the two of them were linked together somehow. Duncan Watt had followed her to Edinburgh and snatched her from the platform. Thomas had never spoken to Jessie about his new patient. He had never told her about his strange interest in her and his comments about her, or about seeing him at the police meeting. Did she know him? How had their paths crossed before?

He had to assume that Watt had some sort of plan for her. He had tried to frame her for the kidnappings. If he was the killer of a child and abductor of another, then Thomas had to assume Watt meant to harm Jessie. He thought about going back to Aitchison with this new revelation. Surely, he would have to do something now, but he heard the detective's voice. It was all circumstantial. Thomas was leaping to conclusions. They needed concrete evidence before he would consider diverting his resources away from the search for Adam Symons.

He had to do this himself. Watt had followed her to the train station and taken her away from the London train. He would not be able to walk through the busy city streets with an unconscious woman. There would be too many witnesses. People would notice and would offer to help. A police officer or a doctor may have seen him and intervened. Watt would not take that risk. He must have moved her some other way. Thomas was sure he had not used a car when he had come to the hospital. Could he have taken her on a different train?

He looked around helplessly. Watt could have taken her anywhere. Thomas felt sick. He could have killed her already. He could have thrown her on the train tracks or left her in a close or at the top of Arthur's Seat or Calton Hill.

Then his eyes alighted on the departure board. The word leapt out at him because he had heard it only recently, when the police had been shouting at Jessie in the kitchen. It wasn't a place he had been to, or even thought of before, until he had heard it then.

He checked the departure times. They fitted. A train left twice a day, once in the afternoon at 3.15pm, and once in the morning, at 10.15am; fifteen minutes after the Scotch Express. Watt could have taken her off the London-bound train and walked along to platform three and put her on this train instead.

It was the place where Jessie had lost her child. In her disturbed mind she had killed her own child there, at the canal. Thomas saw it on the departure board, listed under the stops along the route to the west. Ingliston, Linlithgow, Grangemouth, Falkirk, Denny. Then the train split in two, half heading north to Stirling, the other half continuing west towards Glasgow. On the way it stopped there. It stopped at Castlecary.

21

THURSDAY AFTERNOON, 25 NOVEMBER

1920

It had gone quiet again. She had heard a door open and close and the bolt being pulled and footsteps fading into the distance. She had called out as the man had retreated, but his stride did not falter, though she did notice the odd way one footstep seemed heavier than the other. There had been no sound since then. He had not returned. In the darkness and silence, robbed of daylight, Jessie couldn't tell how much time had passed. She didn't know if it was morning or evening or the middle of the night. She was hungry and thirsty. She sat against the wall until it grew uncomfortable. She curled up on the ground and waited. She thought he must have taken the child away with him as the silence drifted on, but then she heard it wake and cry out for an eternity before it went quiet once more. The crying needled at her brain, crawling insidiously inside her, recalling vivid memories of her own boy in her arms, clutching to her, suckling from her breast, his wide, brown eyes staring up at her. She cradled her chest and felt the ache of her absent boy. She felt the strong grip of his tiny hand around her finger and the soft scalp covered in thin, fine hair. She yearned to hold him and comfort him once more. She yearned to comfort the screaming child in the room next to her, to comfort and soothe and say it would all be alright because she was there to look after him.

Later, she heard the footsteps approaching, the same distinctive stride as before. With its strange rhythm, one foot dragging rather than confidently stepping. Again, the footsteps went to the door next to her room; the bolt was pulled open and she heard his voice talking to the baby in a low murmur. She guessed he was feeding the child. She heard the door being closed and the bolt being drawn again. This time the footsteps stopped after a few paces. He was outside her door. Nothing happened.

She pulled herself up and went to the door and put her mouth close to it. 'Please. I'm thirsty.'

She could sense him there. The metal bolt in her door screeched. She jumped back and heard the lock being turned. Then the handle moved and the door opened. Orange light penetrated the gloom, stinging her eyes, which had been shrouded in the darkness for so long. She took a step back, expecting him to enter the room, but he remained outside. She didn't dare step forward to confront him. She needed him to make the first move. The light flickered and she looked down and saw a hand come through the gap in the doorway at the floor. A metal bowl, such as a dog would drink from, was placed inside the door and his hand withdrew. The door was closed again and darkness consumed her small chamber once more. The footsteps receded into the distance again.

'Thank you,' she called out, her voice a dry rasp, in the hope he might stop and return, but he kept walking. She crouched down and crawled forward, feeling in front of her to find the bowl. Her hands grasped the cool metal and she put her finger inside it and touched the cold water. She had no idea if it was clean or dirty, it could have been scooped from a puddle of rainwater in the street, but her throat was so dry she had no choice but to drink it. She sipped, raising the bowl carefully so as not to spill a drop. It felt refreshing as it slipped down her throat. She splashed a little on her face, on her eyes and her dry mouth and drank the rest.

There was nothing more she could do except wait. She curled up on the floor again and closed her eyes.

The cries of the child woke her. In her dark haze it took her a moment to remember. It wasn't Alexander who had visited her in her dreams once again. It was the boy next door. Adam Symons, she was sure. She went to the wall and did what she could to soothe him.

'There, there, Adam. It's alright. Please stop crying, Adam.' Her pleading grew desperate as his wailing grew louder. She started to shout, using her own voice to block out the unbearable noise from the room next door. She was screaming in a frenzy. She stood up and began pacing wildly around the room and beating the wall and the door. 'Stop it! Stop it! Stop it! Make it stop!'

She jumped at the violent knock at the door. 'Quiet down in there!' the man called. She stared at the door. Once he was sure she had calmed herself, he went to the room next door and his low, murmuring voice soothed the child. She assumed he had brought some milk to the boy. She didn't move, listening intently for any sound. His footsteps left the room and came to her door once more. The bolt was lifted, the door pushed open, and the firelight encroached once more.

The man stood on one side of the door and Jessie at the other, waiting for him to take a step into the room. Jessie backed away as the door opened wider, pushed by his hand. His other hand held the torch aloft. A tall figure entered the room. She put her arms up to shield her eyes from the increasing light and retreated until she felt the cold stone wall at her back. She peered through the flickering shadows to try and see the face of the man who was holding her captive.

Her heart stopped beating, her breath caught in her throat, and she was unable to move.

'Hello, Jessie,' the man said, his deep voice echoing around the room.

The shock gripped her like a vice and the floor came up to meet her and she crumpled in a heap. The darkness surrounded her once more.

She woke with a start as cold water was splashed across her face. A rough hand slapped her cheek and grabbed her by the hair and shook her head from side to side until she came to her senses and feebly pushed it away and sat up. The light was above her now, the torch held in a bracket on the wall. He was squatting beside her. His hands gripped her wrists and restrained her. She couldn't bring herself to look at his face, fearful of confirming what she thought she had seen. She willed herself to confront him, and her breath caught in her throat once more.

The face was older, lined with life. The hair was longer, but thinner than it had been. The eyes were the same colour, but behind them was a malice that had not been there before. His smile was laced with dark spite and was lopsided, pulled down on one side by an ugly scar than ran down the side of his face. The boyish looks she had once adored had vanished. His shoulders were broad; he had grown into a man from the boy she had known.

'Duncan?'

He laughed in response to her bewilderment. It was not the laugh she remembered. His voice was rougher and deeper than before, but still with the west coast accent and enough of his old tone for her to recognise, but the laugh was something new. It made her shiver. It was malevolent and evil and ugly.

'Surprised?' he asked. Jessie was mute. Her mind was trying to catch up with what she was seeing. As it did so, she began to unravel the enormity of it. 'You probably thought I was dead.'

'I never knew what happened to you.'

'That was always your problem. Selfish bitch. You never thought of anyone but yourself.'

'What do you mean?' She was confused at his anger.

'You know exactly what I mean. Running off like that, leaving me. When you knew I would have helped you. You and the boy.'

'That's not what happened. You wanted nothing to do with me. You threw us away. Your family told me to stay away from you.'

He laughed again. His grip on her wrists grew tighter and he leaned in close. She could feel the spittle from his mouth against her skin as he spoke to her through his gritted teeth. 'I heard you ended up in a mental house, and now I know they were right. If you think that was what happened you must be insane.'

22

THE PARK

1903

She was a girl again, sixteen-years-old, in the south of Glasgow, among the upper- and middle-class houses of Battlefield, Mount Florida and Langside. She was two years out of school and working in a local shop on weekdays. She helped her mother at home the rest of the time, raising her younger brothers, while her father worked for a bank in the city. It was the start of spring and fresh buds were on the trees and the first splashes of colour began to decorate the green grass of Queen's Park. She joined her mother walking around the park on Sundays, after attending the church at Camphill. It was there that she had first seen him. It was his height that she had noticed first: taller than six feet, and head and shoulders above his mother, who walked on his arm. Jessie's own father was a short man, barely five and a half feet tall, and she and her brothers followed that family trait. When her father joined them for a stroll around the park and they passed the handsome, tall boy, he towered over him. She smiled at him and he returned the smile and she sensed his interest. Her adolescent mind began to think about him and look forward to the weekend when she would get a chance to glimpse him again. She imagined ways in which she would be able to speak with him. In dreams, somehow their mothers and fathers disappeared and they were alone and it was her arm that was looped through his as they walked around the pond and she picked the flowers as they talked and laughed. She asked her friends about him and found out his name. Duncan Watt. His father worked in the city too, like her own, but with a different bank. The family had a good reputation within the community, even though they had not come from old money. He was expected to attend university in Glasgow after the summer, which did not displease her as he would remain living with his parents in Mount Florida.

Her opportunity came unexpectedly one evening when she was returning home from the shop. It was summer now and the evenings were long. A heatwave had come over the city and the streets had sweltered for a fortnight. She cut through the park to get home. It was teeming with people: children and adults enjoying the fresh, warm air after a busy day cooped up in school or offices in the city, or sweating on the building sites or shipyards or in the grain mills. Trousers and skirts were rolled up and lifted as people paddled in the pond. Younger children stripped down to their vests and splashed each other.

He towered above them all, his mop of brown hair soaked through and plastered to his forehead, his trousers rolled up to his knees and his shirt open as he splashed with his friends in the water. She stopped and watched him, smiling at his casual energy. His height gave him an advantage over his friends in their play fight. He saw her at the side of the pond. Their eyes met and for a moment, the rest of the park faded into the background. The spell was broken when he was tripped up and landed in the water. The boys around him revelled in their unexpected victory.

Later, they walked around the pond together, the sun still high in the evening sky. She knew she should have been back home and soon her mother would start to worry about her. He had left his friends to come and talk to her and they had already completed two laps of the park. His clothes began to dry and he rolled his trouser legs down and she looked away as he tucked his shirt back in and buttoned it up.

She could not remember what exactly they had spoken about, apart from introducing each other. They must have spoken about family, about what school they had gone to, what church they attended, and their hopes for the future. She left him to return home for dinner. They agreed to meet the following evening at the same time. This became their routine. She would find him waiting for her by the pond, always on the same bench. After that first meeting, he was always alone. He spent his days relaxing and reading, preparing for his start at university. She liked to hear about what he was reading. He was to study law and he insisted he would become a fighter for justice for the poor and the downtrodden in the city. He encouraged her to tell him her dreams. She told him she wished to travel the world, to be an explorer like the heroes of Jules Verne. He promised he would take her on adventures to far flung lands. Then they would return and settle down and have a large family. She blushed when he spoke of marriage and children and of sharing a house and a bed. She had never spoken of such things with a boy before. With her friends, sex was whispered about in hushed tones and shy giggles. She became annoyed when he teased her about it and he apologised and told her he would never talk of such things again and she slapped him on the arm.

When they passed each other in the presence of their parents, they could no longer hide their connection from them and her mother guessed what was going on. To Jessie's surprise, she was not angry, but encouraged her to meet with him and told her he was a fine-looking gentleman from a good family. By all accounts, he had a bright future ahead of him and she would do well to cultivate his affections. His mother had not been as encouraging, preferring him to remain focused on his learning and education. There would be plenty of time for girls after he had finished his studies and had made a start on his law career. He reassured Jessie that he would not be swayed by his mother's thoughts. He loved her, and he hoped she felt the same way about him.

Jessie told him that she loved him, too.

'Will you wait for me to finish my studies? Then we can marry and we would be able to afford a house to live together.'

She blushed, as she always did when he touched on this topic. 'Is that a proposal?'

'I suppose it is, if you wish it to be.'

'Then we must consider ourselves to be engaged.' She laughed. 'But we must not tell anyone, least of all your mother.'

'If we are engaged, then I think I am entitled to a kiss.'

They were in a quiet corner of the park, on their evening loop, away from the busy area by the main street and the pond and hidden by a large oak tree. They were holding hands and now he turned to face her and took her in his arms and she felt his strong, lean body against hers as he drew her in towards him. She tilted her head skywards and closed her eyes and waited, unresisting, as his lips found hers. Like the first time they had looked at each other, time stood still and the birdcalls and traffic and chatter of people disappeared. She took in his scent, inhaling him as his nose and cheek brushed against her own, her tongue searching his mouth as his entered her own. For a brief moment, everything seemed perfect to her; she understood happiness and true love clearly and the beauty of life and everything that it entailed.

When they broke apart, he held her and they smiled into each other's eyes. He whispered to her 'Do you like that? You can have it if you want it. We don't have to wait until we're married.' She blushed, unwilling to tell him that she was curious and tempted. He pulled her in closer. She felt his hands move down from her back and she didn't stop him, and then one hand was at the front of her skirt, pressing against her and she felt a sensation like she had never felt before.

Deep down, no matter how much she liked it and wanted it, she knew that it was wrong at that moment. She tried to pull away from him, but he was strong and pressed against her. She tried to talk to him.

For weeks and months afterwards, she tried to remember what she had said. Had she told him to stop? It all happened so quickly. She was a blur of conflicting emotions. Had she been firm enough in her refusal?

His hand clamped over her mouth and she looked into his eyes and saw a stranger. It was Duncan, but it was an unknown version of him. He was no longer charming or handsome. The boy had gone and in his place was a wild animal. She saw lust and selfishness and power.

She remembered the sun dipping behind Camphill and the quiet of the park as people made their way home. Behind the oak tree, they were alone. For the first time in her sheltered life, Jessie felt vulnerable. She smelled his scent from the hand across her mouth. She looked up at the leaves above her, gently swaying in the warm breeze. He held her against the tree with one arm and unbuckled his belt. She was pinned there. She could not get away. She tried to push him away, but she was nothing to him. She scratched and slapped his face but he did not care. She felt him lifting her skirt. She looked into his face and pleaded. His face was a malevolent sneer, a look of self-right, of victory, of owning and using her. She gave up. She stopped struggling and let him have his way with her. She felt the rough bark clawing at her back as he forced himself on her, and she was surprised that it was over so quickly. He withdrew and her skirt fell down. He fastened his trousers. Before she could react, he had taken her hand and they were continuing their walk along the path. He didn't act as though he had done anything wrong. She remembered her confusion. Did he think that was how it was meant to be? Did he think she had enjoyed him forcing himself on her? Was that how he believed women should be treated? They still held hands as though they were young innocents. She didn't pull away from him. She wanted to tell him she had not wanted it to be like that. She had not wanted it at all, but she said nothing.

Neither of them spoke until they reached the gate. He said goodnight to her and promised to meet her tomorrow, as usual. She only nodded and left him and walked home. She went straight to her room and closed the door and lay on her bed and wept. Her parents did not disturb her. They had become used to her solitariness, when she wished to be alone to daydream of her young love. She felt shame and humiliation. She cleaned herself to wash away the sin she had committed. She noticed the spots of blood on her dress.

She was a quiet girl and no one at the breakfast table or in the shop noticed she was more reserved the following day. She did not go through the park on her way home. She took the long way home along the streets and avoided him. Part of her hoped he would come to find her to apologise, and then she could tell him how she felt about what had happened. No one called for her at the house. Days went past and she continued to avoid the park. He never came looking for her. She knew he had used her. He had got what he had wanted all along. She imagined him boasting about his conquest to his friends. She started to become paranoid when customers in the shop would giggle or glance at her. She knew he had told people and word had got round about what he had done. She took her punishment in silence. It was what she deserved for having behaved so disgracefully. She prayed word would not reach her family and was thankful for each day that passed when no one in the household said anything.

Autumn came round. The nights drew in and the heat dissipated from the city. The park was quieter in the evenings and Jessie began to use the shortcut home from work again. He would be in the city; the university term had started. There was little danger of bumping into him around Langside and Mount Florida. He had left that part of his life behind.

Then on one Friday evening, there he was. He was with his friends, sitting on the bench where he used to wait for her every evening. She faltered, but there was no choice but to pass him. She bowed her head and walked quickly. As she passed him, she glanced up and saw him looking at her. She recognised that sneer, that look of power and victory and she was only grateful that he chose not to call out to her. As the laughs faded behind her, she broke into a run.

It was near the end of the year when she knew she was pregnant. She had been concerned when her period had not arrived as usual. By November, the swelling of her abdomen and the change in her body told her there was a life growing inside her. She could not see the family doctor without going through her parents, so had no choice but to confess to them what had happened. She was prepared for their anger. Once they had digested the news, they would support her. Her mother called her unmentionable names in her rage, words Jessie never would have imagined her mother would dare utter. More damaging than her tirade was the silence from her father. He offered no comfort or reassurance. He stood and let her mother abuse her and then left her bedroom without saying a word.

The doctor confirmed the news and recommended rest and a healthy diet. Her father spoke to the Watt family. They denied their son, now achieving great things at university, could have been responsible. They did not believe Jessie. Their son had told them about Jessie. Any number of men could be the father if the rumours about her conduct were to be believed. Her parents viewed her with renewed doubt. The evidence before them suggested what he claimed could be true.

She heard nothing from Duncan.

Jessie overheard the doctor telling her father about Mrs Maguire, a midwife who could help girls who had got themselves into trouble. They could afford the fee. She was known to be discreet and well-practiced. No one said the word abortion. In hushed whispers, it was dismissed as unsafe and illegal and against the teachings of the church.

To spare the family's reputation, Jessie was to be sent to stay with relatives in Dundee for the remainder of her pregnancy. Once the child was born, a suitable adoption would be arranged and Jessie could return to the family home. They did not care if she wanted to keep the child, it was never an option. They reminded her that to be single and with a child would leave her with no prospects at all. They admonished themselves – how could they have brought up such a child? Where had they gone wrong?

The evening before she was due to travel to the east coast, Duncan called at the house. Her father showed him into the living room and left them alone. She was surprised to see him, and by how contrite he was. He admitted he had been a fool and had ruined their relationship. He asked her if there was anything he could do to help. She suggested he admit to being the father, and explain to her parents what had happened. He shook his head. He would admit nothing. He couldn't, not in his present situation. His family would disown him and he would lose his place at university without their money. It would ruin his prospects.

'And what do you think has happened to me?' she replied, anger brimming beneath the surface. 'My family have disowned me. I have no prospects. You took all of those things from me.'

'I cannot take it back,' he pleaded. 'In the future, I can help in some way, once I'm earning a good wage.'

'You think you can buy forgiveness? They want me to give my child away.'

'Perhaps that's best for everyone, especially the child. They could have a fresh start with a good family.'

'Does no one care what I want? This,' she placed her hands round her belly, 'is my child. It is part of me.'

'Women in your situation give up their unwanted children all the time, it's not unusual.'

'Is it what they want to do? Has anyone asked them?'

'There's always the chance that it may not be born. I have a friend studying medicine who says miscarriages are more common than you think.'

She flew into a rage and threw him out of the house. She screamed after him as he went. Her parents found her wild and wretched and put her to bed. She knew they shared his hope. If the baby disappeared, their problems would disappear also, and they could go back to their lives. She decided then and there to defy them. She would go to Dundee and give birth to her child in her aunt's house, away from the prying eyes of their neighbours, but she would never give her child away. She would keep it and raise it herself.

The following March, her son was born. She named him Alexander. She wrote and told her parents they were grandparents to a healthy boy. She told them she could not part with her child. She would return home to live with them and raise him in their home. She gave them one last chance to do the right thing. The reply was terse and uncompromising. She was welcome to return alone, but the child must be given up. If she insisted on keeping the child, then she would be on her own.

As soon as she laid eyes upon the boy, she knew she could not part from him. She could not give him away to be raised by strangers, no matter how convenient it would be for all concerned. She was bonded to him, he was part of her, and she would keep him and raise him no matter what it took.

She did not tell Duncan. He had made it clear that he would rather see his child dead than have it upset his ideal life. She was pleased that Alexander had taken after her looks rather than his father's. He had wisps of dark red hair, and pale skin and dark hazelnut eyes. She did not know if anyone ever told Duncan Watt about the birth of his son.

When she did think of the father, she only saw the ugly face at the moment of Alexander's conception. She looked at Alexander and wondered how something so beautiful could come from such pain.

23

THURSDAY, 25 NOVEMBER

1920

That evil face stared at her now, disfigured and aged and tormented by demons she could only guess at.

'I would have let you be his father if you had wanted to.'

'You never even let me meet him. Your father told me that I had a son out there.'

'Did you come looking for us?'

'Only when it was too late.' He spat in her face. 'Only when you had already murdered him.'

'I didn't murder him.'

He hit her, a sharp slap across her face. 'You took him from me, you took everything from me.'

'I did come back once,' she sobbed, cowering under his firm grip, 'I begged my family to take us in, we were desperate. They refused.'

'Then, after I've dealt with you, I will find your family and punish them as well.' He let go of her wrists and stood over her. 'But you will die first, and when you do, everyone will know you as a child murderer. They will know the truth about what you are. You and all the other disgusting whores out there. Like that silly bitch who got me kicked out of university, or the French whore who did this to me.' He slapped the scar on his face. He was raving now and Jessie knew he was a madman. She could not be sure what had happened to him to make him this way. It had started that fateful night in the park when she had seen the menace in him as he had taken her. It had always been inside of him. Her only fault was not seeing it before it was too late.

'I didn't kill him,' she said. He lashed out, kicking her in the stomach, hard enough that it made her retch. 'How did you find me?' she asked, clutching her abdomen. She had to keep him talking. The longer he was there, the more chance an opportunity to escape would present itself. She wanted to get out. She wanted to save the boy.

'It took me four years,' he answered with triumph. 'You thought you were so clever. You thought no one would ever find you. Well, I did.

'It took me a long time. I gave up often. Once I read about this rich man, Sir William Ferguson. How he'd been murdered and how a woman called Jessie Bruce had vanished into thin air. I knew it had to be you. I thought about going to find you then. I had already been kicked out of university; my family had disowned me. All because of you and women like you. Before I could search for you, I got into a fight. Glassed a bastard in his face. He survived, but I already had a record of minor charges and this time my father refused to bail me out so I was sent to prison. Five years they gave me. Then the war came along and they sent me to France to fight. I got kicked out after that French tart and her jealous husband turned on me. Just another one of you bitches that were determined to ruin me.

'I came home from France with nothing. I should have been put back in prison, where they had taken me from, but in the confusion of the war, I slipped away and no one seemed to care. I went back home. I saw your mother and your father and your brothers. They told me you had disappeared. I wanted to show you how you had ruined everything for me. You had destroyed my life, setting me on this path of debauchery that I could not resist or escape. And you had my son; you had taken him from me when we could have been a family together. Part of me even thought we could still be a family again. You and my son could save me.' He paused and laughed at his ridiculous notion.

'I remembered about Sir William Ferguson and this Jessie Bruce that had been in the asylum. I went there, to Gartloch. Doctor Andrews is still there. That's when I found out you had killed my boy. I went mad with anger. I swore I would find you and destroy you for what you had done to him and to me.

'Doctor Andrews was a nice man, he thought I was a concerned relative. He told me about your friend, Anne. She's still locked up in the asylum, never to be let out. They think she really killed Sir William and the men took the fall for her. Andrews asked her if she knew anything about you, like where you might have gone. All she knew was you'd said you were getting away, far away from Glasgow, in case anyone came looking for you. Edinburgh, she thought she had heard the night you ran away and left her. She wished she had gone with you. Just another ruined life you left in your wake.'

Jessie pictured the fragile woman standing in the bedroom at Dalmuir House. She had been locked up in that asylum all this time.

'I came to Edinburgh. Two more years it took me. I gave up countless times. I went round the poorhouses; I looked on the streets. I knew you would be in the gutter somewhere, but no one had heard of you. Then I found the House for Fallen Women in Liberton. It was in the newspaper that it was closing down. There was some sort of argument about who would look after these fallen women, as though they deserve sympathy or help from anyone. By the time I got there it had already closed, but it wasn't hard to find a local gossiping about the woman from there who had shacked up with the doctor in town.

'You weren't fooling anyone with your good dresses and your black hair, and the airs and graces you put on. I knew it was you straight away. I found you. Now I just had to decide what to do with you.'

'Why didn't you just kill me? Why the children?'

'Don't you understand? I want you to suffer. Like you made me suffer. I wanted to make your life a misery like mine has been. You put a curse on me, with your loose ways. You tricked me into getting you with child.

'Now I've ruined your life. Everyone can see you for what you are. An evil witch. A child killer. You're going to die knowing everyone knows the truth about you now. And I will finally be free from your wicked curse.'

24

THURSDAY, 25 NOVEMBER

1920

It was dusk when the train from Edinburgh Waverley crossed the tall arches of the viaduct and pulled into the station at Castlecary. Thomas stepped down onto the platform. No one else disembarked and he stood alone. The whistle sounded and the train gathered momentum and departed towards Glasgow. To the north-west, across the tracks, four tall chimneys loomed out of the earth, smoke billowing from them like clouds in the dark-blue sky. Between the chimneys were warehouses of various shapes and sizes. Train tracks branched off the mainline towards them. Painted onto the side of the tallest building in huge white letters was written CASTLECARY FIRECLAY WORKS AND LIMEWORKS. The sound of clanking machinery spoke of ongoing industry. From here, bricks and blocks would be taken by train around Scotland and beyond.

Thomas turned his back on the noise and left the platform. There was a sign at the exit pointing to the village of Castlecary to the south. He set off towards the small cluster of houses a few hundred yards away. Thomas imagined this was what Liberton had once been like, before it had been swallowed up by the encroaching city. There was a church with a pointed roof and an adjoining hall, and a row of small shops. A handful of houses lined the main track that ran through the village from north to south. Smaller side streets branched away, with smaller dwellings along them. He assumed the workers from the factory lived in these. Beyond the village boundaries, fields stretched away as far as he could see, sloping dramatically down into troughs before rising again in the distance. The road wound its way along the floor of the valley. He passed a small castle, set back from the main road, which he assumed gave the village its name. At one time a rich landowner would have lived there and owned all the land. Now the industrial factories and kilns ruled the fate of the village.

Unsure of where to turn next, he returned to the church, hoping to find someone who could direct him towards the canal. There was no one in sight. Castlecary had an eerie feeling of emptiness. The dropping temperature and the still air highlighted the sense of isolation. He looked around and saw a signpost next to a path that led across a field. An arrow, with 'Castlecary Inn' and 'Allandale' imprinted onto it, pointed along the path. The inn seemed an obvious place to find locals who could direct him. He felt his left arm shake and jammed it into his pocket. He already knew he would drink when he got to the inn. He had not touched a drop all day.

The path that cut across the field was rutted and rough and in the fading light he stumbled over loose stones and roots and divots. There would be a frost tonight under the clear sky. After ten minutes, there was no sign of the inn. He was on the point of giving up and returning to the village. Then he cleared a hedgerow and ahead saw a light shining in the distance. It must be the inn, sitting alone among the fields that seemed to roll on forever dotted with occasional trees and divided by lines of hedgerows and fences.

As he got nearer, he saw it was a group of buildings. The inn was the largest. It was surrounded by smaller houses and a stable and a barn. The windows of the inn were brightly lit, a welcoming sight for a traveller arriving through the surrounding darkness. He pushed the door open. The noise of men talking escaped into the night. No one paid him any attention as he entered and made his way to the bar at the back of the room. Groups of men were gathered around tables or stood along the walls. A few women were present, mixing among the workers, and one woman was serving drinks from a tray. The crowd was made up of a mix of clean, well-kempt gentlemen alongside workers wearing dirty overalls, their faces covered in grime and dust after a shift at the factory. The banter was lively and from one corner a banjo was being strummed and a song began, shouted lyrics swirling into the mix of voices. There was a stool next to the bar and Thomas settled himself on it and waited for the barman to serve him.

He ordered a pint of beer and savoured the taste of the first mouthful and felt his nerves calm and his hands and arms steady as the alcohol flowed through him. The bartender had other customers to serve. Eventually he returned, running a cloth along the bar surface, mopping up the puddles of spilled beer.

'Another?' he asked, seeing Thomas's empty glass.

'Much obliged,' Thomas nodded.

The barman filled the glass again from the pump. 'Passing through?'

'I was looking for the canal.'

'The canal?' He smiled. 'If you'd kept going another fifty yards beyond here you would've fallen into it. What did you want to look at the canal for?'

'I'm looking for someone.'

The barman placed the replenished glass in front of him. 'Not likely to find anyone at the canal these days. Only get one or two barges passing a day now, if that. Railway has taken most of the freight and passengers away.'

'Are there canal locks near here?'

He nodded, 'Aye, further along, towards Allandale. No one there now though. No lock-keeper in the gate house any more. We send someone up to help anyone who needs a hand with the gates, but most of the barges sort themselves out. Who is it you're looking for, exactly?'

'A woman.'

'A woman ain't likely to be out at the canal on her own in the night, especially in this cold.'

Thomas took the photograph of Jessie from his coat pocket and slid it in front of the barman. 'Have you seen her in the last day or so? Her name is Jessie, or sometimes Louise.'

'What sort of woman goes by two different names?' The barman picked up the photograph and held it up to the light on the wall above. He shook his head. 'Can't say I recognise her. Feel free to ask around if you want.'

'She might have been with this man.' Thomas placed Duncan Watt's army photograph on the bar. 'He'd be a bit older now, with a nasty scar down the side of his face.'

Again, the barman looked at the picture and shook his head. 'Afraid I can't help you. You in the military?' He gestured at Watt's picture and the uniform he was wearing.

'I was, medical corps.'

'Fifteenth Battalion, infantry. Most of the lads in here served too. You and this lad fighting over this woman?' The barman winked at him. 'Stole her from you, has he?'

'Something like that, yes.'

'Well, wouldn't want any trouble round here if you do find him. Take your troubles away and sort it out between the three of you. But like I said, not seen either of them in here.'

Thomas gulped down the last of his second pint. 'Thanks all the same.' He jumped down from the stool and made his way back to the door. There seemed little point in showing the photographs to anyone else gathered in the bar. If the barman had not seen Jessie, then he could be certain none of the other guests in the Castlecary Inn would have seen her. He would go to the canal and find the lock. The lock where Jessie had lost her child.

He circled round to the back of the inn and picked up the path that ran across the grass. He followed it, peering into the night, his way illuminated by the moonlight. After a minute, he saw a black line that ran across the path. On the other side of this black void was a row of trees and a hedge that stretched away to the left and right. When he reached the edge of the void, he looked into the still, black water. The canal. There was barely a ripple on the surface, and on an overcast night, he was sure he would have fallen straight into the murky depths. The path turned and ran alongside the water. He turned to the right, taking him away from Castlecary and towards Allandale. Somewhere along here he would come to the lock gates.

Fifteen minutes later, he finally saw something that broke the monotonous, flat canal. A wood that had shadowed the towpath cleared away and to the south, he saw another small village. This must be Allandale. Like Castlecary, it seemed to nestle in a small clearing of its own. The buildings were modern, built to house more workers from the Castlecary works.

As he exhaled, his breath formed clouds of frost in the night air. The effects of the two pints were wearing off, and he felt the cold creeping in to his body. He pressed on. He felt the path start to slope upwards, following the gradient of the land.

He saw the white paint first, reflecting in the moonlight. It was used to cover the top of the gates and the ends of the large beams that protruded from the canal across the path. He made out the black shadow of the gates rising up from the canal, matched on either side by steep brick walls. The gates were closed on the side nearest to him, which meant on the other side the water was higher, matching the height of the land that the canal continued along. On the other side of the canal, he saw a small house that must have once been the lock-keeper's home.

There was no sound around him. The air was damp and musty, fouled by the stagnant water. He reached the beam of the closed gate. Attached to the side of the gate was the walkway on which he could cross the canal, a ledge that faced into the deep pool of water beyond. There was no railing or safety barrier. One false step and he would be plunged into the freezing water. He was not a strong swimmer, even in favourable conditions. He was certain he would not survive a fall into the canal.

Holding onto the top of the gate, he edged out onto the walkway, his back pressed against the solid wood, his feet shuffling along as he looked down into the black depth. He reached the midway point, where the two halves of the swing gate met. There was a small gap in the ledge as it passed from one side to the other. He slid his foot along and felt the end of the platform and tentatively groped further along until he found the other side. He stood for a moment and took a deep breath, and stared down at the water.

This is where she lost her child. Fresh air and alcohol hit him and the water rose up towards him as he swayed forward. One hand let go of the gate behind him and he frantically waved it about in front of him, trying to correct his balance. He felt he was drawn towards the water. It was inevitable he would fall into it and would drown beneath that black surface. He could feel the last ounce of air leaving his lungs and his body convulsing. He would be submerged forever, lying at the bottom of that hellish dark pool, undisturbed and forgotten. No one would come looking for him. He had told no one where he was going.

He righted himself and pressed himself back against the solid wood and closed his eyes, and the dizziness passed. He opened his eyes again. He was certain Jessie had not been capable of drowning her boy here. In desperation, some may have resorted to such a crime, or paid others to do the deed. Infanticide happened, and the canals offered a way out for those who had nothing left. But he knew Jessie. He knew she could not have done it.

He shuffled along the rest of the walkway and, with a sigh of relief, made it to the other side. The lock-keeper's cottage had fallen into disrepair. White-washed walls were covered in green moss and lichen and were stained brown and black with dirt. The windows were boarded up with wooden planks, which had begun to rot and crumble and fall away. There was no fence around the grounds. The grass and weeds had grown and formed a natural barrier between the building and the canal path. The black slate roof was bowed, with gaps where tiles had fallen off. It had clearly been uninhabited for some time, another victim of the railway and the lack of canal traffic. There was no sign of life. The moon was high in the sky now and a small breeze had risen, causing the water in the canal to lap ominously against the walls of the lock. In the distance, across an empty, fallow field, he heard the sinister call of a crow, cawing in a bare tree silhouetted against the horizon.

He approached the door in the middle of the wall facing the canal. It was boarded up like the windows on either side of it. Thomas managed to get his fingers between two of the planks that were nailed into the surround and pulled, but they did not budge. He looked closer and saw that, unlike the boards that covered the windows, these planks were new and the nails that held them in place glinted with a silver coating, rather than rusted brown. Someone had put them up recently.

He stepped away from the door after another unsuccessful attempt at removing a wooden board. He circled round the building. Evening dew on the long grass seeped through his shoes. There was no window on the side of the house. He came to the rear. There was a narrow garden, beyond which a fence separated the house from a field of weed-covered ruts that stretched away into the distance. Across the field, the crow cawed again. Thomas was sure it was warning him, a portent of doom that sent a shiver down his chilled spine. The rear of the house mirrored the front with a central door between windows on either side. He approached the door. The only sound was the swish of the long grass as he stepped through it. Again, the wooden boarding was new and secured tightly with fresh nails. There seemed to be no way into the house.

Perhaps he had been wrong. He had come on a hunch without any evidence that Jessie had been brought this way. He was certain she had been taken from Waverley train station, but beyond that everything had been supposition. Watt could have taken her anywhere. A day later, they could be beyond the borders of Scotland. They could be on a ship to the continent or to America. He had seen the name Castlecary on the departure board and had felt certain it was the place that held the key to everything – the missing child, the murdered child, Jessie and her lost child, and Duncan Watt. Alone beside the empty lock-keeper's house, next to the silent canal, he began to doubt his reasoning. All he could do was return to Edinburgh or Liberton and let Aitchison and McHarg do their job. He should leave it to the professional police, who would mock him for his crazed dash halfway across the country. He had been a fool.

25

THURSDAY EVENING, 25 NOVEMBER

1920

The shock was still raw. The trauma he inspired still burned. She tried to comprehend it all. She thought of the murdered girl, Lily May. He had brutally slain her. Horror overcame her. Duncan had killed the girl and left her in the tower only to cast suspicion on Jessie. He wanted revenge for the loss of his son. He blamed her for Alexander's death. That much she accepted as true. She was at fault for their son's death. The rest was delusional. He had never wanted his son; he had never wanted to know him and had never tried to find them. In the early months when she struggled to care for Alexander, she had not strayed far from the south side of Glasgow. If he had made a serious effort to find them, he would have. He had wanted nothing to do with her or with his son. The rejection she felt after he had used her for his own satisfaction was real and raw, but she knew she would have reconciled with him if only for the sake of Alexander's health and prospects. She had been that desperate, but it had never been an option.

He came to her again after a few hours. When she heard him

approach, she was determined to confront him. She had little left to live for. If he should strike her down, then what loss would it be to anyone but herself? She had no need to further her existence in this cruel world. If she could have found a way to end her life in the empty cellar, she would have taken it. She contemplated using her dress to make a noose of some kind, but there was nothing upon which to hang it. Had there been a sharp rock or shard of brick, she would have found an artery to cut.

No sooner had she turned her thoughts towards ending her life than she heard a cry through the wall. She had nothing to live for, but the same could not be said for the poor child in the next room. Duncan had killed one innocent child already. She could not allow him to do it again. She would sacrifice herself willingly to save Adam Symons, to give him the chance at leading a fulfilling and better life than she had achieved; to give him the chance that her own boy never had. Her resolve grew, but she had no means with which to act upon it. Their position was hopeless. She was unarmed, weak from hunger and thirst, and she had no idea where they were being held. No one knew they were here. No one would be coming to their rescue. Her only thought was to try and talk to him and make him see the horror of what he had done. She must try to appeal to any remaining humanity left within his scarred and twisted mind. How could she reason with a madman?

His uneven footsteps approached. He came to her first, although the baby was wailing again through the wall. He pushed the door open and stood on the threshold. Jessie stood with her back against the far wall. He said nothing, only stared at her, deciding what further evil he could inflict upon her.

'You murdered that girl in Liberton,' she said. He did not respond, but took a step forward into the room. 'You could have punished me, killed me, without hurting any children.'

His lip curled up. 'I don't want to just kill you. I want you to suffer as I have.'

He held a coil of rope in one hand, and in the other was the glint of a blade.

'You think I have not suffered?' she exclaimed. 'You have no idea how much pain I have lived with since the day you disowned me and your son. You think I do not blame myself for Alexander's death?'

'If you truly believed you killed him, how could you possibly have gone on living?'

'I did not want to go on living. I drove myself mad with the guilt. I tried to kill myself.' She held down the top of her dress and let him see the top of her chest. 'You are not the only one with scars to bear.'

He stopped. 'You admit that you killed him.'

'I did not murder him. I loved him more than any child has ever been loved, but because of that I could not give him away. No one would help us. He died because of my love for him, but I did not murder him.'

'I spoke to the doctor at the asylum. He told me you admitted to killing your own child.'

'I was out of my mind. I blamed myself. Sometimes, when delirium strikes me, to this day, my mind tells me that I killed him, that I drowned him in a canal. But I did not. I did not. He died in my arms. I came to the canal to drown myself, to be united with my son in death because I could not bear to be without him.'

'You liar!' His sudden fury startled her. 'You killed him and felt nothing. You ruined my life, my only chance of a happy existence. You took him from me, my only chance of a family. Look at me now.' He pointed at the ugly scar on his face with the knife. 'No woman will take me for a husband now, after what that bitch did to me. Who would want a scarred cripple for a husband? What child would want this for a father?'

His broad frame crushed her against the wall. He held the knife to her throat. She tried one last time to reason with him. 'What good will this do? Whatever you have planned will not bring

Alexander back. Your son is lost. Why make others suffer as we have? Why take another father's son?'

The blade traced a line along the exposed scar on her chest. She felt it slice through her rough skin and a small trickle of blood ran down her front. 'Because those women are like you. They are not fit to raise children, just as you were not. They destroyed men's lives. Those wretches will not be missed, nor their bastard children.'

'Punish me, but not the boy. Kill me if you must; tell everyone I was the murderer of our child, but let him live.'

The blade paused. She thought she had finally got through to a small spark of humanity that still resided within him. He withdrew the knife and put it in his pocket.

'No.' He uncoiled the rope and looped it over her head and tied it around her waist, her arms clamped to her sides. She was too weak to resist. 'It is too late for you to save him. You must die with him to show the world who you really are. You and all the other women who destroy the lives of the men they trap.' He pushed her to the ground and bound her ankles and wrists and joined them with a length of rope so that they were shackled together. 'When you see what I have planned for you, you will understand why it must end like this. There is no other way.'

He was mad. He was not a man of any kind, but a monster. He was deluded and cruel. And he held her life and the life of the boy in his hands. She was powerless to stop him.

She lay on the cold stone. He left her there. As he got to the door, the torch on the wall flickered and went out. Darkness enveloped them. He cursed and picked up the torch and made his way up the steps. The door to her room was open. She heard a creak as another door at the top of the steps was opened. She tried to loosen the ties that bound her, but they were tight and unyielding. She tried rubbing her wrists against the wall in the futile hope that the rope would break. Her wrists began to bleed, and she collapsed to her knees. It was hopeless.

Thomas was turning away from the dark house when he had heard the faint creak of a door being opened. It was followed by footsteps and the murmuring voice of a man speaking to himself. He heard the soft crackle of fire, conspicuous in the silence of the night. Someone had lit a match. He stopped breathing and stood still and concentrated, turning his head to try and locate the sound.

His heart pounding, he crept forward until he was pressed against the wall, the cold brick and moistness of the damp moss against his hands. He edged along until he reached the window, then bent down and found a small gap between two rotten boards. He put his eye to the gap and saw only black. He moved round, trying to take in the whole of the room behind the boards, and as he did so, he saw an orange glow. It was faint and off to the side. It was coming from the middle of the house, through an internal doorway that led to a hallway. Someone was inside the house.

He slipped back from the window and gathered his thoughts, deciding what he should do. It could be a vagrant seeking shelter from the cold night, but Thomas dismissed this idea. They were in the middle of farmland. The cities that teemed with the poor and homeless were too far away for someone to have made it all the way out here without finding some other accommodation. It could be some other criminal, hiding out from the authorities in the countryside. He would only know if he confronted the person inside.

He steeled himself. There was further movement inside the house. Footsteps moved across floorboards and the creaking door was opened again. The trace of firelight receded, and only darkness remained through the gap in the window. Whoever was in the house had disappeared towards the rear.

He stood up and pulled at one of the planks of wood that had rotted away. It came away easily, as did the two planks next to it, leaving a gap wide enough for him to squeeze through. This must be how the person gained access to the house, pulling the boards up behind them once inside. Thomas raised himself onto the ledge and let his eyes adjust to the gloom inside. The room beyond was empty. He could make out the outline of the doorway through which he had seen the flame. He dropped down as quietly as he could, wincing as the floorboards groaned as he landed. He felt his way along the wall until he reached the doorway. It was a hallway, as he had guessed, with doors leading off it to the other rooms of the house. But all of the doorways were empty voids, no doors hung across them, and there was no sign of light within any of the rooms beyond. Where had the person gone?

He stepped into the hallway and silently moved along. He felt the floor change beneath him. The solid floorboards stopped and he felt a small ridge. Then his foot caught on something sticking up from the ground. He bent down and found it with his hands. It was a metal circle, a handle. He realised what it was and where the person had disappeared to. It was a trapdoor. He raised it, slowly, praying it would not make a noise that would betray him.

He moved to the side and leaned forward with his hand outstretched into the gap in the floor. He felt cold stone. It was a stairway leading beneath the house. He could hear the faint cries of a baby coming up from the darkness below.

Duncan returned with the relit torch. He walked past her room and ignored her. He placed the torch back in the wall bracket and went into the adjoining room. The screams of the child became louder. He spoke gently to the baby and the wailing ceased. She wondered at the delusion that let him act so caringly to a child he intended to murder in cold blood.

She lay on the ground, her head turned towards the door, fearing his return and whatever lay in store for her. Then she saw the shadow appear. It came from the bottom of the stairs and crept across her doorway. Her eyes grew wide when she saw him and she stifled the cry that threatened to escape her lips.

The stairs led down to a narrow corridor. Thomas was in a cellar. The torch was in a bracket on the wall. He could see two doors in the stone wall. They must have been storage rooms at one time, for goods to be kept in before barges took them away, or for the lock-keeper to store the tools of his trade – barge poles and planks and mooring ropes. The walls were damp and slick with moisture, seeping through from the canal into the land from which the cellar had been dug out. He crept along the wall, crouched and silent, until he had drawn level with the first door which was lying open. He saw her lying on the floor, the only thing in the empty room. The second door was also open. Inside he heard the man's voice. He was speaking gently and calmly. Thomas crossed the corridor and went to her, his finger on his lips, urging her to remain quiet and not give away his presence.

Her hands and feet were tied. He touched her forehead. She felt feverish. In the dim light, he could see her dress was torn and her face was covered in dirt with her hair hanging wildly around it. He noticed the scars and scratches on her skin and the slit of blood across the top of her chest. He wiped the hair from her face and they locked eyes. He signalled to her. Are you okay?

She nodded in return. Her eyes glanced towards the adjoining room, warning him.

Thomas understood her fear. He tried to undo the knots around her hands. They would not loosen. He moved to her feet and tried that knot. It was fastened tight and the rope was wet. He needed a knife, or a sharp stone edge, to cut her free. He looked about the room. There was nothing he could use. She gestured to him and he put his face next to hers.

She whispered, 'He has a knife in his pocket.'

Thomas nodded and put his finger to his lips again. Then they both froze as they heard footsteps and Duncan Watt's voice, louder now, speaking to the child. 'Come on, time for you to go upstairs.' Thomas withdrew into the corner behind the open door. Watt passed without looking into the room. He carried the boy, wrapped in a shawl. Thomas waited until he heard the trapdoor being opened and the footsteps above his head. Then he went to her.

'I know him. He is Duncan Watt. He came to see me at the hospital. He lied about his war record. What does he mean to do with you?'

'He wants to kill me, and the boy too. He wants to frame me for the murder of the children.'

'Why you? What is he to you?'

She blinked through stained tears. 'He is the father of the child I lost. He wants revenge for the death of his son.'

The connection was revealed. He showed her he understood. 'Why has he come for you after all this time?'

'He was looking for me for some time. I've tried to talk with him, convince him to let the child go, to hurt me alone, but nothing will change his mind. He will not listen to reason.'

He kissed her gently on her forehead. 'I will get you away from him, but I cannot untie the ropes, they are too tight.' They heard footsteps crossing the hall above their heads. Thomas stood. She shuddered as he left her, lying on the floor. 'Trust me,' he mouthed, then dashed into the corridor and turned towards the second room, empty now that Watt had removed the boy.

Watt came down the stairs and along the corridor and into her room. He said nothing. She looked at him and prayed her eyes would not betray her by straying towards the other room. Watt bent down and lifted her. He held her around the waist and dragged her across the floor and out the door. There was no point in wasting energy by resisting him. He carried her up the stairs. She could not turn her head to see if Thomas was there.

Watt lifted her through the trapdoor and for the first time Jessie saw that they had been kept below an abandoned house. Gaps in the roof let moonlight in. Watt took her by the waist again and dragged her down the hallway and into a room. He lifted her onto a window sill and pushed her through a gap in the boards that had sealed it up. She landed on planks of wood. A nail pierced her shoulder as she landed and she let out a cry of pain. Watt jumped down beside her. She could hear the child crying, somewhere off to the side. She was surrounded by wet grass. Watt picked her up and spoke to her as his large hand clamped around her jaw and turned her head and forced her to take in their surroundings.

'Recognise where you are?' he hissed in her ear.

She could make out a path and a black void and white blocks and gradually the horror filled her and she felt weak and sick. She was at a lock on a canal and she knew which gate it was. She remembered it from that night fifteen years ago when she had last been here, when she had carried her dead son cradled in a grey shawl with her. When she had determined that she would join him. She had looked into this same void and willed herself to jump and let herself be dragged down. How much better would it have been for all if she had succeeded? How much suffering would have been avoided?

'This time no one will come to your rescue. You will die here with the boy, as you should have done with our son. Instead, you killed him and left him alone under this water to rot while you carried on with your life. Not this time. This time they will find you with him and they will know who you really are.'

She saw the boy on the path, only yards from the edge of the canal wall. 'I beg you. Throw me in if you must, but do not punish the boy. I promise you; it is not something that you can live with.'

'You should have thought of that when you decided to live with our son's death on your conscience. Now, others have to suffer in order to show the world who you truly are.'

'I'm sorry for what has happened to you, but can't you see, this makes you no better than me? You have also killed an innocent child.' She had to keep him talking. Where had Thomas gone?

'I am nothing like you. These children, that little girl, this boy, I'm saving them from the pitiful wretches they were born to. Whores not fit to bring a child into this world. I'm saving them from the same fate our son suffered – to be killed by their own mothers in misery, starving and sickly, dragged from poorhouse to whorehouse, from city to city. That is no life for a child.'

'These women have no choice, just as I had no choice. They can only try to survive and hope for better times to come. Do you not think they would do whatever they could for their children, whatever it takes, to keep them safe and alive? I tried to do that for our son. It was others that turned us away, like you and your family. You left us alone and helpless.'

She regretted her words when she saw his reaction. The anger rushed to his face. He squeezed her, the pressure on her body was unbearable. 'You dare to blame me for my son's death? For drowning my son in this canal? You bitch!' Her head snapped back as the blow landed on her cheek. She was dazed, but she managed to stay conscious. She prayed for Thomas to hurry.

Watt dragged her across the grass to the path where Adam Symons lay, wrapped in a shawl. She could see the boy was skinny and weak. He had suffered from neglect in the time since he had been taken, lying alone in the room under the house while Watt had been in Liberton and Edinburgh. No passerby, if there were any, would have been able to hear his screams.

He dropped her next to the boy. She tried to reach out to Adam, but she was bound tight by the ropes. She whispered to him, and began to cry with him. 'There, there, Adam. Sssh, it will be okay.'

'Did you speak like that to my son before you drowned him?' Watt stood over her.

'I did not drown our son!' she cried into the night sky, rolling over to look up at him. She saw the plank of wood swing up from behind Watt's head and shatter across his skull and the giant man crumpled under the power of the blow. Nails protruding from the wood lodged in his back and head as he fell to the ground. Thomas stood behind him.

'Bastard.' Thomas bent down and held Jessie to him. 'Are you okay?'

'Get the knife. It's in his jacket pocket.' Watt groaned and moved beside her. His hands came to his head and felt the nails and plank there. 'Quickly,' she urged Thomas.

He leapt on Watt and tried to find his coat pocket. The sensation brought Watt round and he started to struggle. He pulled the plank free and threw it away. He was taller and stronger than Thomas and he started to writhe around, trying to shake himself free. Thomas found the pocket but just as his hand closed around the knife, Watt grabbed him and threw him off. Thomas landed on his back. Watt got to his feet and turned to see his attacker.

'Doctor Stevenson.' He sneered. 'Come to save the damsel in distress? Do you have a soft spot for all whores or just this one?'

Thomas did not look at Watt. He looked at Jessie and flicked his eyes from her to the ground behind Watt. She saw him and followed his look. The knife had fallen from Watt's pocket. It lay on the ground, unseen by him. Jessie started to wriggle herself towards it.

Thomas crawled away on his back, drawing Watt after him, away from Jessie and the child. If he could give her long enough to cut herself free, she could take the child and escape.

'I know who you are, Watt,' he said. 'You're no war hero. You didn't fight one day in the trenches. You don't have shell shock. You wouldn't have lasted five minutes there. You just abuse those weaker than you. Have you killed before? How many women have you beaten?'

Watt laughed, stalking after the retreating doctor scrabbling along the path. 'You think you are a hero because you fought in the war? You think you are strong? You are a weak, little man. A drunk who cries himself to sleep each night, who can't learn to deal with the horror he has seen. You think you are helping those other weak men who come to you? If you had any sympathy for them, you would put them out of their misery. You should put yourself out of your own misery. Let those nightmares win, Doctor Stevenson. Let the fear and anger inside you free instead of trying to hold it together. You should have ended your own life. I'll gladly put you out of your misery myself.'

Jessie reached the knife and managed to grasp it between her hands. She sat up and began sawing at the rope around her ankles. She kept an eye on the two men. Watt towered over Thomas as he retreated. She felt the rope loosen and, with a final hack, it split open and her feet were free.

'You think murdering an innocent baby makes you a big man? You are evil. What happened to make you this way? You think you are owed something from this world? Why? Plenty of men have suffered worse than you. All those real men who came back from the war, broken and beaten and with nothing, who returned to try and live a normal life despite the true horror they had been through.' Keep him distracted, Thomas thought. 'You are nothing compared to the weakest of those men. You are a coward.' He stopped shuffling backwards as he felt the earth fall away beneath him. He had reached the edge of the canal.

'End of the line, doctor,' smirked Watt. 'All your fancy words and talking cure gibberish won't help you now. I'll show you what happens to weak drunks. Can you swim?' He raised his hands and bent towards Thomas, preparing to push him over the side and into the black water.

Thomas looked behind in desperation. He looked beyond Watt. He couldn't see Jessie. Had she got away? If he could die knowing he had saved her, he could be at peace. That would be enough. He had nowhere else to go. He waited for the fall and the black death to come.

Then Watt arched back and his arms swung round and grabbed at his back and he fell forwards. Thomas ducked out of the way as Watt fell over him, down into the water. He turned in time to see the splash of white froth as Watt hit the surface, and he saw the glint of the knife blade half-buried in his back with the handle sticking out. He turned and saw Jessie standing in front of him.

'Enough,' she shouted, and then she sagged and fell to the ground before repeating it, a sigh this time. 'Enough.'

She ran along the uneven tow path, or tried as best she could in the dark. She could not see the uneven dips and holes in the ground. Three times she stumbled and thought she would fall, but she managed to right herself and carry on. She clutched the screaming child to her shoulder. The screaming was good. It meant he was alive. Not like Alexander. She would not let that happen again. This boy would survive. When the blade had struck Duncan in the back, she had felt the weight lift. A release from his hold, a release from the past that had gripped her for so long. She would run from this darkness and towards a new life, a better life, a life free from her burden. She would not forget Alexander, she could not, but she would carry the memory of him with a new fortitude. She had become too comfortable in Liberton, thinking that she had escaped, when in reality her trauma was only buried below a shallow surface, waiting for the opportunity to emerge and drag her down once more. Duncan Watt had been the physical manifestation of her nightmare. He had awoken the devil in her from its slumber, but at the same time she had rediscovered her determination, her stubbornness. She had forgotten she had to fight for her life, if she stopped, then the demons would creep up on her and catch her again. Her desire to live had been jolted back into consciousness. She had defeated both Duncan Watt and her demons. She was free, running through the night, seeing the welcoming glow of light from windows in front of her. This boy, Adam, would get another chance at life, and so would Jessie.

She reached the door and burst through it, into the blinding glow of life and fell to the floor, cradling the precious child in her arms.

She had won. She had banished the demon. She had left him behind her.

26

SATURDAY, 27 NOVEMBER

1920

MISSING CHILD FOUND ALIVE

KILLER OF LILY MAY FITZPATRICK

IN POLICE CUSTODY

Adam Symons, the six-month-old boy abducted from his mother in Edinburgh four weeks ago, has been found alive and his kidnapper arrested by police.

The extensive police investigation led them to the village of Castlecary, between Falkirk and Cumbernauld, in the late evening of Thursday night. The boy was discovered at an abandoned lock-keeper's house next to the Forth and Clyde Canal. It is believed this is where he had been held captive since his abduction.

A man in his mid-thirties was arrested at the scene and has been charged with kidnapping. He has also been charged with the kidnapping and murder of Lily May Fitzpatrick, the baby girl who was abducted in Edinburgh in late October and whose body was found in Liberton ten days ago. So far, police have declined to name the man. At present, he is being kept in a prison hospital, having sustained a knife injury and catching pneumonia after falling into the canal attempting to evade arrest.

Adam Symons is said by doctors to be malnourished and underweight, and suffering from a chest infection and jaundice, but is expected to make a full recovery. His mother, Sarah Symons, of Edinburgh, expressed her relief at her son being found alive and safe. 'Thank God there is no sign of any abuse or injuries inflicted upon him and I have my son back.' She thanked the police force, led by Detective Inspector McHarg, for their hard work in finding her son. 'They never gave up on finding him alive, even when time went on and all hope seemed lost.'

The police investigation was sparked when three children were reported missing from Edinburgh poorhouses under similar circumstances within a few days of each other. The third child, Roddy MacPherson, was subsequently found safe and well living with a couple in Morningside. His mother, Abigail MacPherson, remains in police custody charged with falsely reporting a crime, wasting police time and selling a child for financial gain.

Detective Inspector McHarg addressed reporters at the Abbeyhill Police Station on Friday afternoon. 'I am delighted at the positive outcome of this case and the safe return of baby Adam Symons to his mother. This result was down to the hard work and endeavour of my officers, who worked diligently day and night under my command, never giving up hope that the boy would be traced alive and well. I would like to thank the public for coming forward with information which helped solve this crime. We remain heartbroken about the killing of Lily Fitzpatrick, but would like to assure the people of Edinburgh and the wider community that we have the perpetrator in custody. He has confessed to the murder, and justice will be served upon him in due course.'

Sarah Symons will be reunited with her son when he is well enough to leave hospital. She has received offers of financial support from private benefactors and from several charities, although at the moment she remains without a fixed address.

The case has once again raised questions about social welfare in our major cities for the vulnerable, including single mothers with children, who are forced to live on the streets. No one from the local city council or the government has responded to our enquiry for their views on the matter.

The man arrested for the kidnapping and murder of Lily May Fitzpatrick and the abduction of Adam Symons is expected to appear before a city judge for sentencing when his health has improved sufficiently. Having confessed to the crimes, it is expected that he will receive the death penalty or imprisonment for life.

Robert Plenderleith finished the article, folded his newspaper and placed it on the bar top. He picked up his pint glass and swallowed the final mouthful.

'Another?' Arthur asked.

'Not tonight.' He stepped down from the barstool and fastened his coat. 'Still no sign of the doctor?' He gestured to the empty table where Thomas Stevenson would usually have been seen of an evening in Liberton.

'Malachy says he saw him at his house, wi' the wummin,' said Joseph from his seat at the window.

'That so?' asked Plenderleith.

'Aye, police cart dropped them off this afternoon. That detective is still there with them just now.' Malachy pointed through the wall in the direction of Kirkgate.

'Surprised she would show her face around here again, after the trouble she has caused the doctor.'

Rose Melchin happened to enter their half of the bar as Plenderleith said this. 'Whit trouble wud that be, Rab Plenderleith?'

'Well, Rose, bringing the police into his house. Her devilish past.'

'But she had nothin' tae dae wi' the polis investigation, or the missing bairns.'

'She had nothing to do with this crime, no, but that doesn't excuse her past. I heard she killed her own child, drowned him in a canal.'

'Ye shouldnae go spreadin' gossip like that aroun' the town, especially if ye dinnae ken the truth a' it.'

'Heard she was locked up in an asylum too,' Malachy joined in.

'An' a prostitute an' aw,' said Joseph.

Arthur sensed his wife bristling beside him. 'That's enough noo, gentlemen. We'll hear nae mare aboot it unless we ken some actual facts, and ah suspect we'll never ken the truth aboot Louise, or Jessie, so ah'll mind ye tae keep yer mooths shut oan the matter while yer in the inn.'

Rose exited through the dividing door. Plenderleith stopped next to Malachy and Joseph on his way to the door. 'The fact she used a false name tells you all you need to know. She must have been guilty of something.'

Joseph nodded in agreement, 'An' why wud the polis be drappin' them hame after Thomas went chargin' aff tae the city tae look fir her?'

Plenderleith shook his head. 'Get used to it, lads. That's what'll become of Liberton now that they city has come to us. Mad women and whores in the streets and police rounding them up and children starving and begging and murderers hiding amongst us.'

'A disaster fir us aw,' Joseph agreed.

'Well, goodnight gentlemen. At least The Liberton Inn hasn't suffered so far.'

'Don't bet against it though,' warned Malachy, 'how long before we're swamped by these city types looking to live away from the smoke and noise, looking for a bit of fresh air. They'll be here soon enough.'

'There's already talk of the tram line being extended to run through the village, and widening the roads for cars and more houses being built. It'll never be the same around here.' With that, Plenderleith left, placing his hat on his balding head and stepping out into the night, his feet crunching on the fresh blanket of snow that had fallen, the first of the upcoming winter. As he marched away, along the road to Mount Vernon, he cast a final disparaging look over his shoulder, along Kirkgate, and saw the glow from the window of Thomas Stevenson's house. He buried his hands in his pockets, spat on the pavement, and carried on his way.

'You are a very lucky man,' Detective Inspector Aitchison said, flipping his notebook closed and tucking it into the chest pocket of his coat. 'You should have come and told us instead of running across the country on your own.'

'Would you have done anything?' Thomas asked. They were in the living room of his house. Jessie and Thomas were in the armchairs next to the fireplace, with a warm fire crackling behind the grate. Aitchison sat on a chair that had been brought in from the kitchen, and Detective Fraser stood at the window. They had just finished recounting the events of Thursday night once again, this time officially. Detective Aitchison had finished asking all his questions.

'We may be slow to react sometimes, Doctor, but we do get there in the end.'

'You had already dismissed me twice.'

'It's easy to say what should and shouldn't have been done in hindsight.'

'Don't worry, Detective Inspector. I have no desire to take issue with you over anything, given the way things have worked out.'

'You realise if Watt had died, you would both be sitting in a cell at the station just now, charged with murder? As it is, you are lucky to avoid any charge for assault and attempted murder. Without

Watt's confession, we have little evidence with which to prosecute him for the murder of Lily. Only circumstantial hearsay. But given the nature of his crime, and the suffering that Miss Bruce has been put through already, Detective Inspector McHarg has decided it would not be in the public interest to muddy the waters around this case any further.'

Thomas was tempted to add that perhaps the police would not want the public looking too closely into how the investigation had been handled, from their initial reluctance to look into the missing children reports, to missed opportunities during the case. The killer had, after all, approached them willingly, not a mile from the crime scene at one point, and the police had accepted his word as a witness, without looking into Watt's history.

They had shared a moment of shock after Watt had plunged into the canal lock. Thomas stared at Jessie, who was looking at the black canal in a trance, the same darkness into which she had once plunged, carrying her dead child, wishing to be dragged down into the depths to join him. Thomas picked himself up and took her hand and spoke softly to her.

'Come on, we must see to the boy.'

'He's still there,' she said. Thomas looked and saw the black shape on the surface. Watt was face down in the water, arms outstretched, the handle of the knife in his back pointing up into the sky.

Was he worth saving? A deranged man who had murdered a child in cold blood, to avenge his long-standing grievance against a woman he had abused. How many other women had he abused? He could not ask Jessie to save his life, not after what she had been subjected to by him. But he was a doctor, a calling he had clung to despite all he had seen and been through, the very worst that humanity could unleash. He had saved men on his operating table in the fields of Europe without asking what sort of men they were, or what sort of past they had. No doubt some of those he had saved had killed men in battle, no doubt some of those scarred and bitter men had gone on to commit other crimes. He had heard the experiences of enough veterans struggling to adapt to life afterwards to know this would be true. If he was to let Watt die, what would that make him? He would have sunk to that same level.

'I have to save him. It's my duty.' She stared at him. He could not read her. Was it anger? Hatred? He urged her to go and this time she did, breaking away from him, their hands slipping away from each other. She took the boy with her and disappeared along the path. Perhaps understanding would come later, if not forgiveness.

Left alone at the edge of the canal loch, Thomas contemplated the water and the body floating in it. Thomas was not a swimmer. Jumping into the freezing water after Watt would only bring certain death to both of them. He ran back to the old house and grabbed the torch that was still burning inside the door. He cast the light around, looking for something that would help him. In the corner, among rubbish and debris, he saw an old barge pole with a hook on the end, a remnant of the former occupant's profession. He grabbed it and ran back out. Holding up the torch, he could still make out the floating body. He lay the torch down and cast out the barge pole from the edge of the lock. After several failed attempts, he managed to get the hook caught in Watt's shirt collar and he dragged the pole back, bringing the body to the side of the canal where he could reach down and grab it. Leaning over the edge, he managed to pull the heavy man out and fell backwards. Watt's waterlogged bulk landed on top of him, his face against Thomas's. He managed to squirm out from underneath him. Watt was not breathing. He removed the knife and rolled him onto his back. He felt a slight pulse in his chest. He positioned him to open up his airway, tilting Watt's head back to open up the throat. Then he started resuscitation: breathing into Watt's open mouth and pressing down on his chest to keep his heart beating. He kept going, he had no idea for how long. He was damp and cold, and it seemed futile, but not once did he stop to question if it was worth the effort. Finally, Watt jerked and spluttered and Thomas rolled him onto his side and water poured out from his mouth. Thomas held him and could feel his shallow breathing, sporadic and weak.

The first men to arrive from Castlecary Inn found Thomas sitting there, next to the canal, holding onto the injured man.

'All's well that ends well, as they say.' Aitchison rose from his chair. 'It's unlikely we will need you to attend any trial or sentencing hearing, but I would ask you to be available should the need arise for witnesses. He may decide to change his plea.'

'There is one thing I would like to ask you to do,' interjected Thomas as Aitchison turned to see himself out.

The detective turned back. 'And what would that be?'

'An apology to Miss Bruce is in order, wouldn't you say?'

'Like I say, in hindsight it's clear to see he was a madman, but at the time I had to take his report seriously and treat it as I would any other information.'

'I don't dispute your intention, Detective, but I do think it could have been handled in a much more delicate manner.'

Jessie interrupted. Thomas saw a hint of a smile on her lips. 'It's quite alright, Detective. Thomas is being facetious. Perhaps instead of an apology, you might see your way to making some restitution to a woman's charity, or raise the matter of policing of the less fortunate in society to your superiors as a matter of interest?'

'That's not really my job,' Aitchison blustered.

'No, of course it's not.'

'Good day, Doctor. Ma'am.' With an awkward glance at Thomas, Aitchison motioned for Fraser to follow him.

'How is the boy?' Jessie asked, just as Aitchison was about to cross the threshold to the hallway.

He stopped and turned back once more. 'As well as can be expected. Still in the hospital. Needs to put on weight, be fed properly and so on. There's no sign of any injury to him.'

'What will happen to him?'

The detective shrugged. 'I expect he'll be given back to his mother.'

'Will anyone look after them?'

'I can't rightly say. I'm sure given their ordeal, the church or a shelter will be sympathetic to their plight.' He shrugged as he placed his hat on his head and left.

Thomas and Jessie let them see themselves out. Thomas got to his feet and watched from the window as the police cart wheeled away, leaving tracks in the fresh snow.

'What chance does he have?' said Jessie.

'Watt? I expect very little. They may try and argue insanity and put him in an institution, but given the nature of his crime, I suspect he will be given the death penalty.'

'Not Watt. I couldn't care less what happens to him now. I wish he had drowned in the canal.'

'Jessie, I—'

'It's okay, Thomas. I understand why you did what you did. You are a better person than I could hope to be. No, I meant the boy, Adam Symons. What chance does he have if he is cast back into this cruel world with his mother, without any care or support, not even a home? Surely, we should do more to help.'

'I'm not sure what more we can do.'

'Not you and me. I mean everyone. Society. How can it be right that young mothers are left to fend for themselves when they have nothing?' She stopped. 'I still think of that poor girl, Lily May.'

Thomas had no answer for her. The image of the small, broken body flashed through his mind at the mention of her name. He knew it was a ghost that he could not leave behind. She was there now, in his head, alongside James Napier for evermore.

Should the government or the council do more? There had been calls during and after the war to do more for those left widowed or crippled or abandoned, but the war was over. That was for politicians to debate.

'I've been thinking.' He turned from the window as the cart disappeared at the junction, turning towards the city.

'Yes?'

'About the future.' Was it too soon to bring this up with her? He had been thinking of nothing else since that night at the canal, as he sat with Watt and waited for help to arrive. He had been thinking about it when he had been pacing along the canal in the darkness, hoping to find Jessie alive and safe. He had been thinking about it when he had jumped onto the train to Castlecary, hoping his gut feeling was right.

'The future?'

'I know it may not be the right time to discuss such things, but I realised something when you went missing.' He took a breath and plunged ahead. 'I realised I didn't want to be without you. That I couldn't bear to be without you.' She did not react. He turned away, fearing the rejection that would follow. 'I fear I have wasted a lot of my time since the war, stuck in that nightmare, and that it is time to start thinking about the future. The world is at peace, the terror is over, never to be repeated again. Lessons have been learned and we will never sink so low again.' He waited for her to respond, but heard nothing. He turned back to her.

She smiled at him. She knew how hard he found it to express his emotions. For all his faith in the 'talking cure', and his work with fellow veterans, he had never come to terms with his own trauma. His only way to cope had been to bury his feelings and not allow those terrible mental scars to drown him. That, and his reliance on alcohol to ease the pain.

He took her smile as encouragement. 'I regret that I have not been a better friend to you, that I never asked about what had happened to you. I would like the chance to make that right, if you would allow me.'

Her laugh startled him, and she saw that he was about to misinterpret it. 'You fool, Thomas. I would like nothing better than to have you as my friend. You are already the friend that I needed.' She laughed again. 'What a damaged pair we are.'

'Then you will stay?'

She shook her head. 'Not here. I think we both need a fresh start, somewhere further away from our past.' They had too many nightmares associated with Liberton to stay there. If she was to heal, she needed to separate herself from her past fully. She needed to leave Alexander behind in peace. Of course, she would never forget him, but they had to learn to live with their demons if they were ever to go on living. There was still a chance for happiness for them both, but not here, not in this country.

'And I will never marry you, you understand.'

He did. She would never allow herself to be under the power of any man, no matter how much she loved or cared for him. He had not considered leaving, but what she said made sense. The idea of leaving behind Liberton, Scotland, Europe, the war. It seized him as the right thing to do. As soon as they were free to do so, as soon as justice had finished with Duncan Watt, they would leave.

'But where should we go?'

She smiled at him again. 'We have time to decide that.'

There was a whole world of possibilities ahead of them. He walked to the sideboard and took a glass tumbler and opened the bottle of whisky. As he tipped it up, she laid her hand over his and stopped him from pouring the whisky from the bottle.

HISTORICAL NOTE

All We Cannot Leave Behind is a work of fiction. However, where possible, the story takes place using real locations, many of which still survive to this day. There have been some slight adjustments to fit the chronology of the story, most notably, the war hospital based at Craiglockhart was officially closed in 1919. I extended its life by a few months into 1920. It was there that the war poets, Siegfried Sassoon and Wilfred Owen, and other officers, were treated for shell shock having returned from the front lines.

The Liberton Inn continued to serve the locals on the corner of Kirkgate and Kirk Brae until it closed in 2016. The dividing wall between the two halves of the u-shaped bar was removed in 2006. The building still stands, although the signage has disappeared. The Industrial School for Boys in Liberton became a care home, and was converted into residential flats in 2017. Alnwickhill House remains in use as residential flats. Liberton Tower is now available to book as self-catering holiday accommodation.

Queensberry House on Canongate is now part of the Scottish Government's Holyrood Campus, while the Abbeyhill Police Station, built in 1896, still stands. It ceased to be used as a police station around 1932, and from 1980 to 2002 became an Armenian restaurant. It is currently unused and derelict. The Craigleith Poorhouse is now the site of the Western General Hospital. Much of the Old Town and Royal Mile in Edinburgh remain unchanged.

The Waverley Steps, which lead down to Waverley Station are still there, tucked behind a retail centre and with added escalators on the side.

Trains running between Glasgow and Edinburgh still cross the viaduct at Castlecary, also known as the Red Burn Viaduct, running alongside the Forth and Clyde Canal. The train station ceased to be operational in 1967 and nothing remains. In 1937, it was the scene of Britain's worst snow-related rail crash: 35 people were killed when two express trains collided. Another accident caused by a signal failure in 1968 killed two people. The Castlecary Lime Works also closed in 1968, and by 1970 the sight had been cleared.

The history of Dalmuir House was adjusted for the story. The original Dalmuir House was bought by the local authority around 1908 and demolished. A new house was built in 1918 on the same site. A house still stands, although the park is now enclosed by housing estates, high-rise flats and a golf course.

Gartloch Hospital continued to be used as part of the NHS for the treatment of mental health patients until 1996. Many of the surrounding buildings were subsequently converted into homes or demolished to create Gartloch Village, but the Category A-listed administration building remains intact but derelict.

Precise records for the numbers of deaths and recovered bodies found along Scotland's canals do not exist, but anecdotal evidence suggests infanticide and suicide took place throughout their history, particularly when they were at their peak during the start of the industrial age. The case of Jessie King, the Stockbridge woman who took money to adopt babies and then murdered them, became notorious and eventually led to changes in the law. Jessie took on all the guilt for the crimes, while her partner, one Thomas Pearson, went free, despite suspicion that he coerced the mentally impaired Jessie into committing the crimes. Jessie King became the last woman to be hanged in Edinburgh in 1889. The inspiration for using the names 'Thomas' and 'Jessie' in the novel came from the names of my paternal grandparents, who lived in the Liberton and Gilmerton area of the city. The notorious baby killers having the same forenames is purely coincidental.

ACKNOWLEDGEMENTS

Thanks to Wendy Kelly, the first reader and first judge of all my novels so far.

Thanks to Chloe, Sophie, Meera, Jane and all the team at The Book Guild and Megan, Hannah, Alex and Jake and all the team at Troubador Publishing for all their hard work, advice and help in getting this book in a fit state to be seen in public and for their continued support.

Thanks to Joanne, Chloe and Caden for putting up with their husband and dad devoting more time than he should to his stories, instead of being with them.

Thanks to each and every single one of the readers who has picked up and read *All We Cannot Leave Behind* and my previous novels. Giving up a few hours of their time to spend it reading the outpouring of my imagination is such a gift to give to a writer.

If you enjoyed reading *All We Cannot Leave Behind*, please tell people about it. Leave a review on Amazon, Goodreads or Waterstones websites, or tell people about it on social media and help spread the word. Your kind words are appreciated more than you can imagine.

ABOUT THE AUTHOR

Iain Kelly lives in Scotland. He works as an editor in the television industry and is married with two children. *All We Cannot Leave Behind* is his fifth novel.

For more information visit his website: www.iainkellywriting.com

Follow on social media:

Facebook: iainkellywriting
Instagram: @iain_kelly_writing
Twitter: @IainK_Writing
LinkedIn: iain-kelly-writing

ALSO AVAILABLE

THE BARRA BOY

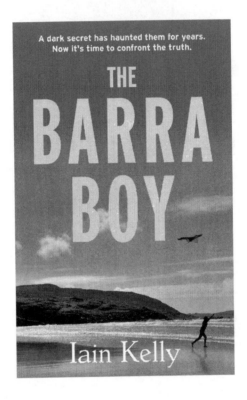

1982. Thirteen-year-old Ewan Fraser is sent to the remote island of Barra, off Scotland's west coast, to stay with his aunt and uncle.

Resigned to a monotonous summer of boredom, he is befriended by local girl Laura Robertson; together they explore the golden beaches and rocky coves of the idyllic island. But a dark secret that connects Laura to the mysterious outcast Mhairi Matheson and her son, Billy, is hidden beneath the tranquil surface... A secret that threatens to tear the small community apart.

Forty years later, Ewan returns to confront the truth about the formative summer of his adolescence, and finally learn the truth about Laura and the boy from Barra.

Praise for 'The Barra Boy':

– '[A] superbly written, character driven story that ranks as one of my favourite reads of the year. The author has a wonderful feel for locations... This is an outstanding novel from an author with a great future.'

– 'rich in description, superbly controlled pace of reveal... we have lots and lots of praise for this book – highly enjoyable setting, utterly pleasurable to imagine, early introduction of suspense that lasted right through to the conclusion, and satisfying answers to the mysteries that you encounter during the storyline. Great, great work.'

– 'a thoughtful combination of literary fiction and coming-of-age novel, and will undoubtedly remain in my memory for a long while.'

ALSO AVAILABLE

A JUSTIFIED STATE

Book One of The State Trilogy

The future.

The socially reformist Central Alliance Party rules unopposed.

Poverty and homelessness have been eradicated, but overpopulation, an energy crisis and an ongoing war jeopardise the stability of the country. When a local politician is assassinated, Detective Danny Samson finds himself at the centre of an investigation that threatens not only his life, but the entire future of The State.

Praise for 'A Justified State':

– 'the action is pacey and exciting, the characters fleshed out, nuanced and believable, the mystery…is genuinely intriguing and alarming.'

– 'the writing brought to mind Phillip Marlow, *Do Androids Dream of Electric Sheep?* the world of George Smiley, and Robert Harris' *Fatherland.*'

– 'This is a superbly well written fast paced, suspenseful mystery. A page turner as the action…makes you gasp.'

ALSO AVAILABLE

STATE OF DENIAL

Book Two of The State Trilogy

Election time in The State, the citizens prepare to vote.

A journalist from the Capital City heads north to report on growing resistance to the powerful ruling Party.

An ex-police detective returns to the city he once fled.

Together they become entangled in a burgeoning opposition movement.

Soon they learn the Party will do whatever it takes to remain in power, and one life is all it takes to spark a revolution.

Praise for 'State of Denial':

– 'Well paced and full of drama. A great sequel.'

– 'Well written, the plot flows effortlessly... A gripping sci-fi that is a little bit horrifying and a lot entertaining.'

– 'Get lost in the pages...through passages that may have you holding your breath.'

ALSO AVAILABLE

STATE OF WAR

Book Three of The State Trilogy

The State is at war at home and abroad. While the global First Strike War continues, a civil war threatens to bring down the ruling Central Alliance Party.

Daniel Samson – Citizen, Traitor, Survivor. Gabriella Marino – Soldier, Assassin, Fighter.

Caught between The State Forces and the rebels, hunted by both sides, they must choose between their own survival and protecting the city and the citizens trapped within the war zone. Are they willing to sacrifice their own chance of happiness to save a city from destruction?

The thrilling conclusion to The State Trilogy sees Danny and Gabriella join forces against their enemies in a fight that will determine the fate of The State, and the lives of all those who live there.

Praise for 'State of War':

– 'A lot of writers could learn how to create a believable future by studying Kelly's novels.'

– 'More action, more emotional stakes and this time the wrong move will not only end their lives but take a city with them.'